CAN'T LET HER GO

CAN'T LET HER GO

Nashville Dreams

Book Two

Sandy James

FOREVER
YOURS

New York   Boston

Copyright © 2018 by Sandy James
Preview of *Can't Fight the Feeling* copyright © 2018 by Sandy James

Cover design by Brian Lemus
Cover images © Shutterstock
Cover copyright © 2018 by Hachette Book Group, Inc.

Forever Yours
Hachette Book Group
1290 Avenue of the Americas, New York, NY 10104
forever-romance.com
twitter.com/foreverromance

First published as an ebook and as a print on demand: January 2018

Forever Yours is an imprint of Grand Central Publishing. The Forever Yours name and logo are trademarks of Hachette Book Group, Inc.

The publisher is not responsible for websites (or their content) that are not owned by the publisher.

The Hachette Speakers Bureau provides a wide range of authors for speaking events. To find out more, go to www.hachettespeakersbureau.com or call (866) 376-6591.

ISBNs: 978-1-4555-9561-7 (ebook), 978-1-4555-9560-0 (print on demand)

E3-20171117-DANF

This one is for Madalyn Grace.
For you, the future is so bright you've
got to wear shades.
Love you!

ACKNOWLEDGMENTS

To my talented, insightful editor, Lexi Smail. Thank you, thank you, thank you!

As I say—repeatedly—I'd be up the proverbial creek without my main critique partner, Cheryl Brooks. Love you!

Thanks, as always, to my wonderful agent, Danielle Egan-Miller!

I wouldn't have survived this last year without my family, each and every one of them. Please know how much I appreciate all your love and support!

CAN'T LET HER GO

CHAPTER ONE

Holy shit. It's her. It's really her!"

Ethan Walker glanced up from the bar in response to his business partner Russell Green's words of awe. "What are you talking about?"

"Not what. *Who*. Chelsea Harris, that's who," Russ said. "She's here."

"Who's that?" Already annoyed at having to cover a Saturday night shift for one of the bartenders, Ethan didn't have the patience for Russ going gaga over some woman. The older he got, the more Ethan hated crowds, and Words & Music was packed tonight.

"*Chelsea Harris.*" Russ leaned against the bar and frowned. "Have you been living under a rock?"

"On a farm," Ethan grumbled as he set two drafts on a waitress's tray, wishing he'd been a little less sloppy with the foam. He wiped his wet fingers on a bar towel and moved on to the next order.

"Thanks, Ethan," the waitress said with a saucy wink before whisking the booze away.

"Welcome," he mumbled in return. The last thing in the world he wanted to do was flirt with his staff. Sure, most of his waitresses were pretty damn cute. But, as his daddy always cautioned him, he kept work and fun separate. He shifted his focus to Russ. "Okay. You've got my attention now. So what's with this chick?"

"Chick?" Russ let out a snort. "You're really clueless. The last thing I'd ever call someone like Chelsea Harris is 'chick.'"

Well aware of Chelsea Harris's fame—and that she'd breezed in with her entourage about fifteen minutes ago—Ethan had some fun by jerking Russ's chain a little more. He shrugged. "Then tell me why I should know her."

"She's only the hottest thing to hit country music in the past five years." Russ's disgruntled tone and emphatic gestures made Ethan fight a grin. "Look over to high-top table eight, dipshit. You can't miss her. Hell, the woman can't seem to get a moment of peace."

Eyes already on the subject of their conversation, Ethan only shrugged again, despite the fact that nonchalant was the last thing he felt.

Chelsea Harris was gorgeous. A mane of long wavy red hair. A curvy figure, the kind he preferred. She seemed entirely unfazed by the way the people around her buzzed with excitement and took her picture with their cells. She was chatting with the two other women sitting at her table, both of whom appeared to be friendly rather than celebrity suck-ups. A rather beefy security guard kept a close eye on her, even though he wore dark clothes and was trying to blend in.

The woman clearly knew her own appeal, and she exuded confidence. From the way she laughed and gave slight nods to anyone who was able to find the courage to make eye contact, she relished her celebrity status.

A queen on her bar stool throne.

Not all stars were that comfortable in their own skin. Many tried their best to hide from press and fans until they chose the time or place to make contact. A concert. An award show. A fund-raiser. In all other aspects of their lives, they usually demanded privacy.

Not the eminent Ms. Harris. One of the reasons Ethan knew so much about her was because the woman lived her life in the open. His famous parents had been of that breed— acting as if every fan should be a best friend.

A person wanted to know where she was, what she thought, who she was with? All he had to do was pull up any social media account. *Bam.* Chelsea Harris was there. Hell, she was playing on her phone at that very moment, probably doing one of those tweet things.

Hopefully she was telling everyone to get their asses down to Words & Music. The business would always be welcome. If word got out that she'd stopped by, fans would be there waiting in hopes of seeing her the next night. And the next.

As though reading his thoughts, Russ said, "She's great for business. Hope social media is eating this up." He let out a low whistle. "She sure is a looker."

Understatement of the year. Her thick hair caught the

lights exactly right, making it appear like waves of fire rip-
pling down her back. Her gaze swept the room, settling on
the bar. When her eyes caught his, he sucked in a breath, unable to stop a physical reaction to the woman.

With a shake of his head at his own weakness, Ethan
turned away and drew another draft.

"Heard she's unattached again," Russ commented. "Kicked
that pretty boy actor to the curb from what I saw." He let
out a chuckle. "Probably wrote a song about it. She has every
other time she broke up with a guy, and they're always hits."

"Saw? Saw it where?"

Russ rubbed the back of his neck and glanced away. "On
Nashville Chat."

"You watch that garbage?" The show was nothing but gossip pretending to be news. Ethan knew it as *Nashville Shat*
since that's what he and his other partner, Brad Maxwell,
called it.

"Sometimes..."

With a snort, Ethan turned his back and sliced an orange
to garnish one of the foo-foo drinks. He was so preoccupied
thinking about Chelsea Harris and that gorgeous hair that he
nicked his finger when a feminine voice broke into his reverie.

"Ethan Walker?"

"Shit." He grabbed the bar towel again to hold against his
sliced index finger. A quick check showed it wasn't serious.

"You okay?"

The melodious voice made him glance up to find himself
face-to-face with the object of his new fixation. She leaned
down, resting her forearms on the bar, giving him a nice view

of her cleavage. Most of the patrons seated at the bar were gawking at her.

He was dumbstruck. Her eyes were to blame. Such a sparkling green, but it wasn't the color that had him transfixed. It was the intensity he found in those depths, an intensity that put him immediately on his guard.

Despite all the people staring at her, this woman was on a mission.

"You're Ethan Walker," she said. "You own this place."

Since she hadn't asked a question, he saw no need to reply.

"I'm Chelsea Harris."

Several people laughed in response to the statement, as though she had stated something so obvious it was comical. He had to resist the urge to do the same.

"I know." Those were the only words he would spare until he figured out her angle.

Her gaze wandered slowly around the cavernous Words & Music. "This place is amazing. I never saw it before—you know, when your parents ran it. But...wow. You've really done well."

"Thanks." Better to let her lead so he could figure out exactly why she was chatting him up and plying him with compliments. While she seemed genuine, he didn't trust someone with her fame.

She gestured to the two women who waited at her hightop table. "We were all talking about how great sound carries in here. And you've got that fantastic dance floor..."

He took a quick look at the people learning a new line dance from one of the club's dance instructors. "Thanks," he repeated.

Her lips drew into an annoyed line, but she quickly obliged a patron who'd worked up the guts to slide a pen and napkin in her direction for an autograph. She even murmured her thanks for the way the lady was gushing over her songs.

The security guard took a few steps forward, but Chelsea stopped him with a quick flip of her hand and a shake of her head. Then she turned her attention back to Ethan. "You really should be proud of this place."

"I am." He pulled a new drink order up on the point-of-sale screen and went about filling it. His partners—his *friends*—often told him he had a way of irritating just about anyone he came across. At that moment, he couldn't help himself. Her increasingly exasperated reactions at his clipped answers were far too entertaining.

Chelsea put her elegant hand on the bar and began to drum her bright red nails against the wood. "Do you tend bar here a lot? Or is this just a one-night stand?"

He snorted. "Definitely not a one-night stand."

"So you're here a lot? Tell me this...do you hire the talent, or is that the Hitman's job?" she asked.

"Brad hates it when people call him that," Ethan cautioned.

"Everyone in the business calls him that."

"Not to his face."

Her fingers quickened their pace.

So there was a temper to go with that red hair.

Time to end the baiting game.

After setting a glass of white wine and a beer on an empty tray, he finally directed his full attention to her. "I'd really like to know something."

"And what is that?"

"What exactly do you want from me?"

* * *

The man couldn't be any ruder if he tried, and something in Chelsea told her that was exactly what Ethan Walker was doing. Trying to aggravate her.

Well, he'd succeeded. Problem was she couldn't show him what she truly felt. Not if she was going to get her way. No, she needed Ethan's cooperation. From what she'd been told, that cooperation would be a hard-earned prize.

She'd tried to learn as much as she could before setting out to tackle her plan for her newest project. Although her assistant was supportive of her plans, she'd told Chelsea that she was crazy to even *try* to recruit Ethan Walker. His aversion to ever being a part of the country music world again was legendary.

From the moment she'd heard the duet he'd sung with Savannah Wolf, Chelsea had known that he needed to sing with her. God, the man had the most amazing voice. Besides, she didn't understand why he should be different than any of the other people she was enlisting. So far, most of the offspring of former stars had been on board and rather enthusiastic about her plans.

Of course, none of them had Ethan's reputation—a reputation that was twofold. First, he hated being reminded that his parents were Nashville stars. Second, after walking away from a budding singing career years ago, he hated anything to do with performing or recording. Period.

And yet . . . he was friendly with Brad Maxwell's fiancée Savannah. She'd gotten her start at Words & Music, and Chelsea had been so mesmerized by the video of Ethan singing with Savannah that she'd watched it too many times to count.

So he *would* perform.

But on what terms? Did he only pick up a guitar for a friend, or would a good cause—a great cause—be enough motivation?

He threw her a fierce frown. "Are you going to answer my question, or can I get back to work?"

The ill-mannered man didn't even wait for her reply and started tapping at the computer screen, all but dismissing her.

No one dismissed Chelsea Harris.

Sidling around the bar, she savored the surprised expressions of the people sitting close enough to watch her. She glanced at the drink order he'd been reading and then plucked two margarita glasses from the freezer under the counter. As Ethan stared at her, she went about preparing the drinks, much to the amusement of the crowd. Muscle memory kicked in as she found the margarita mix and ice, blended the mixture, and then salted the rims of the glasses. After pouring the drinks, she garnished them with lime wedges and set them on an empty serving tray, earning herself a round of applause.

With a smug smile, she touched the screen to pull up the next order. While she wanted to see his startled expression—to savor it—she focused on the libations she needed to make.

"What in the hell are you doing?" Ethan demanded.

Thankfully, his tone was more amused than irritated despite his choice of vocabulary.

"I would think it was obvious." She flashed a smile at a few people who laughed in response.

"I mean, why are you pretending to be a bartender?"

Chelsea let out an indignant huff. "Pretending?" She nodded toward the drinks the waiter was carrying away, wondering if pictures of her acting as the bartender at Words & Music would've hit social media yet. "Those are damn good margaritas, if I do say so myself. You know what? Name a drink."

"What?"

"Name a drink. Any drink. I can mix it."

As he continued to stare silently, she pulled three draft beers, poured two glasses of wine, and whipped up a screaming orgasm. After passing them off to a waitress, she folded her arms under her breasts and grinned at Ethan.

He grinned back, and damn if her stomach didn't plummet to her feet. The man was too appealing for her peace of mind. Her preference went toward long hair on guys, and his dark brown hair was pulled back. If it were loose, it would probably brush his shoulders.

Sublime.

The first thing she'd noticed when she'd approached him were his eyes. Not only were they a warm mahogany, but they sparkled with intelligence. Even better than his obvious physical appeal, she had no doubt that should the two of them match wits, she'd find herself with an adversary who rose to her level.

"Where'd you learn to bartend?" he asked.

"It's how I survived after college until I got my break in the business."

"You've still got the touch. You can work here if you ever need a job." He gave her another stomach-flipping smile.

"Thanks." She poured two more glasses of wine and then whipped up a whiskey sour.

"Hey, Chelsea!" a guy shouted. "Hold up the tray with the drinks so I can take your picture."

With one of her practiced smiles, she obliged the man. "Be sure and say where I'm at! Words and Music, one of Nashville's best hot spots."

"Thanks for the plug," Ethan said, although his voice was devoid of true appreciation. A shame since the man had a smooth, seductive voice.

Always one to possess a wild and far too active imagination, Chelsea had to smile at the thought of how Nashville would react should she and Ethan ever hook up. The son of "Crawfish" and Dottie Walker—Nashville royalty—and the hottest female star in country music?

Reporters would be tripping over one another to get to them the same way people were now crowding around the bar to watch their exchange.

And the charity album would go platinum.

A chuckle slipped out.

Ethan's mouth fell to a frown. "Are you laughing at me?"

"Not at all," she assured him, absentmindedly turning toward the crowd and signing a few more autographs. The action had become so perfunctory, she hardly thought about what she was doing anymore.

"Then what's so funny?"

He'd never understand how happy she was at the thought of her new album being a huge success, so she shook her head.

The frown became a scowl. "Why are you here?"

Knowing Ethan was in no frame of mind for her to even broach the topic of his recording a song with her, she scrambled for something to say. She wished they had a bit of privacy, but that was in short supply whenever she was in public. "I...um..." She nibbled on her bottom lip, flustered that his gorgeous eyes and handsome face had erased every bit of information she'd gathered on the man; information she'd hoped would help her in this important quest. "Let's see...I—"

With a shake of his head, he gently pushed her aside so he could get to his computer.

She'd lost him before she'd even asked for his help. To rescue the situation, she was going to have to lay all her cards on the table at the start of the game. This man wasn't going to be charmed or cajoled, but maybe he could be convinced if she told him the real reason she was there.

The truth was that she needed him, she needed that rich baritone singing his parents' biggest hit with her.

"I came to ask for your help," Chelsea announced.

"Finally!" Ethan set a longneck he'd just opened on a tray. "She *can* answer a question."

The snickering around them made her sigh. Was nothing in her life private?

"All right," she said, a bit peeved at him and at the eavesdroppers. "I deserved that."

"Yep."

His superior tone grated on her. For a man everyone described as kind and helpful, he seemed to know exactly how to irritate her. "My father passed away last year." The memory still felt like a knife to the heart.

"I'm sorry for your loss." Those brilliant eyes found hers, and they were full of compassion. There was sincerity in his tone.

"Thank you."

"What does losing your father have to do with me?" he asked.

"He died of cancer," she replied. "I want to do something big to honor his memory."

Ethan encouraged her to continue with a flip of his hand.

After a bracing deep breath, Chelsea said, "I'm putting together an album to raise money for cancer research. I'm singing duets with the kids of former Nashville stars, and I'd like for you to cover one of your parents' songs with—"

"No. Way." Turning on his heel, he stalked away.

CHAPTER TWO

Chelsea blinked a few times before acknowledging that Ethan wasn't coming back. She'd been prepared for Ethan's initial resistance, but she sure hadn't expected him to act like a horse's ass. Had she hit some kind of nerve?

Most kids of stars had no problem riding their parents' coattails. She'd heard Ethan was different, yet she didn't think he'd be so opposed to singing with her.

There's more than one way to catch a fish.

But was this particular fish worth the effort?

She had a sinking feeling he was going to require a hell of a lot of work.

The sad fact was that if she wanted the album to be a huge success, she needed him. With the exception of the rather cheesy pop tunes he'd released when he was a teenager, Ethan Walker had never recorded a serious song. Sure, there were some pirated copies of a duet he'd performed with Savannah Wolf on his own stage, but to get that man into a recording studio would be a coup that could help her earn a crap ton of money for cancer research.

Three more drink orders popped up on the screen. Her first inclination was to go back to her friends and get out of the place. It would serve him right to leave his customers waiting for their beverages. Maybe it would teach him a lesson about his rudeness. The problem was that if she stomped away angry, she'd lose any chance of Ethan ever changing his mind and singing with her and she'd look like a fool in front of the fans who were now crowed around the bar watching her intently. If she stayed and kept churning out drink orders, he might see it was a goodwill gesture and reciprocate by helping her out.

"As if..." The man hadn't been even remotely coy in his refusal. Her mixing a few mai tais probably wouldn't over-come his rather adamant refusal.

"As if what?" a man asked as he came up beside her.

She glanced up to find a real cutie, although he wasn't her type with his blond hair buzzed into a military cut. His body was a bit too muscular, but his smile was sincere. He'd been talking to Ethan earlier and wore a red polo shirt with the Words & Music logo embroidered over his left pec, so she as-sumed he worked there.

With a glance back to the point-of-sale screen, Chelsea sighed. "As if the bartender is coming back. I think I pissed him off too much and orders are piling up." She scrolled through the six new drink requests and sighed as flashbacks to her old job filled her mind. The scents of the booze and fried food filled her nostrils, giving her a touch of déjà vu. Rolling up her sleeves, she went to work.

The guy came around the bar and frowned at the screen. "Shit." His blue eyes were full of worry when they locked with hers. "Think you can do these?" He glanced at the crowd. "With an audience?"

"I do everything with an audience." She flipped the caps off two longnecks and set them on the bar. "I can do this, but I'll need a little help to catch up. Know much about bartending?"

"I'm a bouncer, not a booze slinger." After staring at the orders for a moment, he went to the small sink and washed his hands. "I'll do what I can, but...the fancy stuff's beyond me."

Chelsea breathed a resigned sigh. Although he hadn't asked in words, he'd practically begged with his puppy-dog eyes. At least this man would appreciate her help. "Fine. You take the beers and wines. I'll do the rest."

"Sounds good, Ms. Harris."

As she grabbed the ingredients she needed for the first order, she addressed the obvious. "Call me Chelsea. Please. But you've got me at a disadvantage. You obviously know my name, but I don't know yours."

He let out a little snort. "Of course I know your name. My name's Russ Green." He set two drafts on a tray. "I'm one of the owners of this bar."

"This place is amazing." The blender drowned out any other conversation as she got down to business.

There was work to be done, and maybe, just maybe if she kept thing running and charmed his partner enough, she'd get a payoff in the form of Ethan Walker agreeing to sing with her.

* * *

All Ethan wanted was a few moments to let his temper cool, so he stalked to the office, went inside, and slammed the door behind him.

"You break the frame, it comes out of your salary."

Scowling at his other partner, Brad Maxwell, Ethan flopped on the couch since the desk chair was otherwise occupied. "I don't get a salary, jackass."

"Okay, your profits then, numb nuts."

The comment didn't deserve a reply. Money wasn't a problem for Ethan. His parents' legacy was more than he could ever spend, even if he was extravagant, which he wasn't. Hell, they sold more records since their deaths than before, especially since the car accident that claimed their lives had seemed so damn tragic. Two of Nashville's biggest stars dying at the same time? Reporters drooled for stories like that.

Ethan scowled at the memory. Had his father not been trying to get away from some bastard photographer, the accident wouldn't have happened. For once, Crawfish wanted a bit of privacy instead of feeding the monster press, and it cost him and his wife their lives.

Fucking reporters. Still running stories after fifteen years—stories about the mess they *made.*

Had it really been that long? He'd bought the horse farm for himself when he was twenty, only a few months after he'd lost his parents. He was never able to show his father that he could make it on his own.

That thought soured his mood even more.

"What's got a bee up your ass?" Brad asked. "You look ready to bite someone's head off. What happened?" He shot a worried glance at the door. "And who's minding the bar?"

Ethan shrugged. "Beats me."

Brad raked his fingers through his hair. "Now, I know I'm only one of the owners of this place, but it seems to me you might've gone to the effort to get someone to fill in if you needed a break."

"Cut the sarcasm."

"I can't, and you know it. Seriously, Ethan...who's tending bar?"

"Maybe that woman will keep it running." That thought made Ethan smirk. No way would a superstar like Chelsea Harris bail him out—especially after he'd turned down her request.

Brad pitched his pen on the desk. "That woman? I should've known. Did you already sleep with whoever it was, or do you just want to?"

"Stop being so judgmental, you sanctimonious—"

"Oh, come off it. You know you're a player."

With an acerbic chuckle, Ethan said, "Takes one to know one."

"Not anymore. I'm a happily engaged man now, as you know."

Dismissing his partner with a wave of his hand, Ethan had better things to think about.

Such as Chelsea and why she irritated him like a bad case of poison ivy.

Women never got under his skin. Never. *Love 'em and leave 'em and don't look back.* That had always been his philosophy.

And Brad's for that matter... The two of them had enjoyed a wild ride through their twenties.

Twenties?

No, their collaboration as the biggest players in Nashville went all the way back to high school. They'd been best friends. Handsome, charming, and damn popular with the girls. Ethan had never seen a reason to change.

Brad had—even before Savannah had waltzed into his life. Now, he seemed devoted to her, loved her daughter, and had become the most boring man on the face of the planet.

It was enough to make Ethan want to hurl.

"So are you ever going to tell me what whoever she is did to piss you off?" Brad asked. "Do you even know her name?"

"As a matter of fact I do. Chelsea Harris."

Silence stretched between them for a few stilted seconds. "Did you just say 'Chelsea Harris'?"

"Yep."

"*The* Chelsea Harris?"

Ethan nodded.

"You slept with her?" Brad's question ended on a high squeak that made him sound like an adolescent in the middle of a voice change.

"I just met her," Ethan admitted.

"Your point...?"

"Stop being a dick."

The insult didn't seem to faze Brad. "So you *didn't* sleep with her. Then you're telling me that the hottest singer on the planet is in our restaurant tending the bar?" He pulled his phone out of his pocket and started tapping the screen.

"I don't know if she's working the bar or not."

"But she's here? We should get some pictures for the website."

Ethan shook his head. "Leave her be."

Brad glanced away from the screen and let out a laugh. "You really left her to pour drinks?"

That comment got a chuckle from Ethan as he pictured her becoming frantic trying to deal with the demanding waitstaff and insistent customers. If she had stayed, she'd be in well over her head by now. "Yeah, I suppose I did."

"I'll be damned," Brad said after a few more taps of his phone. He held up a picture from Twitter "At least the post mentions our bar, so it's good publicity."

Ethan barely glanced at the picture.

"Savannah's been trying to get me to write a song for her—for Chelsea, I mean."

"You don't write for anyone but Savannah," Ethan couldn't help but point out. Once upon a time, Brad had been the hottest songwriter around. But after a dry spell, he'd begun writing again when he'd met the woman who would soon become his wife.

"What can I say?" Brad grinned. "She's my muse."

"You used to write for everyone, *Hitman*." The nickname would set Brad off, but that was an integral part of their relationship—teasing unmercifully.

"You know I hate it when you call me that."

"The press calls you that all the time."

"You know better, though. They're assholes," Brad said.

Done baiting his friend and feeling much less hostility toward the cheeky Ms. Harris, Ethan got to his feet. "I better get my ass back down there. I imagine the servers are hopping mad that I abandoned them."

"I imagine the servers are probably ogling her. But you never told me why Chelsea Harris ended up behind our bar."

"She was trying to con me into singing a duet with her, so I walked away," Ethan said.

"A duet?" Brad snorted. "She doesn't know anything about you, does she? She might as well have asked for a million dollars."

"I'd be more inclined to give her that," Ethan drawled.

"Want me to go down there?" Brad asked. "I can run the bar for a while. Judging from the pictures of the crowd, she could probably use all the help she can get."

With a shake of his head, Ethan headed to the door.

"Can you believe Chelsea Harris is really mixing drinks in our bar? Priceless."

Ethan shook his head again. "The orders are probably backed up like crazy. I'll get Russ to give me a hand so I can catch up."

"Good luck with that," Brad called as Ethan left the office.

* * *

Chelsea glanced up to find a tall, skinny waitress gaping at her. She'd pulled her hair back into a messy bun, had slipped on her glasses since she hadn't worn her contacts, and was probably as wilted as a week-old flower. Definitely not how she normally looked, especially when there were cameras around, but getting Ethan to agree to help her was worth it. Besides, her publicist, Will Laurence, always told her to be more "real" around her fans.

Dropping her empty tray on the counter, the blonde said, "Oh, my God! You're her! You're Chelsea Harris."

"Not tonight, darlin'. Tonight I'm just a bartender." At that moment, all she wanted was to keep churning out drink orders until Ethan finally wandered back and she could rub his nose in how well she'd handled his bar.

The waitress, whose eyes were still big as saucers, nodded. "Can I have your autograph?"

Chelsea waved her off. "As soon as I catch up on these drink orders, I'll give you an autograph and we'll take a selfie." The best tactic to dissuade eager fans was always redirection. "How does your usual bartender split tips with the waitstaff?"

The question had the desired effect as the blonde shifted her gaze to the growing wad of bills stuffed in the tip jar.

Since Chelsea had every intention of giving all the money to the overworked waiters and waitresses, she dismissed whatever it was the waitress was explaining in response. Sure, some of that money probably belonged to Ethan. But in her opinion, he deserved to forfeit it for leaving them all in such an awkward position. He also owed her a new silk blouse since hers was ruined by booze and fruit juice stains because she hadn't been able to locate an apron.

The chatty waitress finally left with a full tray, and for the first time in almost half an hour, Chelsea was able to let her guard down a little. No new orders waited on the screen, so she went about cleaning up the considerable mess behind the bar since her friends had decided to leave not long into her "shift" as bartender. Not a surprise since they were used to her getting distracted anytime her fans gathered around her.

Russ set some dirty glasses in the sudsy water she'd drawn in the sink. "You're a helluva bartender, pretty lady."

She arched an eyebrow at his veiled flirt. "Thanks."

"Ethan should hire you. You're much better at this than he is."

Ethan's voice boomed from her left. "Kiss my ass, Russ."

Guarding her reaction, Chelsea didn't even look at him. She simply kept washing glasses, feeling a bit smug at having done such a great job.

"Where've you been?" Russ asked, his tone demanding.

"I needed a break," Ethan replied.

"If one of our bartenders left on a 'break' without someone covering, especially with this kind of crowd, we'd fire him," Russ said, piquing her curiosity as to the men's true relationship.

"I had someone covering for me." Ethan inclined his head at her.

Russ folded his muscular arms over his broad chest. "You're damn lucky she stepped in to bail you out."

As the guys exchanged a few of what she assumed were friendly barbs, Chelsea finished the dishes and checked the latest order that now waited on the screen. Ethan and Russ were co-owners of the bar. She'd also been told that the Hitman had a share in the place.

Just as she reached for a clean glass, Ethan plucked it up. "I'm back. Thanks, but you can go now." He inclined his head at the people staring at her. "Go sign some autographs."

With narrowed eyes and barely leashed anger, she fisted her hands against her hips. "You're quite welcome that I kept your bar running for the last half hour. I had nothing better to do tonight than fill in for an irresponsible guy who obviously didn't care if his customers had to wait forever to get their drinks."

Russ rushed to her, red-faced. "We can't thank you enough, Chelsea. You were amazing. If there's ever anything I can do to pay you back..."

She kept staring at Ethan, debating whether she would play the "favor" card Russ had dealt her to try to strong-arm Ethan into the duet she so desperately wanted.

Her gut told her to wait. Judging from the way he was roughly handling his ingredients, she'd be wasting her time and breath asking tonight. Much as she hated to admit it, the man might be a lost cause.

With a resigned sigh, she turned to Russ. "Glad I could help. It was kinda fun to relive my glory days. I need to head out now." She gave one last glance to Ethan, thinking it was a damn shame that a man that good looking had the personality of a wet mop.

She signed several autographs, posed for a few pictures with fans, and was almost to the door with her security guard trialing behind her when Russ came over. "Wait. Please."

She dismissed her security with a quick flip of her hand. The well-trained man faded back several paces as Russ grabbed her arm.

Her first response was to level a withering glare at him—purely a conditioned response since fans seemed to think she was public property, making Chelsea react that way whenever someone put hands on her.

The expression worked, as it usually did, and Russ's hand quickly fell away. "You never told me what you said that made Ethan stomp away."

Perhaps the man wasn't entirely a lost cause. She'd see what she could learn by picking Russ's brain. "I'm putting together an album to raise money for charity. I wanted him to sing a duet of one of his parents' songs with me—'When You Were Mine.'"

"Their biggest hit. Now I get it. No wonder he was so pissed."

"Why?"

Russ thought it over before replying. "Ethan's spent his whole life trying to distance himself from Crawfish and Dottie. You might as well have asked him to donate a testicle." He snorted a laugh. "Hell, that might've been easier for him."

So Ethan had a bad case of Celebrity Offspring Syndrome. It had to have been tough growing up in the shadow of his famous parents. She'd been able to convince or cajole the other children of stars she wanted on the album, but she'd been warned by a lot of people that Ethan would never agree. That only made him a challenge.

Chelsea Harris never walked away from a challenge.

"What do you suggest?" she asked.

"Suggest?"

"I really want him on this album. It's for a great charity—cancer research," she explained. "What do you think might win him over?"

Russ rubbed the tawny beard stubble on his chin. "I don't know...I'm not sure it's even possible. The man hates to sing."

"He hates it?"

"Maybe that was the wrong word. He *sings* all the time. He hates to sing for any reason but to please himself."

"You're confusing me," she admitted. "He performed with Savannah Wolf, right?"

Russ nodded.

"Then why won't he sing with me?"

"Savannah was his friend. He sang with her because she needed his help."

"I doubt I can make him my friend in time to record this album, especially after tonight." She considered her options—or lack thereof—for a moment and then resorted to doing what she had to do. "You know him well. Can I call in that favor and ask you to give me some hints on how to get his help with the duet?"

A frown formed on Russ's face. "I don't know..."

Chelsea clasped her hands in front of her. "I'll resort to begging if I have to. This is really, really important to me. Pretty please?"

He let out a resigned sigh, and she knew she'd won. "I'll try to help, but I can't promise anything."

CHAPTER THREE

His horse farm. The only place Ethan had ever found true happiness.

Moving slowly down the wide aisle of the barn, he stopped to greet any horse that poked a head out of a stall. Stroking each velvet muzzle and murmuring to the animals, he let contentment fill him.

The horses accepted him as he was. They didn't give a shit whether he was the son of famous singers. They didn't care if he owned a bar. All these beautiful animals knew was that Ethan took good care of them and loved them as much as they loved him.

Sure, he only owned two of the horses—Truman and Chairman—but he knew the other animals boarded at his stable well. The owners had busy lives, often finding little free time to exercise their pets or sometimes even see to their daily care.

That's where he came in. He and Joe Alvin.

Joe was a veteran of the Gulf War who'd been an employee of his family from the time Ethan had been a kid. The man had done a great job organizing the Walkers' security at their home, which was open to tourists. Seemed Joe was always there whenever Ethan needed him.

When Ethan's parents died, he'd offered Joe a pension and the chance to retire. Joe had told him he'd rather work on the farm Ethan had bought. Grateful for the help, Ethan had a nice little house built for him on the property. Now, he and Joe had an almost symbiotic relationship in caring for the horses.

With Joe's help, Ethan took on the main responsibilities of feeding, grooming, and exercising the animals. People paid him to do exactly what he wanted to do. He was surrounded by verdant fields, warm sunshine, and the scents of timothy hay and fresh straw.

Life was good.

As he led a horse named General to a set of cross-ties, he caught the sound of wheels crunching the white rock on the drive leading to the barn. Accustomed to folks coming and going, he went ahead and hooked the horse's halter to the cross-ties and opened General's tack trunk to retrieve a brush, curry comb, and hoof pick.

"Ready to get handsome?" Ethan asked the bay gelding when the horse turned his head to stare at him.

"I think he already is."

It took all of his self-control not to slam the lid of the trunk when he heard the now familiar voice. The woman was asking the one thing of him he could never give her, and it appeared she wouldn't take no for an answer. "Well, well, well. If it isn't the tenacious Chelsea Harris." He glanced up to see her grinning at him.

Why did that smile of hers hit him like a punch in the gut? The last thing in the world he needed was to be attracted to her.

But attracted he was. More than he'd thought judging by how he was responding to her physically and he hadn't even touched her yet.

"Where's your entourage?" he asked, a little annoyed at himself for the snide tone she didn't deserve.

Instead of reacting with anger, she grinned. "Flying solo today. It's a nice change of pace."

"I already told you I wasn't singing on your album," he reminded her.

She calmly took a seat on one of the trunks and watched him while he did his best to consummately ignore her. Which wasn't an easy thing to do. Her gorgeous hair was in an intricate braid. Dressed in jeans and a pink blouse, both of which hugged her voluptuous figure, she waited patiently as he worked on General.

Neither said a word until Ethan was done and had dropped the grooming tools into the open trunk. Then he spared her a glance. "Are you just here to stare at me all day?"

"Not really," Chelsea cheerfully replied.

"I can guarantee you that if you came to beg me—"

"I won't beg you."

"—to sing with you, you're wasting your time. Even more importantly," he added, "you're wasting *mine*."

"That's not why I'm here," she said. "And I have perfectly good hearing, so you can stop repeating yourself."

He strode over to stand in front of her. Staring down at her from his six-three perch, he tried to use his height to intimidate her. "Then why exactly *are* you here?"

Judging from her smile shifting to a smirk, she found him about as intimidating as a butterfly. "I need your help."

With an exaggerated sigh, Ethan put his hands on his hips and let his head fall back so he could stare at the dusty rafters. "I thought you said you heard me when I said I wouldn't sing."

"I didn't say anything about singing."

His gaze returned to her, and all his irritation vanished in wake of her beauty. The woman was exquisite. "Then what exactly do you need my help for?"

"I'm buying a horse, and I'd like you to go to an auction with me. I heard you were a good judge of horseflesh."

Chelsea couldn't have surprised him more if she'd told him she was retiring from country music. "A horse? You're here because you want a horse?"

She nodded.

"You all of a sudden just up and decided you needed a horse?"

"It wasn't 'all of a sudden,'" she insisted. "I owned a horse when I was growing up, and I miss her something fierce." Chelsea's lips lifted into a half smile as she ran her hands down her legs. "I also miss how firm my thighs were from riding."

Unable to tear his eyes from her shapely legs, Ethan tried

to dissuade her. "There's no way someone like you has time to properly care for a horse."

"From what I've heard," she almost too sweetly replied, "a lot of people who board their animals here with you are in the same boat. That's the other reason I'm here. I'd like to rent a stall—and I'd like you to help take care of my new horse when I can't."

The idea of seeing her every day actually held some appeal, until he realized that her schedule would never allow her that luxury. Although it annoyed him to admit it, he simply enjoyed looking at her.

He let his irritation with himself show, hoping she'd think it was directed at her. "From what I've heard, I'd be taking care of that horse every damn day. You're on the road all the time."

"Not anymore. Just signed a deal that's gonna keep me close to home for a good, long while. I need a rest from touring. As much fun as it can be, it's rather draining."

Ethan realized that he'd avoided country music news and gossip for so long that he knew next to nothing about her. Only a few things came to mind—mostly about her meteoric rise up the charts and her penchant for dating actors. "Nashville's home?"

Chelsea nodded and jumped to her feet to follow him as he led General back into the stall he'd cleaned out earlier that morning. "Born and bred, but my family moved to Illinois when I was in middle school. Even though we moved back here a few years ago, my Tennessee accent has faded quite a bit, but a *y'all* slips out from time to time."

After latching the gate, he turned to find her right behind him, staring up with those incredible eyes. Without a thought, he walked toward her, and she retreated until her back was pressed against the boards. His mouth hovered close to hers.

He'd dreamed about kissing her. Literally. In fact, Ethan had dreamed about a hell of a lot more than kissing Chelsea. His fascination fueled his need. But suddenly worried he might have frightened her, he began to ease back, putting some distance between them before he did something stupid.

* * *

Chelsea couldn't seem to grasp a thought, let alone hold tight to one. At that moment, all she could do was blink at Ethan and wonder what had stopped him from kissing her.

God knew she would have allowed it. How would he taste? Were his lips as firm as they appeared? Her imagination took control, and damn if her whole body didn't grow warm with need.

A logical thought finally formed.

This man is dangerous.

Just as he leaned back, she gently pushed against his chest. Her senses were reeling, and she despised feeling that she'd almost lost control. If something happened between her and a guy, *she* called the shots. She took the lead, and he damn well followed or she quickly left him behind. Whether the connection was emotional or merely physical, she always ran the show.

But Ethan didn't seem to understand the rules.

"We were discussing my buying a horse," she reminded him. His arrogant smile swept away the last of the sensual fog, giving her the strength to walk away. "The auction is this Saturday."

Ethan opened another stall, grasped a compliant horse by the halter, and led him to the aisle. After he placed the animal in cross-ties, he opened the trunk in front of the stall. "I know. I'm planning to go."

"Great. Then we can go together."

He plucked a brush from the trunk and leveled a hard frown at her. "You have no business getting a horse."

She folded her arms under her breasts and returned the scowl. How could the man almost kiss her one minute and then dismiss her the next? "That's not your call, is it?"

"It is if you want to keep the horse here."

"You're worried that I won't take good care of it?" she asked.

"If you don't, I have to pick up the slack," he said.

"A, that's not going to happen. And B"—she swept her arm down the aisle—"you don't seem to have a problem picking up the slack for a lot of other people and you get paid pretty well to do it."

He went about brushing the horse.

Unaccustomed to being so succinctly ignored, Chelsea resisted the urge to stomp her foot. She did, however, bite the inside of her cheek to keep from tossing an acerbic comment Ethan's way. Her plan had been so simple; win his friendship, then convince him to sing with her. That's what Russ had basically suggested, and since he knew Ethan a lot better than she did, she trusted his judgment. If she wanted to achieve her goal, giving Ethan the sharp side of her tongue wouldn't get her a single step closer.

Besides, she'd wanted a horse for a long time. Unfortunately, the last five years had been a brutal schedule of worldwide concerts. Now that she was settling in for what she hoped would be a long time, she could fulfill her wish—and perhaps also be able to use the opportunity to win Ethan over to her cause.

Relaxing her stance, she let her arms drop to her sides. "I'm looking for a nice mare. I went over the info on the auction site, and there are several good prospects."

The frustrating man kept right on grooming his animal.

"I'm willing to outbid anyone, but only for the right horse."

At least she got a response as he glanced her way and gave her an amused snort.

"I just don't want to spend good money on the wrong horse," Chelsea said. "I've got no experience at choosing an animal, so I'm not sure I'd be looking at the right things." She hurried to add, "I mean, I know about stuff like conformation, but..."

"So if the shoes were made to hide a bad leg, you'd know?" Ethan asked.

"Probably not," she admitted. "That's why I need you."

He smoothed the brush over the horse's backside. "I'm not cheap."

A crack in the wall. "I wouldn't expect you to be, but I've heard great things and—"

"From who?"

"Pardon?"

"Who told you these 'great things'?" he asked.

Chelsea rattled off three names, grateful she'd done her homework before she'd driven out to his farm. While the horse would be a means to an end, she would enjoy the animal and want the best care for it. Ethan, according to her sources, represented that "best care."

He took his time before aiming a curt nod in her direction.

"You said you were already planning to go to the auction?" she asked.

Another nod.

"Looking for a horse for yourself?"

"For a friend."

"Then it shouldn't be too much of a pain for you to help me look as well."

The man constantly appeared on the verge of blowing his stack. Or did he only seem that way around her? Everyone spoke of his generosity and kindness. She'd yet to see either of those traits.

With a weary sigh, he finally said, "Fine."

"Fine?" she asked.

"Fine, I'll help you choose a horse, Chelsea."

CHAPTER FOUR

The crowd at the auction was much larger than Chelsea had expected. In her mind, she'd pictured a few dozen people. Instead, there had to be close to a thousand.

She'd also underestimated the drive time, thinking an hour when it had actually taken her almost two. But then again, she had a bad habit of running a bit late, or so everyone told her. At least this once she could blame traffic and not herself.

Worried she'd missed out on the perfect horse, she reminded herself that there were going to be lots of horses sold over the next two days. Only then did she push her concern aside and focus on trying to locate Ethan in the crowd—something she assumed would be easy, considering his height.

She hadn't counted on so many of the people sitting down. Even worse, almost all of them wore hats, everything from well-loved baseball caps to expensive Stetsons. From behind, she couldn't even tell the guys from the girls thanks to the number of men sporting long hair.

How was she supposed to find him and keep a low profile?

Jerking her phone from her pocket, Chelsea texted him using the number she'd wrangled out of him before she'd left the barn. When she'd tried to use it to make firmer plans for today, he hadn't bothered replying to her texts or the one near-desperate voicemail she'd finally left. The prompt had been a computer-generated voice instead of his rich baritone, so she wasn't sure he'd even received her message. For all she knew, some teenager now had a frantic voicemail from "the" Chelsea Harris. With her luck of late, *Nashville Chat* would get a hold of it and play the rambling recording as they speculated who she'd actually been trying to reach.

Just got here. Where r u?

Then she waited and tried to blend in, unsure of whether he could hear his phone in the hubbub and feeling a bit foolish that he might've pulled a fast one to get rid of her and given her a fake number. She tried to position herself so she could see faces instead of the backs of head, but that made her feel too conspicuous. She'd only passed a handful of rows when she started to feel eyes on her. She'd developed a sixth sense for when fans recognized her, and at that moment, she knew there were people watching her.

Suddenly, her hat was pulled lower to hide her head and a familiar voice was whispering in her ear. "Come sit down."

Before she could say a word, Ethan snatched her hand and dragged her down an aisle to where two empty seats waited. "Sit," he ordered.

Instead of reflexively telling him to buzz off, Chelsea obeyed as he took the seat to her left. The less attention she drew to herself the better. "Keep your voice down," she cautioned since he sounded agitated.

He crossed his arms over his broad chest, straining the buttons on his denim shirt. "I thought you'd keep a low profile like I asked."

"Asked?" Every time she talked to him, she felt as though she were playing catch up in a conversation that had already been going on for a while. She wanted to tell him she'd been doing fine with blending in until he'd dragged her through the crowd, but she was too angry at his matter-of-fact statement. "When did you ask?"

"When I texted. Remember?"

She shook her head. "You most certainly didn't text me. I didn't get a single message from you, even though I sent several—and I left a voicemail message."

"I texted you a couple of times yesterday to tell you about the auction," he insisted.

"You didn't!"

"I did!" He let out a scoff. "It's not my fault if you gave me the wrong number."

All his response did was confuse her more. She shoved her phone in front of his face. "I gave you *this* number! It's a new phone. I have to change my number all the time to keep fans away."

"I figured," he explained much louder than necessary.

"Shh," she cautioned, glancing around to see if anyone was watching them. "Please keep your voice down."

"When I tried to return your other texts and calls, the number wasn't shown. The number you gave me must've been wrong since those texts bounced back."

"Then how did you find me now if you didn't get my text that I was here?" Now her voice was getting louder.

"I *got* your texts. Just couldn't return 'em." He flicked the brim of the hat on her head. "Wouldn't matter if I hadn't. That hair is a flashing beacon."

A beautiful woman with coal-black ponytail that she'd pulled through the back of a sky-blue baseball cap leaned over from Ethan's left. "You two need to turn down the volume a little. People are starting to stare."

Taken aback that a stranger had the audacity to scold them, Chelsea bit back a stinging retort when Ethan turned to the woman and said, "It's her fault, not mine, Joslynn."

Every ounce of Chelsea's ire shifted from Joslynn to Ethan. "My fault? *My* fault?" The man had a talent for pushing her buttons, the same talent she seemed to possess in regards to him.

Then a new feeling bloomed, one that was unwelcomed and a bit of a surprise.

Jealousy.

Ethan knew this woman. He'd brought her to the auction. Was she his girlfriend? His wife? She hadn't heard any gossip that he had either, although stories about him were few and far between. His name only popped up when some reporter was doing a tribute to Crawfish and Dottie Walker.

What right did Chelsea have to be jealous? She didn't even know Ethan. They'd only shared short conversations, which were usually quarrels. She only had one true goal—to get him to sing his parents' signature song "When You Were Mine" with her on the charity album.

No, it wasn't jealousy she was feeling. Definitely not.

Thankfully, Ethan got her right back to being irritated at him when he said, "Yes, your fault. Now can I *please* get back to the auction?"

Fuming, but refusing to give him the satisfaction of knowing he'd gotten under her skin, she tried to turn her attention to the palomino being led into the ring. No way she'd let Ethan's ill humor ruin her day.

Joslynn thrust a hand at Chelsea. "I'm Ethan's friend, Joslynn Wright. He's too rude to introduce us." The acerbic comment was given with a cheeky smile.

Chelsea shook the slender hand. "Chelsea Harris."

Another hand came from Joslynn's left. "And I'm Savannah Wolf. I doubt he'll bother introducing me, either."

One glance at the blonde's face confirmed that Chelsea was sitting close to the fastest rising new star in Nashville, a woman who was going to marry Ethan's Words & Music partner Brad "Hitman" Maxwell. It took all her self-control not to slip into fan-girl mode and tell Savannah that her first album was the greatest thing she'd heard in years.

After gathering her wits, Chelsea was finally able to speak. "Such a pleasure to meet you. Are you two looking for horses?"

Savannah was the one who replied. "My daughter wants to learn to ride." She inclined her head at Ethan. "When I told him I was going to search for a camp where Caroline could learn to ride, he pitched one of his typical bossy fits. Told me if anyone was going to teach her about horses, it would be him. So here we sit." She indicated Joslynn with a quick wave of her hand. "Joslynn's my best friend and Caroline's godmother."

Relief at that news shouldn't have felt so good, but Chelsea was thrilled that Joslynn seemed to have no tie to Ethan.

"I'm thinking of getting a horse too," Joslynn added. "Although I might wait a few more months." Her smile was infectious. "After listening to Ethan go on and on about you, Savannah and I had come along to meet you for ourselves."

Chelsea shifted her gaze between the women. "On and on? About me?" She looked to Ethan, who sat there stone-faced, watching the auction.

"Oh, yes. He's told us all about you," Savannah insisted. "How you had a horse when you were a kid."

"That you grew up in Nashville," Joslynn added.

"He was humming along to your CD on the ride here," Savannah said. "You're all he can talk about."

"I am?" Confused, Chelsea adjusted her cowboy hat, which had tilted to one side.

A growl rose from Ethan. "If you would all be quiet now, I might be able to hear what's happening in the auction. If you want me to find a couple of decent horses, I need to pay attention."

Since neither Savannah nor Joslynn appeared at all intimated, Chelsea assumed his anger was nothing but bluster. "I can't imagine what he had to say about me. He barely knows me."

And he sure as hell doesn't like me...

Savannah smiled. "You'd be amazed what he knows."

* * *

Ethan pounded a fist against his thigh, shielding his embarrassment with feigned anger. "I can't concentrate here."

Perhaps the anger wasn't so artificial after all. As the palomino was led away to be readied for the new owner, he realized he'd probably missed some fine animals while he'd been craning his neck to look for Chelsea's arrival.

If he was going to find them decent horses, he needed to concentrate. "Why don't y'all go get something to drink?"

"In other words," Savannah said with a giggle in her voice, "leave?"

"Exactly."

"C'mon, Jos. I could use some coffee." Smiling at Chelsea, she said, "Wanna come with us?"

"No, thanks," Chelsea replied. "I'm good for now." She shifted her gaze to the black mare being led to the front. "I'd like to watch the auction for a bit."

"Ethan? Want anything?" Savannah asked.

"Yeah," he replied. "For you to stop talking. I want to hear what the announcer has to say about this mare."

Although he should have been grateful for the peace that came with Savannah and Joslynn taking a break, he wasn't. The problem was Chelsea sitting beside him. Try as he might, Ethan couldn't focus on the auction. She kept getting in the way.

Her fault for being too damn pretty. She wasn't wearing anything that should be remotely attractive—just an ordinary blouse and jeans. On any other woman, he wouldn't even have noticed. Then there was the hat she'd put on her to cover a lot of that far-too-noticeable hair. A little too large, the hat kept flopping over her forehead. The way she pushed the brim back with her knuckles even made him stare.

At this rate, he'd be going home with an empty trailer.

"Ooh. She's pretty," Chelsea said.

She'd distracted him so much that he had no idea what she was talking about. "Who?"

"The gray mare." She nodded at the ring.

He had a job to do, damn it. Shifting his focus to the auction, he took the mare's measure and quickly saw the problem. "Nope."

"Why not?" Chelsea asked. "She looks great."

"Look how she favors the back right hoof."

And so it went. Horse after horse. If he saw the slightest problem, he kept Chelsea or Savannah from bidding. Ethan wasn't about to let them waste good money on the wrong animals.

A little after noon, the day's offerings began to look up.

"Savannah." He crooked his finger.

Savannah leaned closer.

He inclined his head at a horse. The bay gelding stood in the ring. Flawless legs. Shimmering coat. Bright eyes. Only three years old, the standardbred had been intended to be a racehorse, but was on the small side. Judging from the animal's laid-back temperament, Ethan figured that career wouldn't have panned out. The bay's calm acceptance of the chaos all around and the way he nuzzled the handler for attention both boded well that the horse would suit a newbie like Caroline.

"Jump in on this one," he told Savannah. "Don't you dare lose him."

"How high should I go?" she asked.

"As high as you need to."

The bidding started low, which almost made Ethan smile. He held on to his poker face for Savannah's sake. The timing was perfect since the crowd had thinned as people scuttled to the food trucks. All she had to do now was outlast two other serious bidders.

In the end, she got the gelding for half of what Ethan would have paid.

"One down," he muttered to himself as Savannah hurried off to pay for her new horse.

"One to go," Chelsea said with a lopsided grin that made him want to grab her and kiss her.

He returned the smile.

CHAPTER FIVE

The sun had already set by the time Ethan had finished the last chore of cleaning out his four-horse trailer. He shut the door and breathed a contented sigh.

Both of his new acquisitions were settled nicely in their stalls and he let the satisfaction that he'd done right by Savannah fill him. She and her daughter could now call that sweet bay standardbred gelding their new "pet."

And Chelsea. He'd helped her get a nice black gelding, and he was sure she'd made the best deal of the whole auction. Unlike the other two ladies, she'd followed him back to his barn. Despite his assurances that he could handle things, she was still hanging around.

He had to admit she was a big help, something that had come as a bit of a surprise. The singer could muck out stalls with the best of them. Had he possessed a mean streak, he could have snapped a couple of surreptitious pictures of her as she shoveled horse shit. Some entertainment rag would probably pay him good money for those shots.

It wasn't as if he'd asked for her help. He'd had every intention of getting the new animals acclimated, then he would've finished the short list of chores Joe hadn't completed. As Ethan bathed the first mare, Chelsea had rolled up her sleeves and crossed the first task off the list Joe had scribbled on the whiteboard—cleaning the stalls that Joe hadn't gotten to. Grabbing a shovel, she went to work. By the time he was feeding the new animals, she was closing the door of the last stall.

She walked over to the whiteboard and picked up the blue marker. Then she just stared at the board as if contemplating which task she should work on next.

Ethan led Savannah's even-tempered gelding into his new stall, gave him a couple of affectionate strokes, and then latched the gate to leave the horse to acclimate. When he came up behind Chelsea, it took all his self-control not to wrap his arms around her waist and pull her against him. She looked delightfully disheveled. The hat had been discarded and several strands of hair had escaped the intricate braid, making her look a little less perfect and a lot more human.

"Do you turn any of the horses out in the evenings?" she asked, pointing at the last item on the list.

"No. Too many mosquitoes this time of year," Ethan replied, unable to stop himself from grabbing the end of her braid and rubbing the silken hair between his fingers. "Big enough to carry away small children."

She chuckled softly. Melodically. "Yeah, don't want any

chance of the animals getting sick. Although . . . " She glanced over her shoulder, catching him dropping his hold on her hair. "What are you doing?"

"I was about to ask you the same thing."

"Are you playing with my hair?"

"Yep." He wanted to do a whole lot more than that, but he just couldn't trust her motivations. "Why?"

Chelsea turned to face him. "Why what?"

"Why go to all this trouble?" Ethan asked.

"What trouble?"

He folded his arms over his chest. "Stop acting so innocent."

"I'm not acting anything," she retorted, mimicking his actions.

"I don't care how many stalls you clean out or horses you bathe. I'm not recording a song with you."

"You already said that."

"Then *why*?"

* * *

Chelsea frowned, feeling guilty and not about to let Ethan know it. Sure, her primary motivation had been to get his cooperation with the duet, but she'd enjoyed their day together. The auction had been fun. Caring for the horses had been relaxing in a way she'd forgotten. She would cherish her new gelding.

She wasn't about to tell Ethan she'd begun the venture with ulterior motives. "If you're talking about my new horse—"

"What else would I be talking about?"

"I told you," she said. "I've wanted a horse for a long time."

"And *conveniently* you wanted me to help you buy one and to take care of it at the exact same time you're asking me to sing some stupid duet—"

"First of all, it's not stupid. I told you already, it's one of your parents' best songs."

"Which one?"

"'When You Were Mine.'"

"Figures," he grumbled. "I hate that one."

"It's for a damn good cause."

His arms fell to his sides as he rolled his eyes.

"Second of all, you already told me you weren't going to sing," she said.

"Who put you up to this?" he asked, and damn if that question didn't bring a warm flush to her cheeks.

"You want me to be honest?" she asked.

"That would be a change," he quipped.

"I wanted to see more of you, okay?"

"What?"

Feeling trapped in her own game, Chelsea shook her head and walked away, heading to her horse's stall. She wasn't surprised to hear footsteps following close behind. She put her hands on the stall gate and watched as her new pet contentedly munched on the messy pile he had made of the flake of fragrant hay she'd left in the stall.

Ethan was behind her. "So you really didn't get the horse just to get me to sing with you?"

That had been her plan, and she should never have

dragged Russ into it. It had been wrong to try to manipulate Ethan.

Funny thing was that she'd been telling the truth when she'd blurted out that she wanted to spend more time with him. Not only had she enjoyed hanging around with him at the auction and the barn, but their near kiss still haunted her.

So she chose to keep her original little scheme to herself. It was history and her new motive was now her driving force. If she really wanted to get to know him better, the last thing in the world he needed to know was that she'd ever—even briefly—schemed to manipulate him.

Water under the proverbial bridge. Better to leave it in the past. "No, I didn't get the horse just to get you to sing with me."

He gently moved her over enough that he could stand next to her so they could both look over the gate. "He'll be a good saddle horse once I break him."

"You'll break him yourself? Isn't that dangerous?"

"Nah. Not if you know what you're doing," he insisted. "I've broken at least a dozen other horses. I can handle yours." He inclined his head at the stall. "He shouldn't be too tough. He was a racehorse, so he's used to a harness. A saddle wouldn't be too much of a change..." A shrug. "I'll have him ready for you soon."

Her stomach rumbled loud enough to embarrass her.

A warm chuckle rumbled from Ethan. "Getting hungry?"

"Starving," Chelsea admitted.

"Wanna go get a burger?"

Turning her head, she stared at him. "Why, Mr.

Walker…Are you asking me on a date?" She winked, hoping he knew she was pulling his rather long leg.

His lip twitched as if trying to contain a smile. "What I'm asking is if you want a burger."

Her stomach answered the question before she could.

This time, he did smile. "I'll take that as a yes." Stepping back from the gate, he gestured to her. "C'mon. I know a quiet place with the best burgers in Tennessee."

* * *

Ethan loved that Chelsea ate her food with gusto instead of picking at it like most women. Then again, he was quickly discovering that there wasn't much about her that was like most women. She owned her curves, and damn, she had some nice ones.

Thankfully, the place was all but deserted, which was not a surprise at this late hour. At least she wasn't being constantly gawked at or asked to pose for selfies.

After taking a bite of her cheeseburger, she put her fingers in front of her lips as she chewed. The humming sounds of enjoyment pleased him.

"Told you they were good," he said while dipping one of his home-style fries into the glob of ketchup he'd squeezed onto his plate.

"So yummy," she mumbled through her mouthful of food.

They'd chatted about the auction and sipped their sweet teas while they waited for their meals, but Ethan was champing at the bit to find out more about her. He was wary of her motives, despite the fact she'd claimed her charity album wasn't the reason she sat with him now.

Perhaps he was just being cynical, a trait he'd honed to a fine art. Life as the child of the rich and famous had forced him to look at life—especially at people—differently than most. If someone was too attentive or too solicitous, that person always had ulterior motives. Always.

What had brought Chelsea Harris into his club was one of those ulterior motives, which made trusting her now difficult. Yet as they'd talked about the horses they'd seen at the auction and the two that they'd brought back to the farm, she seemed genuinely interested and quite knowledgeable.

Maybe she really had abandoned her quest to get him to sing the duet.

"When do you think you'll break him?" she asked.

Ethan had been lost in thought, so her question took him by surprise. "Him? Oh...the gelding. I'll start in a few days. Might take a few weeks to make him ready for you."

She huffed out a breath. "Just get him to tolerate someone sitting in a saddle, and I can take over from there."

"I don't know...Some animals need a lot of time before they can handle an inexperienced rider."

"I already told you, I used to have a horse. I've ridden plenty."

"Not in a long time. Plus, that doesn't mean you can handle a green horse that's barely broken."

Her eyes flashed as though she smelled a challenge. "Wanna bet?"

Since he knew she was biting off more than she could chew,

he shook his head. "I'm not letting you break your neck on my farm. Think of the press."

"You seem to have a habit of underestimating me." She dipped a fry in ketchup and took a bite.

"When did I underestimate you?"

"How about when you abandoned me at the bar?"

The memory made him grin. "You're right. I didn't think you could handle it."

"But I did. And I can ride a lot better than you think," she said with a decisive nod.

He shook his head in response. "I'm still not going to let you break your neck on that gelding."

"He has a name," Chelsea said. "You don't have to keep calling him 'that gelding.'"

"You want me to call him Keystone Meadowland Hamlet?" Ethan teased. "That'll be fun to text whenever I need to tell you something about him."

He was rewarded with her beautiful smile. "How about we shorten that to Hamlet?"

"Fine. That'll save me time."

"Where did the Keystone Meadowland come from anyway?" she asked.

"Keystone is the standardbred farm that bred him," he replied. "They always put their farm in the name of any of their foals. Most likely, the Meadowlands came from where his sire raced a bunch."

Chelsea nodded and took her napkin from her lap and set it on her nearly empty plate. "I'm definitely full."

Finishing the last of his fries, he pushed his plate to the

side. "Yeah, I've never gone away from this diner hungry. Guess you don't want a piece of pie, huh?"

"Tempting as that sounds, there's no room left."

The waitress was there only a few moments later, gathering up the empty plates before plucking the bill from her apron pocket.

Chelsea and Ethan reached for it at the same time, leaving them both holding one end of the paper.

"My treat," she said, tugging gently. "My way to thank you for helping find Hamlet."

He shook his head and pulled back. "My way to thank you for cleaning the stalls."

Neither would surrender the bill, and the waitress just stood there, her gaze shifting between the two. After a long period of silence, she cleared her throat, causing both of them to look at her. "Might I suggest you go Dutch?"

Every time he saw Chelsea smile, Ethan wanted to smile in return. The woman was simply too lovely for his peace of mind.

"Good idea," she said, releasing her hold as she reached around to fish something out of her purse.

While she was occupied, Ethan deftly took his wallet out of his pocket, grabbed three twenties to overtip as usual, and handled them to the waitress. "Keep the change."

Chelsea set her girlie wallet on the table. "Hey, no fair! I was going to pay my share."

Sliding out of his side of the booth, he held his hand out to her. "I'll let you have the check next time."

After quickly putting her wallet back in her purse, she took his hand and stood. "Fine. I'll hold you to that."

The waitress headed behind the counter with the dirty dishes. Her absence left Ethan and Chelsea alone in the empty diner.

She slung her purse over her shoulder and turned only to run right into him because he hadn't moved a step. "Sorry." Instead of backing away, she tilted her head to stare up into his eyes as she laid her hands against his chest.

He wondered if she knew exactly how tousled she looked. A large amount of her curly hair had escaped the braiding and there were smudges of dirt on her shirt and jeans. Any reporter finding her now would have a heyday getting pictures of the beautiful Chelsea Harris looking like she'd spent the day in a barn—which she had.

He shouldn't want to kiss her. But he did, and the fact she was less than perfect now made her even more attractive to him. She wasn't some celebrity, some singing sensation. No, she was human, a woman who'd worked side by side with him and didn't freak out over getting a little horse shit on her boots.

Oh yes, he wanted to kiss her.

His arm snaked around her waist and gently pulled her closer against him as he lowered his head and—

The bell hanging on the diner door jingled, the sound as loud as a gong as it rang in Ethan's brain, forcing him to release Chelsea and take a step back. There was no way he was getting involved with a celebrity. Ever.

Her red brows knit and a frown bowed her lips.

"I need to get back to the farm," he said, turning his back to see two men walking into the diner. "It's getting late."

"Fine," she said.

"I need to get up early to feed the horses." Damn if his tone wasn't defensive. He took a calming breath. "Are you coming to the farm tomorrow?"

She shook her head and he was surprised how disappointed he felt.

"Why not?"

Her eyes widened at his demanding tone. "I'm rehearsing with Chuck Austin tomorrow. We're singing his mother's song 'Can't Let You Go' for the charity album. He wanted to run through it a few times before we record in a couple weeks. Then I've got a show at Black Stallion. In fact I'm there the next two nights."

The album. He should've known. That, and she was singing on their biggest competitor's stage. "So you won't have time for Hamlet."

She fisted her hands against her hips. "I'll be out as often as I can."

"I guess we'll just have to wait and see."

* * *

Although it was late, Chelsea called her mother as she drove home. Sure, she might be hovering a bit, but she wanted to help her mother through her loss as much as she could. Chelsea missed her father, and she knew what her mother was going through was even more devastating.

It wasn't like she could count on Tony or Josh to stay in touch. Her brothers were sweet guys, but both lived too far away to see the family much. She had no idea if they called their mom as often as she did, but she was the only daughter. She felt responsible for any nurturing that needed to be done.

Betsy Maddox picked up on the first ring. "Hello, sweetheart."

"Sorry to call so late, I was just thinking about you. Did you have a good day?"

"I'm better today. Sorry about being so needy yesterday."

This sweet, caring woman had lost her husband of thirty-four years, the love of her life, and she was apologizing because she'd called her daughter a couple of times to say she was lonely? "You can call whenever you want, Mom. I only wish there was something more I could do for you."

"You're such a blessing."

"So are you. Guess what?"

"What?"

"I got a horse today," Chelsea announced.

"Oh, how wonderful," her mother said, sounding as sincere as always. "I'm so glad you won't be on the road so much for a while. I missed you so much."

What Chelsea couldn't say in response was that she still nursed guilt for not being home more often when her father had been ill. Breaking stadium contracts was akin to financial suicide. Even though it had cost her, she'd found a way to be with her father those last precious weeks. But then she'd needed to finish her tour and she wished she hadn't felt so bad about leaving her mother.

"You're awfully quiet," Betsy said.

"I was just thinking about all the times you and Daddy came to watch me riding Biscuit when I was little."

"Well, then, I'll have to get out to wherever you're keeping that new horse and see if you remember how to ride."

"That would be nice."

"How are the plans for the charity album going?" her mom asked.

"They're going well," Chelsea replied. "Except...I can't get the Walkers' son to sing with me."

"Why on earth not?"

My question exactly. "He doesn't like performing. I think he hates having been in the public eye when he grew up. He doesn't want anything to do with recording."

"As sweet and charitable as those people were," Betsy said, her disdain plain, "I can't believe their son wouldn't help you out."

"I need to talk to him more about why I'm doing the album," Chelsea admitted. "Next time I go to the barn to see my horse, I'll try to talk to him."

"Why would he be at the barn with your horse?"

"Because he helped me buy it, and it's stabled in his barn."

A moment passed before Betsy asked, "What aren't you telling me, Chelsea Lorraine?"

I like the guy. "Nothing, Mom. I just wanted to spend a little more time with him to try to talk him into the duet."

Her mother let out a disbelieving snort. "I think there's more to it."

Chelsea wasn't about to discuss her Ethan infatuation with her mother. The poor woman surely didn't want to hear about relationships after all she'd been through. "If there ends up being more, I'll be sure and let you know."

Another snort.

"I'm glad you had a good day, Mom. Talk to you tomorrow."

CHAPTER SIX

Standing on his back porch, Ethan took another sip of his black coffee. It was particularly strong this morning because he'd had trouble sleeping the night before. A redheaded temptress haunted his dreams, making him feel like a hormonal adolescent. To get some shut-eye, he'd finally taken matters into his own hand and yet that had only sated his body. Nothing could calm his thoughts.

Tendrils of steam rose from his cup and snaked from his nose every time he exhaled. Autumn was setting in hard this morning, and his backyard was a patchwork of frosted grass. At least the day would warm nicely, as it always did in Tennessee.

About to head to the barn and get his day going, Ethan stopped when he heard the steady rhythm of a horse cantering. Weekends tended to bring owners out to check their horses and perhaps even give those horses a bit of exercise. They just didn't tend to show up so early.

Thinking Joe was starting turnouts or giving one of the animals a ride, Ethan quickly drained the rest of his coffee. Back in the house, he set the empty cup in the sink, grabbed his jacket, and headed to the barn.

Joe wasn't there, and a glance down the long aisle showed the door on the other end of the barn wide open and only one stall empty. Hamlet's. Checking the board, there was no X next to the stall number to show that Joe had taken the gelding to turn out in one of the paddocks. Surely he wasn't stupid enough to ride the new horse without knowing whether he was broken.

Then the black appeared in the open door with a rider on his back. Even though the orange glow of the rising sun was behind them, he knew the person astride Hamlet was Chelsea. Not only was her shape easy to recognize, he knew no one else would have the guts to try to ride an unbroken horse, especially bareback.

At a bouncy trot, she rode up the aisle toward Hamlet's stall, where she slid off the black's back and led him to the cross-ties. Dressed in a denim coat with fur trim, dark jeans, and a pair of tan leather gloves, she didn't seem at all fazed by the October chill. Her nose was red, as were her ears, but she didn't seem to mind. "Good morning," she said sweetly.

Ethan held the bridle as she slipped it off and deftly put on the halter. He slung it over his shoulder and then latched the left cross-tie to Hamlet's halter while she attached the right.

"I thought you said you weren't coming today," he said.

"I changed my mind," she replied with a smile as she doffed the gloves and shoved them in her coat pockets.

"You took a big chance riding him, especially bareback," he scolded.

"I found out he was already broke to bareback." She shrugged. "I don't have a saddle yet anyway."

Hanging the bridle on the hook outside General's stall, Ethan couldn't help but point out, "That didn't stop you from borrowing a bridle."

"Since General's your horse, I didn't think you'd mind. Saddles are another story. I have no idea what belongs to whom in the tack room. Besides, Shellie told me he wasn't saddle broke."

"Who's Shellie?"

"The groom who took care of him at Keystone Farm."

"How do you know that?"

Chelsea went to General's tack trunk. "May I borrow your brush? I need to do some shopping for all his gear soon, if you can recommend a place."

"Why ask? You already helped yourself to his bridle," Ethan replied. His temper had soured, but he wasn't sure exactly why. Maybe he was mad because he couldn't impress her with his machismo by breaking her horse.

"I'm sorry," she said. "But—"

He waved away whatever she was going to say. "If you say 'but' after 'I'm sorry,' then you're not really sorry."

The comment brought a smile to her lips. "You're right. I'm *not* sorry. I borrowed a bridle for half an hour. It's not like I committed a cardinal sin. Add ten bucks to my stall rent to make up for it." She cocked her head to consider him as he sat himself down on one of the trunks. "Why are you so pissy this morning? Not enough coffee?"

He put his hands on his hips. "You don't even know me well enough to know if I drink coffee."

She flicked the brush over Hamlet's haunches. "Lucky guess. I know without enough coffee I'm as mean as a bear whose hibernation was disturbed."

The sweet southern lilt to her voice charmed a grin from him, and he relaxed his stance. "That mean, huh?"

"Probably worse." She brushed her long braid over her shoulder. "In my case, the hair says it all. At least that's what my parents always said."

"So the red's natural?" he teased.

All she did was keep smiling. "Do I look like I got it from a bottle?"

What a ridiculous conversation, yet he loved talking to her. "I have to admit, if it's not yours, it looks pretty damn natural."

"If I had my purse with me," she said, "I'd show you pictures of my dad and my brothers. Then you wouldn't have single doubt."

"All gingers?"

"Oh yeah."

"You still haven't told me how you knew Hamlet was rideable," he reminded her.

"I posted that I'd bought him, and the groom recognized the name. Shellie messaged, and we talked about the things he likes and doesn't like. Which reminds me, I need to get strawberries. According to her, he loves them."

"So she used to ride him?" he asked.

"Yep. Said he loved to trot around at the farm all the time.

She just never tried a saddle. She also said he couldn't get the intensity he needed to be a racehorse, which means you were right about him. He'll be a great pet." Tossing the brush back into the trunk, she grabbed a comb and went about working through Hamlet's thick tail. The horse was docile, even turning from time to time to watch her. Chelsea rewarded him often with friendly pats on his muscular rump. "So where's the best place to get a decent saddle and some tack for my new guy?"

"New or used?" Ethan asked, expecting her go diva and demand the best.

"I'm not particular," she replied. "As long as it's in good condition, I honestly don't care." She ran her fingers along the tattered halter that Hamlet had worn when they'd picked the horse up after the auction. Since all animals were supposed to be provided one by their previous owners, most supplied one that wasn't in the best shape. "Anything's gotta be better than this."

The woman constantly surprised him. Most of his owners were wealthy, and they always bought the most expensive stuff around. A shame when broken-in saddles were often better for new riders. "I know of a friend who's got a great saddle that I think will suit you. Pretty sure she's ready to sell it."

A red eyebrow cocked. "She?"

The note of jealousy in the way she said the word made him happy. God only knew why, but it did.

"Abigail Cameron. Lives down the road. I'll ask her about it. I imagine you'll get a decent price."

"Sounds good." Finished with the tail and mane, she put

the comb back in the trunk. "Can I mooch some fly spray? Sorry to be so needy."

Ethan went to the supply cart by the whiteboard and came back carrying the large bottle of spray that Joe mixed himself from vinegar and eucalyptus oil. "You're not mooching. I'd be spraying him before I turned him out anyway. Besides"— he shrugged—"I don't like the commercial brands around my animals. We use this instead." He thrust the spray bottle at Chelsea.

She gave a delicate sniff of the bottle. "Eucalyptus?"

A grin bloomed as he nodded and admitted, if only to himself, he'd totally misjudged the woman. "Plus vinegar. How many horses did you have?"

"Only one of my own." She shielded Hamlet's eyes and pumped the trigger a couple of times over his head, sending a light mist of fragrant protection over his face. "Do you have a stick for his eyes?"

While she gave the animal a good coating of fly spray, he grabbed the waxy stick that Joe concocted to use around the horses' eyes to keep flies from pestering them while they enjoyed the sunshine. After Chelsea used it gently around the horse's big brown eyes, she gave the stick back to Ethan with her murmured thanks.

"Which paddock?" she asked as he put the spray and stick away.

"I'll show you."

Leading her horse, she followed Ethan down the white gravel road to the grid of large turnout paddocks. He was especially proud of how much room he gave his horses to simply enjoy being horses. They were outside animals that relished their time out of their stall, and he made sure none of them lingered inside unnecessarily, especially on sunny days.

Hamlet started sidestepping when he saw the open areas, clearly knowing he was going to get some free time to romp and was showing his excitement.

Worried that she might have trouble with the large horse, Ethan cautioned, "Hold tight to that lead rope or you'll lose him—or get your foot stomped."

"I know. I've got him." She tightened her grip as he opened the gate to Hamlet's assigned area. Like a pro, Chelsea led the horse through the gate, snapped off the lead rope, and then let the animal go.

After kicking up his back heels, Hamlet loped the entire length of the field as Ethan and Chelsea laughed.

"I imagine being a racehorse that he spent far too much time in a stall," he said.

"You're probably right." She turned to give him a beautiful smile. "He's never going to have to worry about that again."

"You'll spoil him rotten."

"Damn right." A quick check of her watch made that smile vanish. Turning on her boot heel, she marched back to the barn, and he followed right behind. "I need to clean out his stall," she said, "then I gotta run."

"Rehearsal, right? For your duet album?"

All she did was nod and pick up her pace.

Back at the barn, she hung up the lead rope. When she reached for the manure shovel, Ethan put his hand over hers.

"I'll take care of the stall. You don't want to smell like horse shit when you meet Chuck Austin."

She released her hold on the handle. "You know him?"

He nodded as he carried the shovel to the stall and leaned it against the gate. Fetching the empty wheelbarrow, he rolled it up to the stall. "Our paths have crossed."

"Sounds like there's a story there."

There was, but he wasn't about to tell her how he and Chuck—together with Brad—had partied hard on more than one occasion. Although it would be easy for Chelsea to learn all about Ethan's rather colorful past, he didn't want to air his dirty laundry to a woman he was beginning to like.

As a friend, he reminded himself, knowing it for a lie the moment the thought crossed his mind. There was something about her that drew him, and he found himself unhappy that she was leaving, especially to hang out with Chuck Austin.

He had to keep reminding himself that she was a celebrity and that she came with baggage. The press had the power to destroy the lives of people in the public eye. He wasn't about to set himself up for disaster the same way his parents had.

"Did I say something wrong?" she asked.

He glanced over to see her brows drawn together. "Nah. Just thinking about all I've got to do today."

"Well, okay then..." Another look at her watch. "I really should go. I need a change of clothes." She took several steps away before turning back. "Thanks for cleaning the stall. See you tomorrow morning?"

"I'll be here." *Waiting for you.*

CHAPTER SEVEN

Ethan tugged on the brim of his hat, trying to keep a low profile.

Russ, on the other hand, seemed to have something to say to just about every person they passed. The guy was too damn sociable for his own good.

Still having no idea why he'd invited Russ along for the ride, Ethan kept moving through the crowd to get to the empty table waiting for them. All it had taken was a call to the Black Stallion's owner to finagle a reserved table so he could catch one of Chelsea's shows. Lying to himself that he was only there on a scouting trip to determine whether she would make a good headliner at Words & Music, he took a seat and tried to blend into the wall.

But Russ was waving at someone across the way, making a racket as though he had something important to say to anyone he knew. By the time he finally took his seat, the opening act was wrapping up to lukewarm applause.

That didn't bode well. Chelsea was facing a cold crowd, and Ethan felt a little sorry for her. Back when he'd sung—in another lifetime—he'd always had a troop of screaming girls there to watch him. He'd been nothing but a gangly teenager who found himself on the cover of *Teen Heartthrob* every other issue. It was embarrassing even to think about. The mullet. The tight pants. The ridiculous bubblegum tunes. No one cared what songs he wanted to sing or that he truly had talent. All that mattered was whether he looked the part.

The whole thing had been his parents' idea, wanting him to be a teenage sensation. They'd figured it was simply the next step in their legacy, having their only child become a recording star in his own right. So instead of letting him sing the country music he loved, they'd hired some "handler" to look at the other ludicrous guys who seemed to draw adolescent females by the millions. That man had picked everything from Ethan's clothing to his songs.

After two hits that reached *Billboard*'s top twenty, Ethan had threatened to call it quits, despite his mother's protests and his father's displeasure. They'd begged. They'd pleaded. They'd even tried to bribe. Ethan had wanted nothing to do with being a star and had absolutely no intention of living the way his parents lived. They had no privacy. None. Everything they did was covered by the press. "Crawfish" Walker couldn't take a dump without it ending up in some rag of a publication.

Then his parents died. Out for a quiet evening on their anniversary, they'd been hounded by a rude photographer who kept insisting on butting into their time alone. Crawfish had finally gotten so fed up, he'd escorted Dottie to their car and left. The photographer gave chase as though any picture he could get would be worth a fortune.

Crawfish wasn't one to give up easily. In an attempt to ditch the photographer, he'd kept increasing his speed until he lost control of the car and swerved into the oncoming lane. Ethan's parents had been hit head-on by a delivery truck, and the photographer who'd caused the wreck hadn't even been charged with a crime. The cost of fame for his parents had been their bleeding and broken bodies.

And Ethan's father had died before Ethan could show him that his goal of owning a horse farm could be every bit as fulfilling as singing some syrupy songs for a bunch of teenaged girls.

Without his parents around to force the issue, Ethan had put an immediate halt to his singing career. He'd spent the rest of his life trying to distance himself from his musical persona—and his parents' fame. He had no intention of spending his life evading the vultures of the press that had already cost him far too much. It wasn't easy to maintain his privacy. Even though they were gone, their will arranged for their home to continue to provide the annoying guided tours for the Walkers' fans. When he was growing up, he couldn't so much as take a shower without worrying about some rabid devotee drifting away from a tour and trying to corner him when he was butt naked.

Now, every single time he picked up his guitar, he couldn't help but be reminded of his shitty past recordings and what a fool he'd been to follow his parents' orders and sing. If anyone even mentioned his former "career," he bristled like a pissed-off porcupine. Perhaps one day he could look back on that time with nostalgic humor, but even thinking about it caused embarrassment that was close to unbearable.

Fifteen years later, that day still hadn't arrived.

"Ladies and gentlemen..." The MC waited for the crowd to settle a bit. "It's time for our headliner. Back home again, the winner of CMA's Female Vocalist of the Year for two years running, Nashville's own Chelsea Harris!"

The music swelled, the sound of a steel guitar leading the charge as Chelsea came out from stage left, waving to the crowd. Dressed in a red shirt covered in glittering beads, she looked every inch the star. Her hair was loosely pinned up with wisps of curls escaping to frame her face. She'd chosen a wireless mic, barely visible as it snaked from behind her ear to rest to the left of her pretty mouth.

"It's so good to be home again! Let's get this party started!"

Her shout was met by thunderous applause, whistles, and boot stomping. The crowd was no longer cold as she launched into a song, and all Ethan could do was watch.

* * *

Chelsea felt the crowd's excitement thrumming through her, giving her strength and helping her brace herself to sing. The intro to the old Barry Manilow hit "It's a Miracle" filled her. She'd chosen it for two reasons. First, because she was well known for turning old songs upside down, giving them a new country beat and introducing them to a new generation. Second, because the words were perfect. As the lyrics said, she'd been just about everywhere, but coming home meant more to her than the people watching her could know. So she tried to tell them in song.

Heart pounding, she soaked in the smiles and the cheers, letting them fire her blood. There was no high like performing. Nothing else could make her feel so transcendent. Alcohol. Men. Buying the most expensive shoes she could find. None of them matched singing, especially to a crowd so happy to have her with them.

Venues like the Black Stallion were her favorite. Sure, having an arena full of people was thrilling. But to see every face, to hold that eye contact, to toss a wink or a smile at someone close was better. Whenever she saw someone singing along, her heart soared.

The song ended to raucous applause, and Chelsea smiled at the crowd before launching right into her latest hit, "Every Saturday Night," a cheerful song with a strong beat to get the people even more rowdy.

And then disaster happened.

In all her years performing, she'd only stumbled over lyrics once—in her high school talent show when she'd seen her father. He'd told her he had to work overtime again that night, and she hadn't expected him to come. Yet she'd seen him trying to sneak in the back of the auditorium as though not wanting to disturb her. Her next verse had become a muddled mess, but she'd recovered when he gave her one of his grins and a thumbs-up.

Despite her bobble, she'd won first prize.

Now, singing a song she'd warbled close to a hundred times, she lost track of the lyrics when her gaze found Ethan Walker sitting at one of the farthest tables with Russ at his side.

Frantic, she picked the words back up thanks to Jasmine, one of her backup singers. With an almost imperceptible nod of appreciation, Chelsea finished the song, doing her best to ignore the men.

No, not men. *Man.*

On stage, she had a job, and that job didn't include fretting over Ethan and worrying about whether Russ would open his trap and tell him that he'd helped her concoct their stupid plan.

Fortified by the audience's appreciation when she ended the song, she went back to doing what she did best.

She entertained the crowd by singing her heart out.

* * *

After Chelsea sang two encores, Ethan watched her bow one last time and exit the stage. He'd give her a little time to rehydrate and relax, then he'd make the perfunctory trip backstage to offer his compliments. She'd earned it.

"That was a great show," Russ said.

"Yep," was all Ethan would say. The show hadn't been great; it had been the best he'd seen in years. Chelsea was a force of nature, and she blew away the crowd like a category five hurricane.

When Russ started to stand, Ethan grabbed his shirtsleeve and jerked him back into his seat.

"What gives?" Russ asked. "Thought we were going backstage after the show."

"You've got to give her a little time. A performance like that is beyond draining. Let her get something to drink and decompress." Ethan glanced at his watch. "Ten minutes. Maybe fifteen. Then we'll head back there."

The owner of Black Stallion, Robert Campbell, came weaving his way through the crowd, which was rapidly dwindling now that the show was over. When he reached Ethan, Ethan stood to shake Robert's offered hand. Russ followed suit.

Robert leaned a hip against their table. "So what d'ya think? Great show, wasn't it?"

"Hell, yeah," Russ replied. "Chelsea Harris is something else."

"And she's here for one more show next weekend," Robert said, his chest puffing with pride. "Might just give you boys a run for your money."

Ethan had to resist the urge to join the pissing match Robert was trying to start. "Chelsea is quite a ticket," was all he'd concede. The Black Stallion could hold almost as large a crowd as Words & Music, and having Chelsea Harris as a headliner was a coup. But in the long run, Words & Music brought in more people and had a better reputation. No need to rub Robert's nose in it.

Russ wasn't quite so contained. But then again, he never was. "You've got Chelsea two nights. We've got Savannah Wolf the rest of the year. I'd say we have a leg up on you, Robbie."

"Yeah . . . well . . . That's what happens when one of the owners is going to marry his star performer." Looking near a pout, Robbie suddenly perked up. "We'll take you down when we hit the softball field again. We're bar champion three years running." Then he laughed. "Maybe I can get Chelsea Harris to play shortstop for us. What d'ya think?"

It was Russ who replied before Ethan could. "Not happening. She'll be far too busy."

"How do you know that?" Robert asked.

"She told me she's got a lot of work to do on a charity album," Russ said.

Robert cocked his head. "Since when did you get to be her best friend?"

The cocky smile on Russ's face put Ethan on guard. "Since she came to ask my help."

"Help?" Robert asked. "With what?"

Russ cuffed Ethan on the shoulder. "Just needed a way to open the door to my boy here."

A waitress was trying to get Robert's attention. He nodded in her direction. "Gotta go. Need to keep my place running smooth." A motion to the waiter who'd been serving Ethan and Russ. "Give these guys another drink," Robert told him. Then he turned back to Russ and Ethan. "I've got the tab for tonight. Catch you two later." He trotted toward whatever glitch needed his attention.

"What can I get you gentlemen?" the waiter asked.

"Nothing," Ethan replied before Russ could. "We're getting ready to leave."

Plucking a twenty from his wallet, Russ handed it to the waiter. "Tip's on me."

Only when they were alone again did Ethan try to pin Russ down on the things he'd said to Robert. "What exactly did you mean?"

"About what?" Russ looked confused.

"About giving Chelsea Harris a way to me?"

"Oh, that. It was nothing. I was just braggin' to piss off Robbie."

"I've got no problem with that," Ethan said. "But you didn't answer my question. Why exactly did she need to...as you put it...'open the door' to me?"

As if he suddenly was uncomfortable answering the question, Russ pushed his chair back and popped to his feet. "She's got to be ready to see us by now."

Ethan was quickly losing his temper as an icy fear began to inch up his spine. He'd allowed himself to become friends with Chelsea because he'd trusted her when she said she had no ulterior motive in being at his farm. All she wanted was a horse.

Seemed as though he might have been wrong. Dead wrong.

If the train of thought racing through his head now was correct, she'd lied right to his face. "She wanted your help to get me to sing with her, didn't she?" Ethan asked.

"Ah, c'mon, Ethan." Russ took a step toward the stage. "Let's go tell her what a great show it was."

"Answer the question." Ethan regretted his demanding tone when several people turned to stare at him.

Russ frowned. "She's doing the album for charity. For her dad."

Anger churned Ethan's stomach and it dawned on him he

wouldn't be so pissed off if she hadn't gotten under his skin. Normally, he'd brush an episode like this aside and chalk it up to something a typical Nashville phony would do—try to pretend to care for him just to get his voice on some album.

Problem was that he'd thought Chelsea Harris was different, that she honestly wanted to get to know him better. For the first time in just about forever, he'd given someone his hesitant trust only to have it stomped into the mud.

While his first impulse was to get the hell out of Black Stallion and go home to down a few beers, Ethan decided it would be more fulfilling to confront her now, after such a great show. With any luck, he'd be able to get to her enough to ruin her night. Then he'd tell her to take her horse and get the hell out of his barn—and his life.

"You coming?" Russ asked.

"Wouldn't miss it for the world."

* * *

A knock on her stage door didn't surprise Chelsea. Ethan had to know etiquette dictated that he stop by and commend her on her performance. With the exception of her bobble of the second song, she was pretty sure she'd left her fans satisfied. Yet she found she was more concerned about whether he'd enjoyed her show than she was about anyone else in that audience.

"Come in," she said, finding herself a bit breathless at the thought of Ethan coming to her. This little infatuation could easily get out of hand if she didn't nip it in the bud. Yet it had been so long since she'd found a man who liked her simply for being herself rather than being *the* Chelsea Harris. If she was infatuated, so be it. She'd take the time to see exactly where that road would take her.

The door opened to Russ, who had an enormous smile on his face. He strode across her dressing room and shook her hand hard enough to rock her whole shoulder. "You were great."

"Thanks."

Her gaze drifted over his shoulder to see Ethan standing in the doorway, his shoulder casually leaning against the frame. His arms were folded over his broad chest, and his face was an unreadable mask.

"Hi, Ethan," she said. "Did you enjoy the show?"

The only reason she knew he'd even heard her was because he gave her a curt nod.

Russ gushed like a longtime fan. "You sounded great. And damn, you picked some great songs."

Ethan gave his eyes a roll, probably at Russ's inability to find any adjective other than "great." His silence weighed heavy on her.

"Thanks, Russ. I appreciate it." She had to gently extract her hand from his enthusiastic grip. Then she carefully stepped around him to move closer to Ethan. "Would you like to go someplace quiet and have a drink with me after I get changed? Helps me unwind after a performance."

She hadn't planned to be so brazen in asking him to spend time outside the barn with her, but something about the way he was looking at her—*glaring* at her—made her uneasy. So far, she'd been convinced they could become friends. Perhaps even something more if she bided her time and slowly got him to relax that tight guard he kept on himself.

He arched a tawny eyebrow. "A drink? You want to have a drink with me?"

Chelsea nodded, although the unusual tone of his voice made the hairs on the back of her neck rise in warning. "Sure. We can talk horses and—"

Ethan's rude snort interrupted her.

"What?" she asked, her gaze shifting from Ethan to Russ, who now seemed agitated.

"Chelsea," Russ said, laying a hand on her arm. "Ethan's a bit . . . miffed."

"Miffed? At me?" Her stomach plunged to her feet.

His eyes on his shoes, Russ put his hands in his back pockets. She'd seen naughty children who appeared less guilty. "Yeah . . ."

"Russ told me everything." Ethan unfolded himself to his full height, arms at his side with his hands fisted.

"Everything? What are you . . ." As she closed her eyes, she felt as though someone had shoved a hand into her chest and squeezed her heart. "About my getting the horse to get closer to you."

"To get me to sing with you," Ethan said through a clenched jaw. "That was fucking sneaky of you. I'd expect no less from a . . . *star* who always gets her way."

Regret was a tough bite to swallow and it nearly choked Chelsea. There were so many times when she could've been honest with him and told him why she'd started this little game—and that somewhere in playing that game the rules had begun to change.

Taking a few steps toward him, she held her breath in hopes he wouldn't storm away before she could explain. "Ethan . . . if we could go somewhere and have a drink, then we can talk."

"There's only one thing we need to talk about, *Ms. Harris.*"

Hating and yet deserving his snide tone, she recited the question he was prompting her to ask like some line in a play. "And what exactly is that, *Mr. Walker?*"

"Your horse. You've got two choices."

The raw anger in his voice hurt, but she accepted it as her due. This man valued trust above all else, and although it had only been a venial sin, she'd lied to him. Oh, yes it was her due.

But she also deserved a chance to explain herself. "Ethan, please . . ."

"First, you get your horse the hell out of my barn."

"Or?"

"Or you sell him to me. I'll give you what you paid plus five hundred for your troubles."

"I don't want—"

Ethan wouldn't let her finish. "You've got twenty-four hours to decide."

And then he was gone.

CHAPTER EIGHT

Ethan was still angry when he greeted the rising sun with a cup of coffee. Still angry and...

Hurt?

No. Not over a woman he'd only known such a short time. Women. He could take 'em or leave 'em. And he'd never let one get to him. Ever.

But this one had, and look what he got for it. Angry and...

Hurt.

Chelsea deserved his anger. He'd believed she'd been different than the other fakes in Nashville. Thinking she was something unusual. Something special.

He'd been wrong.

Why was he still so bitter? Hell, he was ready to punch something. Last night, he'd come home and needed to burn off some energy. Joe had left the four-horse trailer full of bags of pine chips that he was going to start using in stalls, so

Ethan had hauled every stinking one of them into the barn, piling them in an empty stall. Sweaty, but still far too pissed to think about rest, he'd cleaned out the tack room, the office, and then sprayed down the floor mats that ran the entire length of the barn.

After all that work and a hot shower, he'd finally been able to sleep. And damn if he didn't have another erotic dream about that redhead who'd bewitched him.

The sound of a car coming up the gravel drive drew his attention. His frown deepened when he saw it was Chelsea's Land Rover. The woman had to be stupid to come and confront him. Everyone in the city knew he had a scorching temper and she was a fool if she thought he'd keep a rein on it for her.

He tossed his coffee cup at the sink, not caring whether he cracked it or not, and stomped out to the barn. By the time he got there, she was already walking up the other side of the aisle, stopping to pat any of the horses that stuck their heads out of the stalls to greet her.

"You've got some nerve, lady," Ethan said when Chelsea reached Hamlet's stall close to where he stood.

"You told me I only had one day to decide," she reminded him sweetly. "I came here to figure out what I want to do."

The woman had no idea how angry she'd made him or she wouldn't be goading him. "I want you off my farm."

"Ethan...I..." After a weighty sigh, she sat on a tack trunk. "Can we talk? Please?"

"I'd rather eat nails. Are you taking my offer to buy Hamlet?"

"No."

"Then you've found a new barn for him?" Why did that thought cause a flicker of regret to lessen his anger?

"No."

He put his hands on his hips and glared at her. "Those were your choices."

"Ethan..."

"I'm not changing my mind," he insisted. "I want you off my property. If you need some help finding a new barn—"

"Ethan, please. I'd like a chance to explain." She closed her eyes for a few seconds. "We need to talk. *Please.*"

"What exactly do you think we need to talk about? The fact you lied right to my face?" His shout was loud enough to make most of the horses poke their heads over their gates to see what was happening.

"You're right," Chelsea said, getting to her feet. She moved closer, forcing him to take a step back. "I lied. I'm sorry."

A scoff slipped from him as he sternly crossed his arms over his chest.

"Won't you at least let me explain?"

"You lied. What's there to explain?"

"How about *why* I lied." When she tried to lay a hand on his arm, he jerked his shoulder so she couldn't. Her hand fell to her side. "Can we sit and talk? I want to explain. I do. This wasn't... I didn't..." She let her head fall back as she closed her eyes. A moment or two passed before she leveled her gaze at him again. "I guess all I can do is apologize. If you won't listen to me or even give me a chance to explain, then I'll see what I can do to find a new home for Hamlet."

Although he cursed himself a fool, Ethan was affected by the defeated tone of her voice. "If you need more time..."

With a shake of her head, she said, "I'll have my assistant—"

"You have an assistant?"

"Well, yeah... The phone calls alone are practically a full-time job."

"An assistant. Figures. What's her name?"

"Her name's Addie, and she's amazing. As if you care. Look, I'll find someplace today and see if we can get him transported. I don't want to be a bother to you anymore." Turning on her heel, she started to walk away.

Fighting the urge to tell her to stop, he watched her slow steps and wondered if he was making a huge mistake letting her walk right out of his life. He was prepared to open his mouth and ask what her explanation was, but he kept quiet when she whirled back around, anger plainly written on all her features.

"I can't believe you're just gonna let me leave! God, you're a stubborn son of a bitch." Her hands were fists at her sides, and color was high on her cheeks. "I told you a little white lie. That's all. One stupid little lie about my original intent for buying Hamlet. So what? Is it worth throwing away... Gah!" She covered the distance between them in long, irate strides. She poked him in the chest. "Why can't you just be reasonable?"

"It's reasonable to let you lie to me?" he asked, utterly fascinated by her change in mood. "And since when did I get to be the bad guy here?"

"Since you won't even let me explain. Did you ever think I might've had a good reason for fibbing?" He didn't even have time to answer when she answered for him. "No! People aren't perfect, Ethan. I'm not perfect. I made a mistake. Okay? One stupid mistake."

Anger now easing, he couldn't help but be fascinated with her. The woman was spitting mad, but she was the one who'd screwed up. "At least I'm not a liar."

"No, you're not. But you are a coward."

"Coward? What the hell are you talking about?"

"I might be a liar, but I'm *not* a coward." Throwing herself against him, she looped her arms around his neck and pressed her lips to his.

In his mind, he tried to will himself to stay still, to keep from responding. Only he couldn't. His lips softened as he wrapped his arms around her waist.

Everything about holding her in his arms felt right. Her curvy body tight against his. The taste of her. The little whimpers from her throat. He wanted to consume her, to keep feasting on those full lips. Accustomed to being the aggressor, he had to adjust as she was the one who thrust her tongue into his mouth, sending fire racing through his body.

Backpedaling with her in his arms, he was able to sit on a trunk, then he lifted her onto his lap. He stroked her back as she kissed him with more raw passion than he'd ever been kissed. Her hands moved to his chest as she kissed her way across his check. Her tongue tickled his ear before she whispered, "I'm no coward. I take what I want. And I want you." Then she buried her face against his neck.

A shudder raced through him as he smoothed his hands down her back to cover her backside.

* * *

Chelsea smiled against his neck, giving his beard-roughened skin one more lick before pushing against his chest and easing back. Now, she had his full attention. "So can we talk now?"

"Later." Ethan cupped her neck and pulled her into another heated kiss.

She gave him what he wanted—what *she* wanted—trying to weave a haze of desire around him to keep him rooted to one spot long enough for her to explain.

Her own desire soared, and when his tongue slid between her lips, she sighed in pleasure.

Before things got too out of hand, she broke the connection again. Hands pressed to his chest—or was she caressing him?—she tried to put a little distance between their greedy bodies. "Before this goes any further, we really need to talk."

With a resigned sigh, Ethan nodded.

Aware that being in his arms would muddle her thoughts, Chelsea got to her feet. "Why don't we go inside? I'll fix us some coffee, and we can sit down and talk this out."

"What exactly makes you think I want to listen?" he asked.

There was no malice in his expression or his tone, so she smiled. "Because you kissed me back." She stepped back, taking his hand in hers and tugging gently. "Please?"

He stood, and without dropping her hand, he led the way from the barn to his back porch. After holding the door open, he followed her into his kitchen and then set himself down at the table.

Taking that action as his tacit permission to brew some coffee, Chelsea went about finding what she needed. A filter. Coffee. There was next to nothing left in the still warm pot, so she poured it out, filled it with fresh water, and quickly got a new batch brewing. Fetching two clean cups from the cabinet, she set them next to the coffeemaker and then took a chair opposite Ethan.

"My father died six months ago," she said. Even speaking the words aloud still felt like a knife to her heart, but she needed to open up to get Ethan to understand why this album was important enough to her to have lied.

"You told me, and I'm sorry for your loss. But what does his passing have to do with you lying to me?" His face was back to being a mask of indifference. Had he not kissed her so passionately, she might have believed he didn't care at all.

She knew he did. "He had colon cancer. Do you know there really aren't a lot of good treatments for that type of cancer?" The memories were hard, but she owed him the truth. "I couldn't do anything. I could only watch as he went through chemo and radiation and..." With a deep breath, she pushed forward. "I've got more money than I can ever spend, and there wasn't a damn thing I could do that wasn't already being done. I've never felt so helpless in my whole life. Mama did everything she could for him. She handled his meds. Took care of his personal needs. I was all thumbs. All I've ever been able to do well is sing." Her hand rose to wipe away a tear from the corner of her eye. "So I'm going to help people with cancer by singing. Every penny this album earns is going to research better treatments for colon cancer. It's more important to me than anything I've ever done before."

Feeling vulnerable and sad, she pushed herself out of the chair to get their coffee.

* * *

Never in his life had Ethan felt like such a selfish schmuck. All he'd thought about was himself and how much he didn't want to record again. He couldn't even think of what to say in the wake of what she was revealing to him.

"I lied to you," Chelsea continued with her back to him, "because I knew having you sing on this album would generate *so* many sales. But you turned me down flat without even hearing me out. I was desperate. I asked Russ what I could do that might convince you to record a song. He said you would if you liked me as a friend, and the best way to get to know you was to spend time with you." She glanced out the window. "You spend all your time here. With horses. So I got a horse. I got Hamlet."

"Make mine black, please," he said in a near whisper as she started to sprinkle a pink packet into one of the cups.

"And here we are." Picking up the cups, she returned to the table. She set one cup in front of him and then she held her own while she took a seat. "I just didn't expect to end up liking you so much. That was a bit of a... " She let a smile bloom. "Let's just say it was a surprise."

What does a person say when he's made a jackass of himself? Yes, what she'd wanted of him was something he hated. But that didn't mean he had to be so short-tempered with her. "I'm sorry I was such a jerk to you."

"No, Ethan. I'm the one who's sorry. When I started all this, I never expected...Look, I'll find a new place for Hamlet. Okay?"

He finally found his voice. "You don't have to move him. You can keep him here. You'll need help taking care of him because you're so busy."

"Thank you," she said quietly before sipping her coffee.

Following suit, he had to admit she did a better job making coffee than he did.

Chelsea set her cup down. "Now, we have one more thing to talk about."

Ethan quirked a brow.

"We kissed."

The memory made him smile. "Yes, we did."

Her chin rose. "I don't regret it."

"Neither do I."

"Well, then...What are we gonna do about it?"

Always one to play his cards close to his vest, Ethan shrugged. While he wanted to let her know exactly how much the kiss had affected him, he couldn't help but be wary. He wanted to tell her he liked her too, that she was starting to matter to him, which was why that little lie had pissed him off so much and he'd overreacted. Yet he couldn't ignore the fact that she was a star. A genuine star.

Having her around was inviting himself into the light of scrutiny that he'd sooner avoid. He'd had his fill of that grow-

ing up, and his parents' death still haunted him. Although
the crash had been seen as a tragic accident, he knew better.
That photographer's flash had killed them.

The last thing in the world Ethan wanted was to put
himself in the path of reporters. And to watch Chelsea be
hounded? Unbearable.

Her smile slowly died. "You really are a coward. I thought
after..." With a shake of her head, she stood. "I'm going to
the barn to take care of Hamlet."

Ethan caught Chelsea's hand when she tried to walk past
him. There was one thing he could do to make this up to
her, and although he was still wary, he would give in this one
time. "I'll sing with you."

Her eyes stayed fixed ahead of her. "Thanks, but no." She
tried to pull away.

He wouldn't allow it. "Let me do this for you."

Her gaze caught his. "I don't want your pity."

"Good, because you won't get it."

"I should go."

Getting to his feet, Ethan refused to release her. While
she stared at the hand that held hers so tightly, he took
advantage and drew her into his embrace. He kissed her
before she could protest and before he could talk himself
out of it.

She kissed him back, winding her arms around his neck
and gently tugging on his hair. There was no hesitation when
he slipped his tongue between her lips to coax a response. She
let out a moan and pressed herself closer against him, mold-
ing her body to his.

Kissing this woman was playing with fire, and he was ready to get burned.

He picked her up and backpedaled until he could set her on the kitchen counter. As he kissed her, his hand rose to cover one of her full breasts. Her contented moan made him smile against his lips.

She knew how to kiss, and her hand smoothed down his chest, resting against the fly of his pants. He was hard and eager, pushing his groin against her hand. All he wanted to do was carry her to his bedroom and ravish every inch of her. He had a feeling that if he made love to her he might never be able to let her go.

That thought sobered him, and he eased back. "I've got chores," he said in a voice husky with his desire.

Her smile revealed that she knew exactly how much she'd affected him. Taking his hand, she led him toward the door. "C'mon. I'll help you."

CHAPTER NINE

Chelsea stopped when she saw a short man with a long gray ponytail standing at the gate to Hamlet's stall, stroking the horse's muzzle. "Um...hi."

The man didn't even turn his head to look at her, seemingly enraptured with her horse. "You gotta be Chelsea. Ethan told me this be your horse."

"He is. His name's Hamlet."

"Fine-lookin' animal. Standardbred. Don't see no racehorse in his eyes, though," the man said.

Ethan strode to her side. "Joe Alvin, this is—"

"Chelsea Harris," Joe said. "I know. Thanks to you, we don't listen to much else 'round here no more."

"You listen to my music?" she asked, a smile blossoming.

"The boy has it blastin' in the barn almost constantly." He finally turned to face her. "Pleasure to meet ya."

Swallowing a gasp, she willed herself not to react. The right side of the man's face was a mass of scars, burns most likely. But his blue eyes held intelligence, and his smile seemed genuine.

She held out her hand. "The pleasure's all mine."

After he gave her a firm handshake with a callused hand, he turned back to Hamlet. "This one's too gentle. No wonder he didn't make a good racehorse."

Something in the authoritative way he made that claim made Chelsea curious. "Have you been around a lot of race-horses?"

Joe let out a chuckle and stepped to the next stall as she followed. "More than my share. Worked as a groom 'fore I served. Trained some after. Thoroughbred, standardbred. Was damn good at it too."

"Why did you stop?"

Inclining his head at Ethan, Joe said, "This one's daddy begged me to work for him after I got burned in that barn fire. Couldn't refuse Crawfish nothin'. Came to the Walkers when Ethan was barely walkin'."

"Uncle Joe..." Ethan heaved a sigh. "Please don't start telling 'good ol' days' stories."

"They're mine to tell, ain't they?" Joe said with a smirk.

"*Uncle* Joe?" Chelsea quirked a brow. There was a lot about Ethan she had to learn.

"Yep," Joe said. "Raised this boy while his daddy and mama were on the road."

This endearing man was going to be a fountain of infor-mation about Ethan, and she planned to fish for every story she could. Knowing about his past would help her understand him. "I can't wait to hear all about his childhood."

Joe grinned. "Well, there was this one time when he weren't no more than five—"

"Enough of that." Ethan took her hand and dragged her down the aisle of the barn. "We need to see about a saddle."

Tripping to keep up with him, Chelsea said, "I thought you knew where I could get a good used saddle."

He didn't stop until they were in the tack room. "I already got it for you." Pointing to a beautiful leather Western saddle, he said, "Bought it yesterday. Was going to tell you last night, but... Screwed that up royally, didn't I?"

She lightly ran her fingers over the floral tooling on the chestnut-hued leather. "It's beautiful." The middle of the seat and pommel were smooth black leather, and the underside soft sheepskin. "Was this your friend's?"

"Yep. She was happy to sell it to someone she knew would use it. Said it was too pretty to sit around gathering dust."

Had she searched for weeks, she couldn't have found one half as perfect. "How much do I owe you?"

Ethan shook his head. "There's a matching bridle. Reins and a breast collar, too. But you'll have to get a good saddle pad when you get your tack. We need to shop for that soon. You can borrow any of mine 'til then."

"We?" Then she processed what he'd said. As if she'd let him buy her a saddle, especially one so expensive. "I can't let you pay for this."

"Too late."

"Ethan..."

* * *

Ethan shrugged, feeling a little like some boy with a crush who'd just handed the object of his affection a wilting rose. "It's only a saddle, and it's not like I can't afford it."

Having expected an argument, he was again surprised at Chelsea Harris when she turned, pushed her arms around his neck, and kissed him.

The simple kiss didn't stay simple for long. Every time he touched her, he went a bit crazy. Didn't even matter that they were only a few feet from Joe or anyone else who might stop by the barn. He kissed her long and deep, loving how her tongue glided over his, sending heat racing through his veins. If they finally came together...he had no doubt it would be amazing.

She eased away first. "Since Joe's here to help you, I really should be going." A yawn slipped out that she tried to hide behind her hand. "Didn't sleep much last night."

"Me, either," Ethan admitted. "Sorry I was such an ass."

"You had every right to be mad. I'm glad we can start over."

He shot her a sly smile. "Are you coming to visit Hamlet tomorrow?"

"I wouldn't miss it for the world."

He followed her out of the tack room, watching the sway of her long hair as Chelsea walked back up the aisle. "We should talk about the duet and—"

Turning to face him, she shook her head. "That's a dead issue, Ethan."

"Not to me, it's not."

"Who's dead?" Joe asked.

Having spent his whole life respecting the man, Ethan had to bite back a sarcastic remark about Joe's penchant for butting into conversations. "No one's dead."

"The duet is dead," Chelsea said.

Joe cocked his head. "What duet?"

"The one I'm singing with her for her charity album," Ethan explained, hoping she would realize that once he was on board, he would see his commitment through.

Obviously not appeased, Joe said, "Charity? Which charity you singin' for?"

"He's not singing," Chelsea insisted.

Getting a bit aggravated that she wasn't being grateful he'd agreed, Ethan turned to face her. "I *am* singing."

She shook her stubborn head. "You were so adamant before that you didn't want to sing with me. It's clear you don't want to do the song."

Singing his parents' signature song wouldn't be easy. There were just so many bad memories of all the times they'd left him when he'd been too young to understand why they always had to be on the road. But after the way he'd treated her, he would find the strength to sing the duet. "I changed my mind."

"I changed my mind, too," Chelsea insisted.

"I can't believe you're arguing over this when I'm giving you what you want."

"But it isn't what *you* want."

Joe watched the exchange, his gaze switching back and forth between two of them until the poor man had to be dizzy. He finally put his fingers to his mouth and let out an eardrum-piercing whistle. "For the love of... Will one of you *please* answer my question? What charity?"

"It's for cancer research," Ethan replied.

"Colon cancer," Chelsea added.

"The boy don't like singin' much," Joe said, slipping his hands in his back pockets and rocking on his heels.

"Which is why he's not doing the duet," Chelsea insisted. "After what Russ said—"

"Oh, hell," Joe said. "Russ stuck his nose in this? What did he say?"

"He didn't stick his nose in anything," she explained. "He was working at the bar when Ethan up and left and he told me Ethan reacted so rudely because he hates singing."

Ethan heaved a sigh. "I don't hate singing."

"You've been adamant from the moment I brought up the duet that you wouldn't do it."

Hands on his hips, he glared at her. "I will."

"You should," Joe said. "Good cause and all."

Ethan nodded. "See? Even Joe thinks I should sing with you."

Her eyes found Ethan's. "You're sure you want to do this?"

"I'll admit, I hate recording—"

"Then you shouldn't—"

"Oh, for shit's sake... will you let me finish?" At least she had the sense to bite her lip and stop talking when he was close to blowing his stack. *"But...* it's for your father's memory, so I'll sing with you. Okay?"

Joe cuffed Ethan on the shoulder. "My boy always does the right thing." On that pronouncement, he headed into the tack room.

"Are we agreed now?" Ethan asked.

Still not looking convinced, Chelsea chose to put the discussion off. "We can talk about details later." Taking his hand, she moved close enough to rise on tiptoes and brush a kiss over his mouth. "I should go."

After a squeeze of his hand, she hurried out of the barn. A few moments later, the roar of her Land Rover's engine signaled her departure.

Not surprisingly, Joe came out of the tack room, grinning in his goofy way. "That one's a keeper, boy."

Since he'd been "boy" to Joe all his life, Ethan didn't bother scolding him for the rather derogatory nickname. He'd learned a long time ago that Joe had his own way of doing things and changing the man was impossible. "You think so, huh?"

"I do," Joe replied, stepping out into the barn. He stared down the empty aisle the same way Ethan was. "But she's a singer."

"She is."

"A good singer judgin' by the music you been playin' lately. Is she as big a star as your daddy and mama?"

"Pretty damn close."

Joe glanced over to Ethan. "Think you can handle that, boy?"

"That's the million-dollar question, Joe."

"I'll tell you this... it's past time you settled down and started havin' some babies."

With a scoff, Ethan shook his head. "For God's sake, Joe. I'm not looking for a wife."

"Why the hell not? What are you now, forty-nine? Fifty?"

"You know damn well that I'm thirty-five," Ethan said, putting his hands on his hips and trying to get Joe to back off with a frown.

As usual, Joe wasn't the least bit fazed even though he was a good eight inches shorter and thirty pounds lighter. "I'm sayin' you're close to past your prime. Better grab this one while she's still available. Won't be long, I reckon."

"Past my prime?"

"Hell, you wait any longer," Joe insisted, "and you won't be able to get your pecker hard no more."

Chuckling at the absurdity of the conversation, Ethan said, "My pecker works just fine, old man."

"Then marry this one. Give her some little ones. She'll make ya happy."

"Why are you so hot for me to get married all of a sudden?"

Rubbing his beard-stubbled chin, Joe lost himself in thought before he replied. "I ain't gettin' younger, neither. Need me some grandbabies before I'm too old to teach 'em to sit a saddle proper."

Since Joe didn't have any children of his own, Ethan couldn't help but be touched by Joe's easy acceptance that any of Ethan's kids would be Joe's surrogate grandchildren. But that sentimentality wasn't enough to make Ethan go out and buy Chelsea a ring. Hell, he'd barely begun to accept that they were going to be spending time together. "I'll take things at my own pace, if that's okay with you."

With a snorted laugh, Joe grabbed a halter and started to open General's gate. "Think hard on what you'll lose if you let this one walk away. How many other women would understand the kind of life you've led and be willin' to put up with the infernal baggage you seem intent to drag around with ya?"

On that, Ethan walked away to drown his troubled thoughts in hard work.

CHAPTER TEN

After nearly a week of seeing Chelsea for only short snatches of time when she came to visit Hamlet, Ethan missed her company so much that he found himself at Black Stallion to catch her Friday show.

Her show tonight seemed different, but just because she'd chosen an entirely new set of songs made it no less entertaining. The woman knew how to perform, reminding him a lot of Savannah. Both the women could capture and hold a crowd in a way that could only be called a God-given talent.

He didn't want to look too deeply into why he needed to be there for her second Black Stallion performance. Yet something inside told him that she'd appreciate the gesture. So here he sat, wondering how she'd managed to reach him so quickly and so completely. Would she be surprised he'd shown up?

Ethan had to smile as he watched Joe nodding along with the beat. Even though Joe barely knew her, Chelsea had captivated him every bit as easily and completely as she had Ethan. When he'd told Joe he was heading into town to see Chelsea's show, Ethan hadn't expected the man to tag along. But Joe had insisted, even changing into his "dress jeans" for the occasion. Then he'd talked Ethan's ear off the whole trip, singing her praises in his twangy accent as if he were trying to sell Ethan a good horse.

Great teeth. Perfect conformation. Pleasant temperament.

Ethan didn't need to have Chelsea's finer qualities touted to him. He was already infatuated. His only concern at that moment was how to get her out of Black Stallion without Joe or the press tagging along. Brad had invited him to a late-night cookout. After Savannah's performance at Words & Music, they were heading to Brad's enormous house to eat and enjoy a roaring bonfire. While he might not have asked if Chelsea could tag along, Ethan knew his friend would make her welcome. Besides, she'd already met Savannah, and they'd seemed to click.

Now he only needed to get Chelsea out of there with no one tailing them.

Joe leaned closer. "Sings like an angel."

Ethan nodded.

"Likes horses too," Joe added.

Resisting the urge to roll his eyes, Ethan merely nodded again.

Thankfully the conversation was interrupted when the crowd rose in a standing ovation as Chelsea ended her last song on a note that seemed to go on forever.

* * *

Chelsea couldn't keep her eyes from drifting to the table where Ethan sat. Again. Tonight, his presence had been a comfort and gave her more passion as she sang instead of causing her to lose her lyrics. When the last song of her encore was still ringing in her ears, all she could think about was whether he would come to her dressing room to see her.

The press had been hanging around, and she knew how Ethan felt about being cornered by photographers and reporters. She wasn't sure how they could get away from Black Stallion unscathed.

Assuming he even wanted to leave with her...

Feeling the energy still flowing through her, she hurried to her dressing room. She whipped off the scratchy sequined shirt and tossed it on the dressing table chair. The sweaty black pants followed. She wanted a shower, but that would have to wait until she got away from the bar. Settling for a trucker bath, she washed up in the sink, slapped on some more deodorant, and donned the fresh clothes she'd brought along. She'd barely finished dressing before there was a knock at the door.

"Coming!"

It wasn't Ethan's smiling face that greeted her. Instead, Joe stood there, grinning.

"Um...hi." She tried to look around him. "I thought Ethan was with you."

"Oh, he is. Got stopped by that fancy guy that runs this place. He'll talk the boy's ear off before he turns him loose."

"I see..." She opened the door a little wider. "Please come in."

Settling on the couch, Joe kept smiling.

"Did you enjoy the show?" she asked, trying to break the silence.

"Yes, ma'am. You're quite the singer. You'd make Ethan's mama and daddy proud."

"That's quite a compliment," Chelsea said, touched at his emphatic praise.

"Not many can work a crowd like Crawfish and Dottie," Joe added. "No, ma'am."

The door opened, and Ethan came in. Nearly slamming the door, he leveled a frown at Chelsea. "Now I know why there's press crawling all over this place." He pulled his phone from his front jean pocket when it signaled a text.

"There really were a lot of them." Normally, a couple of reporters or photographers might hang around a smaller show like this. Tonight, she'd been informed there was a crowd waiting at the stage door.

Ethan was still texting, which she found incredibly rude until she saw the anger on his face.

"What's wrong?" she asked.

"I told you, I know why there's a gaggle of reporters tonight," he announced as he worked on his phone.

"Then tell *us*, boy," Joe said, showing where Ethan had learned his impatience.

Instead of replying, Ethan turned the phone to them.

Squinting, she needed a second to figure out what she was looking at. Then the picture registered. It was a shot of

Ethan sitting at the table in the Black Stallion. "Who took that?"

"Not sure," he replied. "But that's only one of a shitload. Russ said we're...what's the word? Trending?"

She couldn't contain a gasp. "We're trending?"

"Someone recognized me. I guess lots of people took pictures." He took his phone back in his hands, touched the screen a few times, and then showed them another picture. This time, it was him going into her dressing room, her red hair clearly visible over his shoulder.

"Someone close is doing this," she said, feeling angry and a bit sick to her stomach. No matter how many times she'd dealt with media storms like this, she always felt as if her privacy were being raked across the coals. Normally, she would handle the press with skill and a note of nonchalance, but knowing how much this had to be annoying Ethan made her typical calm disappear. "I have no idea who could've taken that picture."

"Probably Robert," Ethan said. "Drumming up business, as usual."

As her father had often told her, there was a price for success. The more triumph, the higher the cost. Sometimes it just felt like she might be paying a bit too much.

"I guess people are speculating that we're a couple," he grumbled.

"Well ain't ya?" Joe asked.

Chelsea wasn't about to answer that. With this stupid social media bullshit, Ethan was likely to want to leave skid marks getting away from her.

Ethan shrugged in reply.

"Security is going to have to escort us out," she said with regret.

"Nonsense. You just need plan B," Joe said. He turned to Chelsea. "That leggy brunette who was singin' for you still here?"

She'd never thought about either of the singers backing up her performance as a "leggy brunette" before. "Do you mean Kallie?" The moment the question was out of her mouth, she realized how stupid it was.

"Don't know her name. The one with the wig."

Chelsea picked her phone up and texted Kallie, asking her to pop over from next door. A moment later, there was a knock.

Ethan opened the door and Kallie practically skipped inside the dressing room. She stopped short when her eyes found Joe's face and she gawked at his scars.

If the man had to put up with those kinds of rude stares all the time, it was a wonder he was so kind. Chelsea cleared her throat loudly to get Kallie's attention.

Thankfully, her gaze shifted to her boss. "What's up, Chel?"

Before Chelsea could reply, Joe pointed at Kallie's shoulder-length dark brown hair. "That's a wig, ain't it?"

With a giggle, she put her hand up and lifted it off. Her real hair was almost military short and had been dyed a brilliant magenta. She splayed her right hand over the top of her head, making the trimmed tresses stand up.

Chelsea couldn't help but gape. "How have I never seen that before?"

"Only did it two days ago," Kallie replied. "I didn't want to show it on stage 'til you approved, so...what d'ya think?"

"It's cute," Chelsea replied. "You'll have to get a couple more ear piercings and really show it off." Then she shot Kallie a wink. Since the girl already had an eyebrow ring and three hoops in each ear, she was sure to acquire a few new holes in her head.

"Can we borrow that?" Joe asked, pointing at the wig.

She held the wig out to him. "If Chel says I'm okay to sing like this, then I won't need it anymore."

"It's okay to sing with your pretty pink hair," Chelsea said with a smile.

After handing the wig to Joe, Kallie cocked her head. "What's it for?"

"It's a wig," Ethan drawled. "What do you *think* it's for?"

"It ain't just a wig. It's also your lady's ticket outta here." He shook his head. "Didn't your parents teach you nothin' about how to handle pesky reporters?"

A lopsided grin filled Ethan's face. "I guess not."

"Is that all you need?" Kallie asked. Then she grinned. "Got a hot date."

"Thanks," Chelsea replied. "I'll pay you back for the wig."

"No worries," Kallie said before she skipped out of the dressing room.

"What else do we need to do?" Ethan asked.

"Get that little weasel who runs this joint in here," Joe ordered. "We need him."

Chelsea let out a chuckle at his characterization of Robert. He really could be a little weasel. She was about to text him when Ethan jerked his phone from his pocket and started tapping the screen.

"Got it covered," he said. A few minutes after texting, he was rewarded with a chime. "He says he's busy and wants to know what I want."

"Tell him to stop postin' them pictures and to bring a couple of the black T-shirts and baseball caps his staff wears," Joe said. "They need to fit you and Chelsea."

Seeing his plan, she nodded. "We're going to try to sneak out of here pretending to be waitstaff."

"No sneakin' needed," Joe said. "With that red hair of yours covered, you two could tap dance outta here, and no one would notice, not if you go one at a time. Then you get in Ethan's truck and... zoom. You're outta here."

Ethan frowned. "How will you get home?"

Smiling at Chelsea, Joe said, "I can take the lady's car. Will piss off the reporters to see an old scarred codger like me instead of her."

Chelsea obediently went to her purse, grabbed her keys, and handed them to Joe. "It's the Black Land Rover. I parked close to the stage door." She started texting. "I'm telling security to pretend I'm going to leave that way."

"What makes you so sure this will work?" Ethan asked.

Joe let out a resigned sigh. "Boy, you can be thick sometimes. Reporters ain't the brightest crayons in the box. If you don't look like a star, they ain't gonna notice you. A waiter and a waitress leavin'? They'll pay you no more attention than you would a fly buzzin' by. Just a couple of nobodies leavin' work. Reporters don't care about nobodies."

"Mom and Dad did stuff like that?"

With a snort, Joe replied, "All the damn time. Got to be a game for 'em. Those two could get in and outta anywhere without no one noticin' it."

There had been a few times Chelsea had gone to great lengths to sneak out after a performance, but only a few. Normally, she enjoyed the rush after a concert but after years of paparazzi attention, she was weary of their constant intrusion. While she was picking Joe's brain for stories about Ethan, she could also learn some of the tricks he could teach them to help avoid the press.

Robert stuck his head in the dressing room. "I've got the shirts and hats. What d'ya need them for?"

Joe snatched them out of his hands.

"Thanks, Robbie," Ethan said.

"You're the one who started that online business," Joe said as he handed one of the shirts and a hat to Chelsea.

"What online business?" Robbie asked.

When the man's cheeks reddened, Chelsea frowned. He had guilt written all over his features. "You posted that Ethan was here to see me."

Robert shrugged.

"Damn it, Robbie." Ethan narrowed his eyes. "You know I hate the fucking press."

"Figured it couldn't hurt business," Robert replied, his gaze shifted between Ethan and Chelsea. "You two really *are* an item, aren't you?"

With a disgusted grunt, Ethan pushed Robert out the door and slammed it shut. "Give me that shirt, Joe. I'm getting Chelsea outta here."

* * *

Leaving Chelsea behind had been a lot more difficult than Ethan had anticipated. He'd exited the dressing room first, working his way from backstage to the restaurant floor without a single backward glance. Ethan felt like they had a reasonable chance of sneaking out without leechlike reporters following.

Weaving through the tables, he avoided eye contact so the guests wouldn't stop him to ask for things like drink refills or ketchup. He tugged on the brim of his baseball cap, walking quickly but avoiding the appearance he was doing anything more than hurrying to do his job.

He had to steel his nerves to stop himself from looking over his shoulder to see if Chelsea was behind him. Until she joined him in the truck, he wouldn't know if Joe's little plan had succeeded.

Memories of times his parents had shuffled him through side doors or had asked him to put on a hat or get the hood on his jacket up came rushing forward. His parents had been celebrities. Genuine stars. As he'd grown up, it had seemed as if everyone wanted a piece of them—and their only child.

Now that he and Chelsea had made peace, Ethan wanted to see where this thing between them could go, even if that meant he was going to have to jump back in the deep end of fame. And damn, he wasn't sure he wanted that kind of shit in his life again.

The kitchen was still bustling, and he marched right through it without anyone so much as sparing him a glance.

Once outside the door, he headed to the parking lot, glad he'd parked his truck far away from the entrance. Hopefully, she'd be able to find it when she made her way out of Black Stallion.

Silencing the alarm, he pulled his phone from his pocket and slid into the driver's seat. Then he texted Brad.

Ok to bring a guest to cookout?

Brad immediately texted back.

Sure. Bring her.

A bit miffed that Brad could so easily figure out he was with Chelsea, Ethan sent another message.

Maybe I want to bring Joe.

Brad's answer was swift.

Bullshit. You would ask to bring Joe not a guest.

"Touché, my friend," Ethan muttered. The passenger door suddenly opened, startling him as Chelsea slipped onto the bench seat.

"I can't believe that worked so well," she said, her hand reaching for the brown wig she wore.

Grabbing her wrist, he shook his head. "Not yet. Wait 'til we're away from here."

"Oh, good idea." She buckled her seatbelt and turned her

head to offer him a lopsided smile. "Or do you just want me to leave the wig on to fulfill some fantasy of yours?"

"I like your hair better."

"I believe that's the first compliment you've ever given me." A couple walked past her window, and she sank down a little. "We should go before someone catches on."

He pushed the starter button, bringing the engine to life. A few moments later, they were joining the flow of traffic and heading away from the Black Stallion.

"I'm starving," Chelsea said. "I know a couple of good places if you need any suggestions."

"Actually, I was wondering if you wanted to go to a cookout."

"A cookout?" She glanced to her watch. "At this hour?"

Ethan nodded. "Brad and Savannah like to unwind after her Friday show by throwing some stuff on the grill, lighting the fire pit, and listening to eighties music."

"It sounds great, but...I shouldn't intrude."

Reaching over, he picked her hand up and cradled it in his, resting their joined hands on her lap. "I let them know we're coming. Besides, it'll give you a chance to get to know them better."

"I'd like that," she said. "I was hoping Savannah and I would see more of each other at the barn."

"Well then..." He signaled a left turn. "To Brad's we go."

CHAPTER ELEVEN

Chelsea stayed close to Ethan's side, still a bit concerned that Brad and Savannah might not appreciate Ethan dragging her with him to their home. She was getting cold, but she wasn't about to complain. Had they worn their jackets, they would never have pulled off the ruse of being employees.

The house was beautiful, at least what she got to see of it. They'd skirted around the side through a gate in the wrought-iron fence. Once they reached the backyard, the place came to life with tiki torches, music, and smiling people.

Savannah, who'd been playing corn hole with Russ, tossed her beanbag and then came hurrying across the lawn. By the time Chelsea was standing on the deck, still holding Ethan's hand, Savannah had jogged up the stairs to greet them.

"Chelsea!" Savannah said, smiling at her. "I'm so happy Ethan brought you."

"Thanks for having me," Chelsea replied, relaxing after such an enthusiastic greeting.

"It's chilly tonight," Savannah said, rubbing her hands together. "Let's go sit by the fire."

"Great." Turning her gaze to Ethan, Chelsea said, "Coming?"

"I need to talk to Brad first," he replied. "I'll join you in a minute." After dropping her hand, he headed toward where Brad was playing chef over an enormous stainless-steel grill.

"C'mon." Linking her arm with Chelsea's, Savannah led her down the stairs toward a stone pit that held an inviting fire. "It was getting too cold to keep beating Russ's butt anyway." She motioned to Russ, who tossed aside the last beanbag he held and picked up the little girl who'd been standing at his side.

Long pigtails bouncing, the girl squealed in delight as he ate up the lawn in long strides before joining them at the fire. After he set her down, he settled in on Chelsea's left while the little girl sat by Savannah.

Savannah stabbed a marshmallow with a long skewer and handed it to the girl. "Not too long, Caroline. Don't burn it. After a couple of marshmallows, it's bedtime for you."

Caroline pouted her lip but nodded. Then she glanced to Chelsea. "Hi."

"Hi," Chelsea replied. "I'm Chelsea."

"I know," Caroline said with a smile. "Mommy and I sing some of your songs."

"I'm flattered."

Cocking her head, Caroline asked, "What's flattered?"

Russ was the one to reply. "It means you made her feel happy." The cold evidently didn't affect Russ since he seemed quite toasty in his T-shirt and jeans. It was hard not to gawk at his muscled arms. The man clearly wasn't a stranger to a gym.

"Oh, okay." She grinned. "I like to make people feel happy."

"Want one?" Savannah asked, holding the stick out to Chelsea.

"Sure." She took the offering and held it out so her marshmallow could get toasted by the fire.

"Russ? Want one?" Savannah held out another skewer. "Careful, Caroline. Not too close to the fire."

Caroline nodded and eased her stick back.

Russ shook his head. "No, thanks. Waiting on the steaks." He grinned at Chelsea. "So Ethan was brave enough to drag you here, huh?"

The fire was so intense that Chelsea had to keep her gaze on the marshmallow so it wouldn't burn. "Brave?"

"Yeah. He's tells everyone we embarrass him."

Savannah thrust her spear over the fire. "Can't say I blame him there. We can get a bit...rowdy."

Chelsea let out a chuckle. "I can't imagine you're any worse than my friends." No sooner was the statement out of her mouth when she realized that talking about "friends" could be a bit sad. She had Kallie andJasmine, her backup singers, but they were so much younger. The girls were barely in their early twenties and didn't enjoy the same things as a close-to-thirty woman. And there were the guys in the band. Problem there was that they partied a hell of a lot harder than she cared to, so she'd learned quickly to decline any of their invitations.

She did know a couple of great girls who liked to go grab a drink or hit a club from time to time.

But friends—*true* friends?

Not in years.

Not since she'd become "the" Chelsea Harris instead of plain old Chelsea.

"You like 'em that scorched?" Russ asked with a laugh.

A quick look at her marshmallow and Chelsea groaned. The thing was aflame, so she jerked it out of the fire and blew on it until all that remained was a dripping mess of black shell with a gooey white interior rapidly falling off the skewer.

"Uh-oh," Caroline said. "You burned it."

Ethan's voice sounded behind Chelsea. "I prefer my marshmallows not looking like a lump of charcoal." He settled his hands on her shoulders.

"Yeah, I prefer mine a little brown rather than dark as death," Chelsea said, glancing up at him with a smile.

Caroline dropped her stick and jumped to her feet. "Uncle Ethan!" She reached both arms up to him. Scooping her up, Ethan smiled, his expression so full of love it made Chelsea's breath catch in her throat.

Caroline looped her arms around his neck and hugged him tightly.

"Isn't it past your bedtime, squirt?" he asked.

"Mommy said one marshmallow." She pouted her lip. "I dropped mine."

"Well, then. We'll just grab you another." After setting her back on her feet, he helped her get a fresh marshmallow on her stick.

"So did this guy finally agree to sing with you?" Russ asked.

"I'm singing with her, Russ," Ethan insisted.

Chelsea shook her head at the same time.

"Chelsea..." There was warning in his voice. "I told you—"

"And *I* told *you*," she interrupted. "I have more than enough people." A bit of a lie, but she'd be able to fill seven songs, which would be enough to generate some sales. She simply couldn't bring herself to take up Ethan's offer.

Once Caroline finished her marshmallow, Savannah took her skewer and set it aside. "Bedtime, sweetheart."

"Do I hafta?" Caroline asked, rubbing her eyes in clear fatigue.

"Yes, ma'am, you do." Savannah inclined her head toward the double doors leading from the deck into the house. "Go get your pj's on, and Brad and I will be up to tuck you in soon."

"Fine." The walk to the deck seemed to take forever since Caroline dragged her feet the whole way. She stopped to say a few words to Brad before she went inside.

Brad joined them at the fire and tossed a couple of hoodies to Ethan, who handed one to Chelsea. "What makes you two think I'd let you run around my place with Black Stallion shirts?" They both donned them as Brad took the seat beside Savannah, grabbed a marshmallow from the bag, and popped it in his mouth. Ethan squeezed Chelsea's shoulders. "Add my song to whatever you've got so far."

"Tell me about this album," Brad said. "Ethan only gave me the bare bones and whined about you wanting him to sing a duet."

"I didn't whine," Ethan insisted.

"Look, we can talk about something else," Chelsea said. "I'm not about to make Ethan do something that he was dead set against."

"Chelsea..."

"Oooh. Careful," Savannah said with a chuckle in her voice. "Ethan's starting to growl."

Like Chelsea would let him intimidate her. "Can we change the subject now?"

"Who's doing the capture and mixing for you?" Brad asked, clearly not paying attention to her request.

"Red Barn," she replied. "So what do you guys think of the Titans this year? Not sure we got much help in the backfield after the draft. That last game was—"

With a snort, Brad said, "Red Barn'll charge you an arm and a leg."

"Probably," she admitted. "But they're willing to work odd hours and with short notice since so many of my duet partners are touring."

"But the album's all for charity?" he asked.

"Cancer research," Ethan replied. "Colon cancer, since that's what got her dad."

"That's sad," Savannah said. "My grandfather had colorectal cancer. He passed away about ten years ago."

"I've seen all the commercials about getting scoped to check for it," Russ added.

"A shame Joslynn's not here." Ethan looked down at Chelsea. "She's a nurse. Could tell us more about it."

"I've really got to meet her one of these days," Russ insisted. "How come she's not here tonight?"

"She's on night shift," Savannah answered. "Nothing like a Nashville emergency room on a Friday night. Besides, you'll see her at the wedding rehearsal if nothing else."

The conversation was entirely out of Chelsea's control now, but she tried one more redirect. "I like the new backup quarterback the Titans signed."

"I could record the duet with Ethan for you," Brad offered.

"What a great idea!" Savannah smiled at Chelsea. "If Brad records it, Ethan won't be so crabby about singing."

"I'm not crabby," Ethan said.

"Which is why I should handle things. Hell, I'll do the whole album." Brad grinned. "No charge, either. I can use the tax deduction."

With a shake of her head, Chelsea said, "I can't let you do that. The scheduling will be a nightmare."

"Oh, please," he said. "I own a bar. I'm used to nightmare schedules. Besides, I'd do it just for a good charity anyway. And if it makes Ethan less crabby—"

"I'm *not* crabby!" Ethan bellowed.

"And on that note..." Brad stood. "After Savannah and I tuck the munchkin in, it's time to eat!"

* * *

Brad came to stand beside Ethan. Russ had left to help with closing up Words & Music right after he'd eaten his steak dinner.

"She's not what I expected," Brad announced.

The men had known each other so long that Ethan understood exactly what his friend meant—that despite her fame, Chelsea didn't act like a typical diva.

"Dove right into helping," Brad added, nodding at Chelsea as she stood by the sink, feeding dirty dishes into the dishwasher. "Savannah didn't even ask. Chelsea pushed up her sleeves, stepped up, and started working."

"She's like that at the barn. Shovels shit. Gets her hands dirty."

"She's good for you."

"I suppose so."

"I think you ought to bring her to Jekyll," Brad said.

"To your wedding?"

"Yeah. I mean, it'll be private. No press—at least I hope not. Besides, weddings are *so* damn romantic." Brad elbowed Ethan. "You just might get—"

"If you say 'laid,' I'll punch you right in the nose."

The notion of taking Chelsea to the island resort in Georgia that Brad and Savannah had chosen for their wedding was inviting. Although the event was only two weeks away, he warmed to the idea of inviting her. There would be plenty of privacy since Brad had rented out the entire place even though there would only be a handful of guests. With any luck, the press wouldn't find out about the marriage until after the happy couple enjoyed a nice honeymoon and was back in Nashville.

Chelsea would probably love having a few days away from prying eyes.

"There probably aren't any seats left on the plane," Ethan couldn't help but point out.

"Savannah let me charter a flight. Figured that might keep things quiet."

"She's getting harassed?"

Brad frowned. "Not as much as someone like Chelsea, but she's 'Nashville's Sweetheart' now, remember?"

"I know she hates that album title," Ethan said.

"Allied wouldn't give it up." With a snort, Brad frowned. "They're pretty good with other stuff she wants, but that title..." He shook his head. "Can't always get what ya want, right?"

With a chuckle, Ethan said, "But like the song, she seems to get what she needs from them."

"She's resisting their push to do a stadium tour next year."

"Can't blame her."

"So you'll ask Chelsea to the wedding?" Brad asked.

"There's room on the flight? Those charter planes are mighty small."

"There's room. And I imagine we'll be able to find her a room at the resort since we've got all of 'em rented for the weekend."

"She'll stay with me," Ethan blurted out.

"I imagine she will." With a slap on the back, Brad said, "Now you've just got to get her to agree to go with you."

* * *

Chelsea turned off the water and picked up the towel. All the dishes were in the dishwasher, and the few things that needed to be hand washed were done. After drying her hands, she turned to find Ethan and Brad staring at her. "What?"

"Wanna see the studio?" Brad asked.

"Absolutely!" Setting the towel aside, she followed him as he opened a door and flipped on a light switch. Then he motioned for her and Ethan to go down the stairs he'd revealed.

Brad called to his fiancée. "Savannah? You coming?"

"I'll be down in a minute," she replied from the other side of the big kitchen island, where she was wrapping up the last bowl of leftovers.

Down the stairs, Chelsea found a professional recording studio. "Wow." She gaped at the place. "This is nicer than Red Barn."

"Thanks." Brad pulled out the chair at the master board. "You and Ethan should go in the booth and look at the new mics."

Ethan opened the door to the booth and let Chelsea enter first. Even though the studio was in a basement, it was huge, and all the equipment was up to date. The microphones Brad had mentioned were nicer than the one she'd used when she'd recorded her last album.

If he really was willing to help with her charity album, she was thinking about taking him up on that offer. Out of habit, she picked up one of the sets of headphones and put them on, and Ethan mimicked her actions with the second set. While he put them on, she leafed through the sheet music that rested on the music stand in front of her. The title was "In Another Life," which was unfamiliar to her, making her wonder if it was a new Hitman tune.

Brad's voice came booming through her headphones. "Want to take the new mics for a test drive?"

She smiled at him through the glass that separated the recording equipment from the sound booth. "You haven't used them yet?"

With a shake of his head, he shifted his gaze to Ethan. "Would you mind? Just a quick a cappella to see if they're worth what I paid for them?"

The heat from Ethan's glare could've melted the glass separating him from his friend, so Chelsea said, "I'll do it. What do you want me to sing?"

"Your choice," Brad said. As if he were immune to Ethan's glare, he said, "You start, and I'm sure Ethan will join in."

"Yeah, right..." She adjusted the mic the hung closest to her so that she could sing into it. "How about 'Amazing Grace'? It's got a good range of sound to see how the mic works."

"Whatever the lady wants." After fiddling with the equipment, Brad gave her the sign for "tape rolling," so she launched into one of her favorite songs.

Surprisingly, Ethan was right there with her, singing in a baritone that near to took her breath away. As they sang the first verse, Savannah slipped quietly into the booth, put on a set of headphones, and joined Chelsea at her mic for the rest of the song.

Damn, but it was a pretty trio. The sharp tones from her soprano, Savannah's rich alto, and Ethan's husky baritone blended beautifully, bringing a tear to Chelsea's eye as she remembered singing it at her father's funeral service.

"That was *awesome*," Brad said. "Give me a minute and I'll play it back for you guys."

"You two blew me away," Chelsea said with a smile.

"Oh, please," Savannah said with a dismissive wave. "Your voice is so pure. You could sing anything and make it fantastic."

"Back at'cha, lady. No wonder you're hitting the charts with every new song."

Rolling his eyes, Ethan said, "You two can stop trying to be humble. You both know you're the best singers in Nashville."

"Says the guy who could knock us both down a peg," Chelsea countered. "You have such a great voice."

"He really does," Savannah added before the playback of their song stopped the meeting of the mutual admiration society.

Once again, Chelsea was moved by the song. If Ethan was willing to sing on the duet, she had no doubt their collaboration would be every bit as melodic.

"What do y'all think?" Brad asked, displaying a bit of his Nashville roots.

All three of them began to sing each other's praises again until Brad interrupted. "Any objections to putting it online? I figure I can put a note about how Chelsea's working on a charity album that'll include Ethan. Will drum up some buzz."

"Songs without videos are boring," Chelsea couldn't help but point out. When both Ethan and Savannah started laughing, she frowned. "What?"

Savannah pointed to a camera in the corner of the ceiling, then shifted to a second camera. "Just for future reference, my darling fiancé records *everything* in his studio, both sound and video."

"So noted," Chelsea said. "Pretty shrewd, considering how many times I've done a great cover in practice and wished I'd recorded it."

"So are we Internet bound?" Brad asked.

"Fine with me," Ethan replied.

"Go for it," Savannah added.

"I'm afraid I'll have to be the wet blanket," Chelsea said with a frown. "I promised my publicist nothing goes public without running it by him. It's not like I have my contracts memorized, either, and my label might have some clause about putting something out without their permission."

She felt better when Savannah nodded. "I hadn't thought of that, but you're right. My label might have a fit."

"Sorry, guys," Chelsea said.

"What about the charity album?" Brad asked. "Will they let you post any of those?"

"Oh, yes," Chelsea replied. "We've had a lot of discussions about what I can do with those songs."

"Well, then." Brad rubbed his hands together. "When we record the duets, we'll get snippets of some of those songs online and drum up publicity."

Chelsea gave him a smile through the glass. "If it raises more money for the charity, then I'm all for it."

CHAPTER TWELVE

Can we please talk about the duet now?" Chelsea asked, hoping to put the issue behind them once and for all.

The drive back to her home had been so quiet that she was worried she'd done something to offend Ethan, perhaps in refusing his continued offers to participate. If they could stop disagreeing over whether he'd sing on the charity album or not, she might be able to relax and simply enjoy that they were together.

"That might be a good idea," he replied. For the first time since they'd left Brad's house more than fifteen minutes ago, he seemed to relax. He even reached over to hold her hand.

"First of all, your voice is amazing," she said.

"Thanks." His hand squeezed hers.

"I really think we sounded good together, and I would love for you to sing on the album. But..."

"No 'but' about it, Chelsea. I don't mind singing, espe-

cially since Brad's recording it. He won't screw it up like..."
He shrugged. "I trust him."

"Can you tell me why you hate singing so much? I'd like
to understand why you were so angry at first."

A weighty sigh slipped from his lips, and although he kept
his eyes on the road, she could tell he was thinking hard about
whether to answer her.

"If I'm being too nosy..."

"Nah," he said. "You know, I actually love to sing, I just
don't like to think back to all that bullshit."

"What bullshit?"

Ethan let go of her hand and put both of his on the wheel.
"My parents made me record an album when I was seventeen.
I hated every minute of it. Hated even more that by the time
their producer was done, I didn't sound like me at all."

"What did he do?"

"You name it; he tried it. Echo chambers. Synthesizers.
Overdubbing. He couldn't decide if he wanted me to sound
like a robot or Donald Duck. The songs were a fucked-up
nightmare. My parents thought they were 'timely' and released the album anyway, no matter how much I begged and
pleaded with them not to. They also wanted me to tour, so I
had to do a couple of shows. Those were even more of a mess."

"No wonder you were so mad."

"The reporters were relentless," he added. "They hated
every single song, and they were quite happy to tell the whole
world what a talentless hack they thought I was."

Having had her own share of merciless reviews, Chelsea
could sympathize. "They can be pretty brutal."

"It's in the past," he said. "I just have a hard time leaving it there." A few moments passed before he spoke again. "It's more than that, though."

"Tell me. Please," she coaxed, wanting to know exactly what that "more" was.

"Do you know how my parents died?"

"A car accident, right?"

A weary sighed slipped from his lips. "Do you know why they had the accident?"

Searching her thoughts, Chelsea couldn't remember much about the Walkers' deaths. Crawfish was a well-known heavy drinker—that much she recalled. But she had no clue whether he'd been drinking the night of their wreck. "No, I don't."

"It was because they were famous."

"I don't know what you mean."

"They were being chased by some zealous photographer and Dad was trying to lose him. He lost control of the car, and . . . I can remember it like it was yesterday."

Her heart went out to him, not only because she knew the pain that came with losing a parent but because her own life had been touched by relentless paparazzi far too often. "I'm so sorry, Ethan."

No wonder he shunned the limelight. After being taunted by the press for singing songs he hated, he also blamed them for costing him the two most important people in his life.

They came to the interstate, and Ethan headed up the southbound entrance ramp.

Chelsea tried to stop him by reminding him of the directions she'd given him to get her home. "I thought I told you to head south."

"You did."

"Then why—"

"Your car's at the barn," he said. "Remember?"

No, she hadn't remembered. In fact, she was so tired that she doubted she'd even given him the correct directions. Before she could answer, a yawn slipped out, so deep she shuddered. "Sorry."

"You must be beat," he said as he eased the truck into the flow of traffic that still buzzed on I-65 despite the fact it was close to three in the morning.

She nodded as she covered another yawn with her hand.

"I shouldn't have made you stay so late," he said.

"I had a great time. Besides, I can catch up on my sleep when I get home."

"The way you're yawning? Not gonna let you drive. You'll wrap your pretty little Land Rover around a tree."

"Oh, please." About to tell Ethan all about the number of times she'd had to endure exhaustion and still look great and sing well, she was interrupted by yet another yawn. "I'm fine."

"*Of course* you are. I can see that for myself." Turning the volume on the radio down, he said, "Why don't you lean back and close your eyes? We've got a good twenty minutes before we get to the farm. Take a short nap."

"I should've thought about how far apart our places are when I let Joe take my car. I was focused on getting outta there so I could spend time with . . . I wasn't thinking."

"Yeah, it might've helped if I told you how late we always stay at those Friday cookouts," Ethan said.

The steady passing of the white lines on the interstate had the same effect as a lullaby. "You don't care if I close my eyes? Just for a few minutes?"

"Why don't you come over here?" he asked, patting his shoulder.

That was an offer she couldn't resist. Anytime she could get closer to him, she'd jump at the chance. No man had ever captured her senses and her thoughts the way Ethan had.

Popping her seatbelt, Chelsea scooted across the bench seat. "Sure I won't bother you?"

In a singsong voice, he replied, "Put your head on my shoulder."

And she did.

* * *

In all his days, Ethan had never seen a person fall asleep that quickly. One second, Chelsea was talking. *Boom*, those eyelids shut and her head lolled against her chest.

He would have wrapped his arm around her, but he was afraid to wake her. Instead, he kept his right hand on the wheel and reached across his chest with his left to lift her chin and gently move her head to rest better against his shoulder so she wouldn't get a stiff neck.

As he drove through the darkness, he thought about how well she'd gotten along with Brad, Savannah, and Russ. They all acted as though they'd been pals their whole lives, especially Chelsea and Savannah. But then again, they shared a career that tons of people swore they wanted but few understood. Empathy for stars was often an unavailable commodity. After all, bona fide stars had everything they'd ever wanted, right? At least that's the mantra Ethan had heard his whole damn life. Since his parents were rich, famous celebrities, his life was supposed to be golden. Perfect.

Oh, how wrong people could be.

Brad seemed every bit as taken with Chelsea as Savannah was. In all the time Ethan had been friends with Brad, which was close to forever, he'd never sought Brad's opinion on a woman. Then again, Brad had never taken Ethan's advice, either. Probably because the two of them had played the field too damn much. None of the women they dated were worth getting to know better.

None of them was Chelsea.

For a moment, he was more than a little ashamed of his past. Although he'd been tested and was clean as fresh snow, he could easily have picked up something nasty—even potentially fatal—if he'd screwed around with the wrong woman. He and God didn't have much of a relationship, but Ethan did send a quick prayer of thanks that he'd avoided that horrible scenario.

She let out a little sigh and rubbed her cheek against his arm.

Never had he anticipated feeling for someone the kinds of emotions this woman inspired. He'd always thought his parents were a bit much, the way they always held hands and called each other those lovey-dovey pet names. Having thought those actions were just for the benefit of their image, he now felt ignorant about how to make a relationship work—especially to get one to be as great as what his parents shared.

For the first time in his life, Ethan was thinking about things he swore that he would never be a part of his life. Monogamy. Devotion. Shit, he'd even had a passing thought about how a kid would look, one that he and Chelsea shared. A little girl with her mom's flaming hair.

And if that wasn't enough to make him want to finish off a bottle of whiskey...

Leaving behind the interstate and the lights and noise, he headed for home. First the main roads, then the county roads. As he always did when he turned to ease up the long gravel drive to the barn, he released a sigh of relief.

Home.

Only this time, for the first time, he wasn't alone.

Ethan drove past the barn, stopping long enough to glance out the window at the big board and see that Joe had completed the last of the evening chores as he'd promised. Then he parked the truck outside the kitchen door next to where Joe had left Chelsea's SUV.

Although he hated to wake her, even if only to help her get inside and into a proper bed, Ethan nudged her. "Chelsea, baby. We're here."

She woke up as quickly as she fell asleep. Lifting her head from his shoulder, she blinked a few times. "I should get going then. Got a long drive home."

He shook his head. "You're not going anywhere. Not when you're this exhausted."

"I need to go home, Ethan."

With another shake of his head, he opened the door and climbed out of the truck. Then he held his hand out to her. "You're staying here tonight."

Why was she hesitating? Damn, if she wasn't tugging on her bottom lip with her teeth.

"What's wrong?"

"I really should leave," she replied.

"I won't be responsible for you driving off the road and into some ditch."

"But..." Her eyes finally found his. "I know what you're thinking, and I'm not ready to sleep with you."

"Oh, for God's sake... Is *that* what's bugging you?"

* * *

"It's not *bugging* me, I just..." Chelsea let out a huff. "It's kinda soon in our relationship for me to spend the night with you."

There. She'd said it. And she hadn't even blushed.

There was something special happening here, between her and Ethan. She wasn't going to derail it by having sex with the guy before there was a stronger emotional bond. That road was a dead end, a lesson she'd learned well in her past.

The stakes were higher now that people might know they were a new couple. Any blip on the radar of her love life made it straight onto the airwaves or the Internet. Usually both ad nauseam. One false move, one wrong step, and she would never live the humiliation down. She didn't want to jump the

gun with Ethan only to become more fodder for tabloid jour-
nalists.

His past was another reason. It seemed as though his history was littered with one-night stands and she wasn't about
to add her name to that list. She needed more time to figure
out her own feelings and hope he learned to feel something
for her in return.

Hands on his hips, he glared at her.

Wishing she could read his mind, she slid across the seat
and left the truck to stand in front of him. "I should go." A
yawn tried to slip out, but she did her damnedest to try to
smother it. The yawn won anyway.

"You're staying here," he insisted. "To *sleep*. And that's all."

Before she could argue, he swept her into his arms and
marched to the back door.

She had to admit, the man was talented. He was able to get
the door open without putting her down, then he carried her
straight to a bedroom—his from the looks of it. Then he set
her on her feet. With his back to her, he rustled through the
closet before turning around and tossing her a flannel shirt.
"You can wear this if you don't want to sleep in your clothes."
There was no mistaking the hard edge to his voice.

Holding it to her chest, Chelsea knit her brows. "Why are
you so angry?"

"Gee, I wonder why...You made it quite clear that you
wanna haul ass getting out of here. I promise I won't lay a finger on you."

So that was it. His pride was bruised because she'd insisted
it was too soon to make love. He thought she didn't want him.

She'd have to show him otherwise.

After tossing the shirt on the bed, she went to stand directly in front of him. "Ethan?"

Looking down at her, he cocked a brown eyebrow.

"C'mere." Circling her arms around his neck, she kissed him, letting loose all the desire the man inspired in her.

Afraid he'd be stiff with anger, she smiled against his lips when his passion seemed to ignite. He wrapped her in his embrace and pulled her hard against him.

There would never be a time she'd tire of his taste or how the light scent of his cologne seemed to fill her senses. His tongue teased hers, enticing it to follow into his mouth where he gently grasped the tip with his teeth and tugged.

Ethan's hands covered her backside, lifting until their groins aligned, and at the moment, Chelsea was ready to abandon her earlier request that they wait until they knew each other better.

Surprisingly, he pulled back first. "Get some sleep."

"Where will you sleep?"

"The couch."

"Why not here? With me?"

"I thought you said..."

"We could just snuggle," she admitted. "Unless you think that flannel shirt will make me far too sexy to resist." Then she winked.

He grinned. "It might, but I'll behave. Let me go check the locks. You get changed. I'll be back in a minute."

Chelsea jerked off her shirt and bra, tossing them on the wooden rocking chair that sat in the corner. The shirt he'd given her was so soft, she sighed when it brushed her skin. She peeled off her jeans and left them next to her other clothes. Turning back the sheets, she crawled into bed, socks on her cold feet.

His scent was on the pillow, so she rubbed her cheek against the fabric and closed her eyes, weary and ready to rest.

* * *

She was sound asleep, hugging his pillow.

Why did it seem so right to see Chelsea in his bed?

Ethan shook that thought aside, yawning the same way she'd been doing before he'd insisted she stay. Dragging his shirt over his head, he shoved it in the hamper. After tossing aside all the junk in his pockets, he stripped off his jeans and socks, lamenting the hole where his big toe had been sticking out. The raggedy socks joined the shirt in the hamper.

Wearing only his boxers, he slid between the sheets to join Chelsea. Her back was to him, which made it convenient to roll to his side and haul her up against him. Fitting his thighs to hers and slipping his arms around her waist, he set his chin on the top of her head and breathed in the scent of flowers.

Shampoo? Perfume?

Didn't matter. She smelled wonderful. Enticing.

They fit together quite well, in his opinion.

She let out a sleepy sigh and wiggled her backside against his already semi-hard cock.

She might be able to get a good night's sleep with him snuggling her, but the more his mind wandered down the road of erotic thoughts, the more Ethan realized sleep would be elusive.

He wanted her too damn much.

* * *

"Wake up, sleepyhead," Ethan coaxed. "I've got lunch in bed for you."

His voice pierced the haze of Chelsea's sleepy thoughts. A bit disoriented, she rolled toward him. "You mean breakfast in bed."

A warm chuckle slipped from his lips. "No, I mean lunch. It's almost one."

"One?" Her gaze darted about the room, trying to find a clock. "Seriously?"

"Hope you like pancakes," he said, coming to the bed. He held a wooden tray full of food that smelled so good it set her stomach to growling.

"Love 'em, although I probably shouldn't eat so many carbs."

"What?"

"I'm trying to limit carbs," she explained as she stuffed the pillow behind her and leaned back against the headboard. "I'm a little too chunky."

Ethan let out a derisive snort.

"I am! I can't stand to see myself on video lately. Stupid camera adds *twenty* pounds in my case."

"You look great on video," he insisted.

"I look like Jabba the Hutt," she said, mostly teasing. The

women in her family were uber-curvy, and she'd resigned her-self to being exactly what she was. A girl with big boobs, full hips, and a booty. Whenever her clothes got a little too tight, she'd simply stop sugar and bread and drop a few pounds. But there was no way in hell she'd ever be anything but curvy, not unless she starved herself. No way would she do that.

Skinny was for other girls.

"I like you just the way you are," Ethan said.

All she could do was sit and stare at him. Was this man for real? "Did you steal that line from *Bridget Jones's Diary?*"

His brows gathered. "I don't know any Bridget Jones, and I sure as hell have never read her diary." He set the tray down so the wooden legs straddled her thighs. "Eat. Fuck the carbs."

"Yes, sir."

The man could cook. That much was plain the moment she put the first bite of syrup-covered pancake into her mouth.

"So..." Sitting near the end of the bed, Ethan laid a hand on her shin. "I was hoping you might want to go to Brad and Savannah's wedding with me."

Between bites, Chelsea said, "They barely know me."

"It was Brad's idea."

"Really?" While Brad and Savannah had been nothing but welcoming at their home, she didn't want to intrude on their special day. "I don't know if it's a good idea. I mean, if the paparazzi knows I'm there...it would ruin their wedding."

"Got that covered. It's two weeks from now on an island down in Georgia. Some resort that specializes in destination weddings or something. Figured we could all do some explor-ing before the rehearsal."

Her appetite fled. "I can't go to some touristy place without a lot of planning. I'd get mobbed."

"Brad rented out all the rooms. There won't be anyone on the grounds who isn't an invited guest."

"That part sounds wonderful," she said. "But... that exploring you're talking about? That might have to get nixed. Like I said, I hate getting mobbed when I'm recognized. Spoils everything."

"Fine. No exploring then. Just sitting by the pool all by ourselves, drinking fruity drinks, and catching some rays."

"Which airline?" she asked. "Would there be a first-class seat still available on such short notice? I can't sit coach, not unless—"

"You don't want to get mobbed," he drawled, the humor clear in his tone. "It's a charter. No worries."

"Wow. Then a trip to their wedding sounds like heaven." An incoming call ended that topic. Chelsea checked the ID. "Hi, Mom. I'm sorry I didn't call yesterday."

"I was a little worried," Betsy's voice buzzed in her ear. "I'll admit I've gotten used to talking to you every day."

Ethan gave Chelsea a nod and then left the room, probably to give her a little privacy.

"I went to a cookout after the show last night."

"A cookout? Where?"

"I went with Ethan Walker to one of his friend's houses."

"Ethan Walker? I thought you were angry at him."

"Not angry," Chelsea said. "We've gotten to know each other a little better, and... well, I like him, Mom."

"Like him? Are you two dating?" Betsy asked, her tone concerned. "I can't imagine how the press will take that."

"We're trying to keep it out of the press."

Her mother let out a scoffing laugh. "Good luck with that, sweetheart."

"Yeah, I know. It's not gonna be easy, but we both want to keep things as private as possible."

"So when do I get to meet him?"

Chelsea wasn't at all sure that her relationship with Ethan had reached the meet-the-mother stage. "Soon."

"In other words, not yet." Betsy chuckled. "You're both welcome to come for a visit anytime you want."

CHAPTER THIRTEEN

A week later, Chelsea finally got away from the recording studio long enough to spend some quality time with Ethan. They'd talked and texted, but she'd missed him more than she thought possible after knowing each other for such a short time. After four days apart, they'd snatched enough time to have some lunch at Words & Music, but she craved being able to be with him for longer than an hour at a time.

Now, she walked at Ethan's side as he led Hamlet to one of the riding paddocks. The fact he was going to try to saddle break her horse weighed heavily.

If he got hurt...

She reminded herself that Ethan was an experienced horseman and that Hamlet was the sweetest gelding. She'd ridden the horse bareback more than once. When she'd visited the barn the day before, Ethan had placed the beautiful saddle on Hamlet's back and tightened the cinch. The animal hadn't even twitched in response.

When they reached the corral, Chelsea wasn't surprised to see Savannah sitting on the top fence rail. "You came to watch."

"I did," Savannah said with a smile. "Right after I dropped Caroline off at my parents' house. Didn't want to miss the show."

While Savannah might be eager about seeing Ethan do something considered exciting, Chelsea stressed over the danger. Even worse, once he saddle broke Hamlet, he had plans to do the same for a horse that one of his other owners had purchased a few days ago. Thankfully, Chelsea wouldn't have to endure any more than two ordeals today. Savannah's gelding had been ridden with saddle before it came to the barn.

Chelsea closed the paddock gate behind them and hurried to the fence to climb up and sit next to Savannah. Ethan led Hamlet to where Joe waited, holding a lasso. The man fiddled with it as if he knew how to use it. No doubt it was a precaution if Ethan got thrown and Joe needed to catch Hamlet.

While Ethan talked with Joe, Chelsea turned to Savannah. "This shouldn't be a big thing, right? I mean, Hamlet lets me ride him bareback. A saddle shouldn't be much of a change, right?"

"You're worried?" There was a teasing lilt to Savannah's voice.

Chelsea replied with a brusque nod.

"I'm sure Ethan knows what he's doing."

"I'm just not in the mood to drive him to the hospital."

Savannah let out a chuckle. "I'm sure that's *exactly* what you're worried about. Look at it this way, at least Joslynn's working the ER tonight. She'll be happy to patch him right up. Knowing Ethan, even if he broke a bone, he wouldn't let you get him help right away. He'd sit around and try to tough it out first. You know the 'be a man' stuff guys always try to pull."

"Most of the men I've known are big babies," Chelsea said.

"They *are*. But complaining about aches and pains is a lot different from getting treated. They usually bitch and moan but refuse any help offered. Besides, he wouldn't want to look like a wuss in front of you."

When Ethan glanced over his shoulder, Chelsea tried her damnedest to give him an encouraging smile.

He was a handsome devil, something even more apparent when he wore leather chaps over his faded jeans. Those long-fingered hands were covered by well-used gloves and his cowboy hat made him look even taller. Most women would be drooling at the masculinity he exuded.

She practically was.

Two fingers to the brim of his hat, he saluted the women. Then he waited while Joe took a firm hold of Hamlet's bridle and nodded. Reins in hand, Ethan gripped the pommel and swiftly and smoothly got onto the saddle.

What she'd feared would be a traumatic ordeal ended up being a nonevent. Hamlet didn't so much as twitch. After Ethan was in the saddle, the horse turned his head as though checking who was on his back. Seeing it was one of the men who took good care of him must have put him at ease, because all Hamlet did was stand there.

Joe led Hamlet to the middle of the paddock and then

turned the horse loose. With gently prodding from Ethan, Hamlet started walking. A little more nudging from Ethan's heels and soon Hamlet was trotting around the large oval, following the fence line. As Ethan trotted past, he tipped his hat while they applauded.

After a good thirty minutes of putting Hamlet through his paces, Ethan trotted the horse back up to Joe, who took the bridle and held tight while Ethan swung down from the saddle. Together, they walked to the gate, Ethan opening it to let Joe lead Hamlet back to the barn.

"If you'll excuse me," Savannah said to Chelsea. "I need to hit a bathroom. I'll be back in a few minutes."

After Savannah crawled down from the top rail, Chelsea said, "Don't be gone long. The next one's not supposed to be as easy."

"So I've heard," Savannah replied. "I'll hurry."

With a cocky cowboy swagger, Ethan came over to where Chelsea stared down at him from the fence. "Told you it would be fine."

She smiled, not at all surprised at the pride in his voice. "Are you saying you told me so?"

"I am."

"Fine, you were right. *But*...there's one more animal for you to break. Maybe he'll get the better of you."

"There's yet to be a horse that gets the better of me," Ethan said. "Where's Savannah?"

"Bathroom."

"I need some water." He held his hands out to her. "Go back to the barn with me?"

When she took his hands, he jerked her off the fence rail. As she let out a squeak of surprise he caught her and crushed her against his body. After slowly lowering her to the ground, letting their bodies press together, he covered her mouth with his.

Chelsea wasn't sure if her heart was pounding from the shock of nearly falling or from the way Ethan's tongue was rubbing against hers so deliciously. She liked this new side of him and found there was something about how uninhibited he was—how freely he expressed himself—that made her feel free too.

After a few long moments, he eased back, grinning at her. His hat was pushed back, near to falling off his head from their kiss. He set it back firmly where it belonged, took her hand, and started toward the barn.

"We should go out for steaks tonight," he announced when they reached the small refrigerator he kept in the tack room. He plucked out a bottle of water, handed it to her, and grabbed another for himself. Twisting off the cap, he chugged big gulps, no doubt thirsty from getting Hamlet broken, even though it seemed as if the horse had done all the work. "Some nice rib eyes," he said, "and a bottle of cabernet?"

"Sounds like heaven," Chelsea replied. "I'll have Addie grab some groceries, then we can cook at my place. Or here, if you'd rather. Who gets to do the cooking honors?"

He shook his head. "I'm taking you to Tennessee Roadhouse. I haven't been there yet and everyone keeps telling me how great their food is."

"Ethan, I'm not in the mood to be hounded tonight." Sometimes she loved being a celebrity. Tonight, she just wanted to be alone with Ethan. Besides, from what she'd learned and everything she'd seen, he'd sooner have all his wisdom teeth pulled without anesthetic than be recognized in public. A place as popular as the Tennessee Roadhouse? She'd be signing autographs and posing for selfies instead of enjoying a nice meal with her boyfriend.

Boyfriend. Girlfriend. Such odd terms to describe two people their age sharing a relationship. Surely there were other words that suited them better.

Lover? Not yet.

But soon...

"Then we'll go to Pancho's," he said. "It's been around forever and not trendy at all. No one cares about celebrities there. No rib eyes, but fantastic tamales."

Although she wasn't so sure, she decided to let him have his way. "Fine. Pancho's sounds great."

A loud whistle from outside the barn forced a sigh from Ethan. "Joe's got the next one ready."

"By all means, then. Let's go so I can watch you break your neck."

* * *

The bite in Chelsea's tone shouldn't have made Ethan happy. But it did.

She was worried about him. Truly worried. He couldn't help but smile at that realization. "I'll do just fine." Taking her hand in his, he led the way back to the paddock. "I've broken plenty of horses."

Exactly as he'd suspected, Hamlet had been easy. Not only was the horse docile, but it was also used to weight on its back.

This one might be another story.

As Chelsea climbed the fence again to plop herself next to Savannah, he directed his attention to Thunder—the palomino one of his old friends had bought that needed to learn a new role as a saddle horse.

Thunder was a tall son of a bitch. Heavily muscled, too, considering he was only three years old. Probably a good thing the horse was gelded, because as a stallion, breaking would be a war. Joe had done an admirable job walking the horse around to calm him. The animal looked as ready as he would ever be.

Ethan made a quick glance back to Chelsea and Savannah, wishing they'd left after Hamlet's saddle debut. The women were going to have to accept that he was going to get tossed on his ass a few times before Thunder figured out that Ethan wasn't giving up. The last thing he needed was a hysterical female overreacting and bursting into tears the first time he got thrown. Plus, he didn't like the idea of Chelsea crying.

With a shake of his head, he dismissed them. He had a job to do, damn it. Since when did he fuss and bother over whether a woman let a tear or two fall?

Turning his attention to Thunder, he approached slowly, talking in a low voice to the palomino. "Whoa there, boy. We can do this the easy way or the hard way. Now me? I prefer easy." He stroked the animal's thick neck and then gave it a pat.

The horse let out a snort and tried to toss his head back, an action stifled by the tight hold Joe had on the bridle.

"Think he's tellin' you it's gonna be the hard way, boy," Joe said with the chuckle clear in his voice. "Let me work on him for a minute. Gonna calm him down some more." He began leading Thunder and coaxing him in that low, rumbling voice of his.

"Figured as much," Ethan said mostly to himself. Since the best way to approach a task was to just get at it, Ethan waited until Joe led Thunder back. While the animal seemed calm, Ethan grabbed the pommel, stuck his foot in the stirrup, and threw himself into the saddle.

Things happened pretty quickly. With an enraged squeal, Thunder reared, jerking the bridle right out of Joe's hands. Before Ethan could even get his foot in the right stirrup, he was tumbling off the horse's muscled rump.

He slammed into the ground hard, his back hitting with such force that it knocked every bit of air from his lungs as stars dotted his vision. Pain followed right behind, and for a moment, he feared he was going to pass out.

Feminine screams seemed to hang in the air, but there was nothing he could do except lie there. Breaths wouldn't come, and there were a few long moments of panic. As Chelsea and Savannah suddenly fell to their knees on either side of him, more panic racked him in unrelenting waves. With it came a new fear, one he'd never faced before.

He was mortal.

It wasn't as though his life flashed before his eyes. And it wasn't as if he'd thought he would live forever. But to take a fall while breaking a horse? A fall that made it impossible for him to even twitch a muscle?

Ten years ago, he would have gotten up, dusted himself off, and crawled right back in the saddle. He'd broken two fingers once upon a time while working with a skittish colt. All he'd done that day was tape the fingers together, pop a few aspirin, and down a cold beer. Then he'd gone right back to whatever he'd been doing.

Now, he was lying in the dust and wondering if someone should be calling the paramedics.

"Oh God, Ethan," Chelsea said in a panicked exhale. Her hands were suddenly all over him. "Did you break something?"

As if he could answer her. He still couldn't draw a decent breath, and the few he could manage sounded like asthmatic wheezes.

"Shake it off, boy," Joe said, the words piercing Ethan's haze of pain and further wounding his pride. "Got a job to do. Needs to get done."

So Ethan obeyed. Since breathing was becoming easier, he pushed himself up on his elbows with a groan.

Chelsea immediately pushed against his chest. "Don't you move!"

"I'm fine." He brushed her hands away and then noticed that Savannah was fiddling with her phone. "Put that thing away."

"You need an ambulance," she said.

"Don't you dare." Ethan sat up, his anger and wounded pride overriding his aches.

"But—"

"I'm fine," he snapped again. "I've got a horse to break."

* * *

Chelsea sat back on her heels, not at all convinced Ethan was *fine* by any stretch of the imagination. His face was still pale and drawn, his lips nothing but a thin line. At least he was breathing better, but she could tell each lungful caused him pain. "Ethan... you might have cracked ribs or something." She reached for his hand.

"Enough," he barked.

She jerked her hand back as her concern shifted to anger. And hurt. "Okay, then..."

"I told you I'm fine. Stop fussing at me."

Fussing? Since when was caring for someone, especially someone who'd just taken a bad fall? Narrowing her eyes, she bit her tongue to keep from unleashing the irate words that wanted to fall from her mouth.

Never had someone frustrated her the way Ethan Walker could. Never.

He didn't want her help? Well then... she'd let him have his way. Getting to her feet, she glanced down at Savannah. "Let him be. Tough guy wants to sit there with a couple of fractured vertebrae? More power to him."

Still holding her phone, Savannah knit her brows. "Are you sure?"

Joe was the one to speak. "He don't need no ambulance. On your feet, boy. Get back in that saddle."

With a low growl directed at the men, Chelsea turned away. If Ethan didn't want her help, fine and dandy. He could listen to Joe and let his macho flag fly, but she had no intention of sticking around and watching him break his stupid neck. "Couple of idiots," she muttered at she marched toward the gate.

Savannah jogged to catch up with her. "You're really leaving?"

"Damn right, I'm leaving." Chelsea tossed her head at the men. "I'm not staying here and watching Ethan kill himself on that horse."

"Maybe we should stick around."

Deep down, Chelsea wanted to stay if only to be the one to say "I told you so" when Ethan got thrown on his sorry ass again. Then she'd let Savannah call first responders while Chelsea took her first ride in an ambulance as she accompanied him to the emergency room.

The press would have a field day.

But she couldn't stay. At least not up close and personal. Seeing him fall again would be too much for her to bear. And if that didn't speak volumes for her growing feelings for him, nothing would.

She cared. A lot. Had from the moment she'd met him.

When she got to her SUV, Chelsea hugged herself and leaned back against the front fender. "I'll wait, but I can't watch."

Savannah mimicked Chelsea's actions. "He'll be okay. He's done this before."

"Joe told me it's been years since Ethan broke a horse."

"Your point?"

"I think that fall hurt him more than he'd expected," Chelsea replied.

"Yeah, he did look a little...surprised."

"More than a little." The noise coming from the paddock made Chelsea sneak a peek over her shoulder. Damn if Ethan wasn't in the saddle, keeping a firm grip on the reins. "He's doing it."

Craning to watch, Savannah let out a chuckle. "He sure is. Guess he showed us, huh?"

After a few moments of watching Ethan weathering a rough ride, Chelsea snorted and made herself stop watching. "Yeah, he showed us. And he's going to hurt like hell later."

"I imagine he's going to realize he's not twenty anymore." Turning away as well, Savannah dropped her arms to her sides. "Can I ask you something?"

"Go ahead."

"What's bugging you so much about this?"

"About what?"

Savannah shrugged. "I'll admit I was upset when he got bucked off, but Ethan's a tough guy. Trust me, I've heard plenty of stories. Breaking a horse isn't really that big a thing compared to lots of other stuff he's done. I just wonder why you're so upset over a fall." A few stilted moments passed. "You've got it bad for the guy, don't you?"

There was no getting around it, and since she really didn't have anyone but her mother to talk to about her situation, Chelsea nodded and opened up. "Yeah, I've got it bad. I think

I'm falling in love with him, and I'm not sure that's a good idea at all."

"Why not? You two seem great together."

"I'm not sure us being great together can overcome the problems we face."

"Problems?" Savannah asked.

"First and foremost . . . I'm a celebrity. There's no way around that and Ethan hates publicity. The press gives him hives."

"You're right. That might be a problem, but . . ."

"No 'but,'" Chelsea said with a disgusted shake of her head. "He'd never be able to handle how I live. Touring. Recording. Dodging the paparazzi. He'd be miserable. Absolutely miserable."

A sly smile crossed Savannah's lips. "You're already thinking about a life together."

Chelsea sighed. "Yeah, I am. Much too often."

"Why is that a bad thing?"

"Because there's no way Ethan and I could ever work."

"I disagree." Savannah turned to face Chelsea. "Look, I know it wouldn't be easy."

"Not with my life, it wouldn't."

"I'm not talking about you; I'm talking about Ethan. He's not an easy person to love."

Chelsea cocked her head. "Why not?"

Holding up her index finger, Savannah said, "He's stubborn."

"So am I."

A second finger extended. "He's never had a relationship that lasted longer than a month."

"My longest was three," Chelsea admitted.

A third finger joined the count, and Savannah grinned. "He likes things his way."

"So do I."

Savannah's smile grew. "Then it sounds like a match made in heaven."

CHAPTER FOURTEEN

Even getting out of his chair seemed like an impossible task. Which was a damn shame, because Ethan wanted a couple of shots of whiskey to help kill the pain. He couldn't muster the energy to even try to get to the liquor.

He hadn't broken a horse—especially a horse as ornery as Thunder—in almost longer than he could remember. Evidently getting bucked off at thirty-five was a hell of a lot different than at twenty-five.

His afternoon had been nothing but an internal battle, a fight between the part of him that wanted to believe he could still do whatever he wanted and the part of him that realized he wasn't a kid anymore. The sane part was winning, which only pissed him off more.

Hard for a man to admit he might be past his prime.

A conversation Ethan had with Brad a few months back came slamming back into his thoughts. Brad had been teasing him one day after a night of rather excessive partying.

Ethan had been pretty pitiful, nauseated and dealing with a headache that felt as though his brain was too big for his skull. Evidently, Brad saw great humor in Ethan's misery, and he'd droned on and on about how Ethan might have finally reached the age where having a night of debauchery cost him too dearly.

Since he'd been too queasy to do anything except lie on the office couch and take the lecture, Ethan had tried hard to ignore Brad. Seemed now that many of his friend's points had taken root in his brain. And damn if those points weren't making a lot of sense in light of Ethan's current predicament.

"Be kinder to yourself, Ethan," Brad had said. *"You're not gonna live forever. Hell, keep up the way you are, and you're not gonna see forty."*

Chelsea had stuck around long enough to watch him finally ride Thunder, but then she'd driven away before they'd had a chance to talk much. That was probably a good thing, because she'd looked ready to scold him, and he hadn't been up to hearing any more of what she thought about his tumble.

The crunch of gravel alerted Ethan that someone was driving up to his house. *Uncle Joe, no doubt.* He'd found far too much humor in how stiff Ethan had gotten as the afternoon wore on. Not that Ethan would tell him, but the walk from the barn to the house had been utter agony.

Once inside, he'd groaned like an old man, made his way to his recliner, and all but fallen into it. After finding just enough strength to flick up the leg rest, he'd somehow gotten his boots off and his feet up and hadn't moved since. That was almost an hour ago.

How was he going to be able to pull himself together, get a shower, and then drive to Chelsea's so they could go out for that dinner he'd promised? Yet the idea of calling her and telling her how badly he hurt wounded his pride to the point he was almost able to get up.

But not quite. At least not yet.

A car door slammed. Someone was definitely here. Good thing he'd left the back door unlocked. Joe could just let himself in, which meant there'd be more teasing. At least the old man could pour Ethan a drink, so a visit wouldn't be a total waste of time.

Someone knocked.

"Shit." That meant that it wasn't Joe, because he would've barged right in.

The door opened with a squeak. "Ethan?"

Chelsea. What was she doing back here?

"Can I come in?"

"Sure." He'd be damned if he'd let her see him looking like a crippled geriatric. Problem was that his body wouldn't obey his commands as he tried to get up. A loud groan slipped out when the muscles in his lower back seized into a tight ball of agony.

Footsteps hurried through the kitchen until she was standing next to his chair. "Oh, my God. Are you all right?"

"Fine." He settled back in the chair, wishing there was a heating pad or two or ten behind his sore body. "Just resting before we go out."

Her snort told him she didn't buy it for a moment.

"I *am.*"

"Sure you are." Turning on her heel, she headed right back to the kitchen.

"You're leaving? You just got here."

Another snort echoed back to this living room followed by the crinkly sound of sacks being unpacked. The refrigerator opened and closed a couple of times, as did the pantry door. When she came back, she carried a carton of Epsom salts and a large jar of Instant Heat. "I'm going to draw you a hot bath. You can soak for a bit while I work on our supper. Then we can eat, I'll rub you down with this"—she held up the jar—"and then you can get a good night's sleep." As though she suddenly remembered something, she set the salts and ointment down and scrambled back to the kitchen. She returned with a glass of water and a bottle of ibuprofen.

At her insistence, he swallowed four tablets and handed her back the empty glass. His pride took a huge blow when he had to admit the truth. "I'm not sure I can get up."

"Figured." Chelsea put the glass on the end table before reaching down and slowly lowering the footrest. "Here." She held out her hand.

Ethan grasped it and allowed her to help him up. He was sure every joint in his body popped before he was able to get on his feet.

"Can you make it to the bathroom?" she asked.

"I think so."

"Then let me get the bath started." Grabbing the Epsom salts, she rushed ahead of him and disappeared into the master bedroom.

By the time he lumbered his way through the hallway and

into his room, the sound of running water greeted him. The closer he got, the more he relished the idea of sitting in that old claw-foot tub and letting the heat soothe away his aches and pains.

As he reached for the buttons on his flannel shirt, she was suddenly there, brushing his hands away and unbuttoning his shirt. "Let me." Her voice was husky and low as her nimble fingers worked their way down until she tugged at the shirt-tail tucked inside his jeans.

Although he was pretty sure he could manage to undress himself, Ethan let her have her way. Despite how bad he felt, his reaction to her nearness and that fact she was taking off his clothes was swift. She smelled of clean skin and shampoo and he wanted her. Surely she'd notice.

As she nibbled on her bottom lip, she worked on his belt buckle. To his disappointment, she moved back after that task was complete. "I should go check the water. Why don't you finish up?" On her way back into the bathroom, she grabbed his robe, brought it to him, and draped it over his shoulder. "Put this on, or you'll never make it into that bath."

"Why?" he asked as she hustled away.

No reply, which Ethan found horribly disappointing. On the other hand, he wasn't exactly at his best, and when he made love to her, he wanted to firing on all cylinders.

So he obeyed her and finished undressing before donning his robe.

* * *

Chelsea ran her hand through the steaming water. It was hot enough to help Ethan relax, but not hot enough to burn him. Before pulling her arm out, she scrunched her sleeve up to reached deep and stir around the last of the Epsom salts that hadn't quite dissolved.

After watching the fall he took from Thunder, she'd known he'd be hurting something fierce by the time their date rolled around. Instead of holding him to his promise, she'd put on the brunette wig and run out for a few supplies so that Ethan could get some TLC and still have a nice dinner.

She'd never wanted to take care of a guy the way she wanted to help Ethan. The few men that had come and gone from her life never touched her heart in a way that brought out her softer side. All she'd been able to think about all day was how much she wanted to ease his pain, to comfort and care for him. She suddenly understood why her mother had insisted on doing so many things for her father herself instead of leaving the tasks to his nurses.

Ethan needed her, and she wasn't about to bear any guilt for not being there for him.

He was even more pitiful looking than she'd expected by the time she got to his house. The lines on his face were testament to how much he hurt. All she wanted to do was take that pain away.

Ethan appeared in the bathroom door, wearing the robe she wished she hadn't given him. Ever since she realized he wanted her as much as she wanted him, she'd been plagued with the desire to see if that body that had held her so tightly was a muscular as it felt. As she'd undressed him, she couldn't ignore the hard ridge pressed against the front of his pants. She'd had the nearly overwhelming urge to drop to her knees, free that erection, and lick it. Then she'd drag him to his bed and pounce on him.

Now was the wrong time, though. He needed to recover, and she needed a little more time to be sure she wasn't diving headfirst into another lousy relationship. God knew she hadn't made the best choices where her personal life was concerned. In her world, it was so damned hard to figure out whether a guy liked her for who she was rather than for what she was. So far, she'd guessed wrong every single time.

With Ethan, Chelsea had hopes that things would be different this time. He didn't covet her celebrity; he hated it. No wonder after all he'd told her about his teenaged foray into recording and the story of his parents' deaths. What she was discovering was that his distaste of her celebrity status was every bit as frustrating as someone who only wanted her because she was Chelsea Harris.

Would she ever find anything approaching happiness, let alone love?

Shaking her head at her own uncharacteristic melancholy, she let her eyes rake Ethan from head to toe. A smile bowed her lips. The man was delicious to look at, and the anticipation of seeing under his robe gave her a bit of a thrill, especially since he was pitching a rather nice tent that threatened to part the front. "Bath's ready. Why don't you get in and have a nice, long soak?"

"Join me?"

"Tempting," she said, followed by a contented hum. "But not today, I think."

"What's for supper?"

The fact he hadn't argued with her was enough to tell her she'd made the right call. He wasn't ready for anything physical tonight. "Why, tamales of course! Wasn't that what you promised me?"

A smile was her reply.

"Need help getting in the tub?" she asked as she got to her feet and headed to the door.

"No, but you could stay and wash my back." The grin he gave her sent heat straight to her core. "And then you could wash my front."

If only that smile hadn't been followed by a grimace when he bent to feel the water temperature.

"I'll take a rain check on that."

"Promise?"

"Oh yeah, I promise."

* * *

By the time Ethan got out of the tub, dried off, and got his clothes on, he was exhausted. The way his stomach rumbled when the smell of Chelsea's cooking hit his nostrils made him believe he might just have enough energy to eat before he was down for the count.

He tried to keep from groaning as he made his way to the kitchen. Chelsea had done so much to help ease his pain, and he didn't want her thinking her efforts had been ineffective. The bath had been heaven. The ibuprofen had taken a little of the edge off. And if she rubbed his back and shoulders with the Instant Heat like she said she would, he'd be able to sleep until the worst was over.

All this over proving to her exactly how macho you are, his conscience taunted.

Fuck off, Ethan replied.

Chelsea pulled the stuffed corn husks from the steamer. "Good timing. Dinner's ready."

Since Ethan considered himself a pretty good chef, he started to tease her about skills. "I don't suppose you remembered the chile sauce. They'll be boring without it. *I* would never forget it." He winked.

Her lopsided grin showed that she was on to his game. "Good thing I brought everything I needed with me then." She nodded at some discarded chile pods in a bowl. "Even added onion and garlic."

"Any sides, or were the tamales difficult enough for you?"

"Stop mocking me and sit down, Ethan. Let me get the rest of this on the table." She put the oven mitts aside. "I'm sure you'll be pleasantly surprised."

She was right; he *was* pleasantly surprised. Dinner consisted of expertly cooked tamales, refried beans, and Spanish rice. She even made cinnamon-coated churros for dessert. He caught himself looking around for take-out containers from some ritzy place where she could have grabbed everything on her way over. Instead, he saw the discarded plastic wrap and containers of the ingredients she'd used to prepare him a meal he'd be hard-pressed to duplicate.

How long had he soaked in that tub?

Long enough his skin had pruned and the water had been chilly.

Conversation through dinner was light, and he enjoyed the easy way they found many different things to talk about. He'd never been that comfortable in a woman's company before, especially one he desired as much as he wanted her.

"That was an amazing meal, Chelsea," he said before he set his napkin aside.

"Considering what Savannah told me about how well you cook, I'll take that as the highest compliment." She picked up her empty plate and rose to her feet. "You go park it in your recliner and let me handle cleanup. When I'm done, I'll rub some of that goop on you and we can watch some TV."

"Let me help."

"Nope. Go find us something good to watch. I'll spring for pay-per-view if there's a good movie and you're a cheapskate." She favored him with a sexy wink. "Look for something from Marvel. I'm a sucker for superheroes."

Instead of sitting in his chair, Ethan grabbed the remotes and dropped onto the sofa. As stiff as he was getting, he figured he'd just sleep there tonight anyway. Getting up again was about as appealing as facing a bunch of his parents' fans.

Thankfully, the latest Marvel movie was available, so he ordered it, laid his head back against the cushions, and waited for Chelsea to join him. Although he felt guilty for letting her cook and do the dishes, he vowed he'd return the favor just as soon as he was human again.

* * *

Chelsea smiled when she found Ethan sound asleep on the couch. A glance to the television showed a great movie waiting, but she wouldn't wake him to watch it. When a yawn slipped out, she realized she was every bit as tired.

She sat next to him and put the jar of Instant Heat on her lap. Then she went about unbuttoning his shirt. He didn't wake up until she pulled the two sides open, revealing a chest with the perfect amount of light brown hair.

"Are you taking advantage of me while I'm incapacitated?" he asked, his voice drowsy.

"I'm putting this heat rub on you to help you sleep."

"I was sleeping just fine," he pointed out.

"This will keep you from getting so stiff you can't move in the morning."

"You rub that on me, I guarantee I'll be *stiff*."

She chuckled, opened the jar, and scooped up some of the minty-smelling balm with her fingers. "How about you quit sweet-talking me, take that shirt the rest of the way off, and turn around so I can do your back?" When he obliged her, a gasp slipped out when she saw the bruises already forming on his shoulders and back. "Thunder got the best of you today."

He huffed out a breath. "I rode him, I'll remind you."

"Yeah, but he doesn't have bruises from head to toe."

Chelsea let her hands glide slowly over his broad back, lingering on his muscled shoulders and arms. The man was about as close to perfect as any she'd ever known. When her fingers and palms grew warm, she ended her little game and went to wash the Instant Heat off before she was stuck with burning hands the rest of the night.

By the time she got back to the couch, he'd gotten his shirt back on and looked ready to fall asleep again at any moment. She took her place on his right, propped her feet on the coffee table, and patted her lap. "Put your head down, honey."

The wary glance he gave her before obeying raised her radar a notch.

"I promise I won't bite, Ethan."

He finally obeyed, moving slowly until he was curled up and resting his cheek against her thighs. A small contented sigh slipped from him when she began to comb her fingers through his hair.

"I could get used to this," he said.

Since she couldn't see his face, Chelsea had a hard time reading his emotion. His tone gave nothing away. "Get used to what?"

"Having someone do stuff for me. You know, take care of me."

"I'm sure your mother babied you when you were sick. That's what moms do."

"My mom was always on the road when I was little," Ethan said matter-of-factly.

She knit her brows. "Who watched after you?"

"The staff, I suppose. I kinda ran wild."

"You didn't go on the road with your parents?"

"Only a few times. They were in their element performing. They didn't want some brat chasing after them. Or so dad used to say..."

"You didn't have a nanny or anything?" she asked, growing angrier by the moment.

"Nah," he replied, his voice flat. "The housekeeper got my food and stuff. Then I hung around Joe a lot as I got older."

The more he told her, the more Chelsea disliked Dottie and Crawfish Walker. She thought about Ethan as a small boy, having a sore throat and runny nose with no one to give him medicine or wipe his nose. When kids were sick, they needed coddling and hugs and tons of love. Who kissed his booboos or chased the monsters out of his closet when he was afraid? She was near tears over what his childhood must have been like.

No wonder Ethan could be as frosty as a January morning. He hadn't known love growing up.

"This is nice," he said, his voice heavy with sleep.

"Shh," she said, stroking his hair. "Get some rest. I'll take good care of you."

Always.

* * *

Ethan blinked a few times, not sure what time it was. The room was dark, but he didn't recall turning the TV off.

Then he remembered the evening. He was still sleeping on Chelsea's lap, although she'd somehow managed to get him covered with the afghan Savannah's mother had made for his couch.

Gently lifting his head, he saw that Chelsea was asleep. She'd be so worried about him getting stiff by sleeping sitting up, yet she seemed to have no care at all about whether she suffered the same fate.

All because of him, she'd gone to great effort. The bath. The dinner. The cleanup. Even the pampering. None of which in any way was she required to do. She owed him nothing but gave everything.

A warm feeling wrapped around his heart as he lay his head back down. He wasn't teasing when he said he could get used to the attention. No one had ever gone to that much trouble for him. Not even Joe, although he cared in that gruff way of his.

Chelsea cared. A lot.

That thought helped Ethan relax and drift back into a peaceful sleep.

CHAPTER FIFTEEN

The smell of coffee brewing woke Chelsea. She instinctively reached for the night table where she always kept her phone before she remembered she wasn't at home.

Pushing up on her elbow, she caught the afghan that had been draped over her before it slid to the floor. She didn't remember lying down, which probably happened whenever Ethan got up. She didn't remember him covering her, either.

A quick look around revealed no clock, and she wasn't wearing a watch. Light streamed through the windows, so it wasn't early.

How long had she slept?

"Crap." She was supposed to meet Chuck Austin at Brad's house this afternoon so they could lay down the first track of the charity album. It was still surprising that Brad was so willing to do so much work on her behalf. The time factor alone should've made him withdraw his offer. He not only had Savannah and her daughter in his life, he also had his composing and, of course, Words & Music.

Then he'd surprised her once again and told her he was writing a new song for her to debut on the album. When he'd called and asked her a series of questions about her father, she'd been curious about his purpose. Brad had grinned and told her that her father deserved a special tribute.

The title he'd given the song was "Through Daddy's Eyes," and the moment he revealed that fact, Chelsea had burst into tear—so had her mother when Chelsea had told her about the song. Recording the new song wouldn't be easy, but she vowed to control her tumultuous emotions and make it the best she'd ever sung.

"You're up," Ethan said, coming into the room while holding two cups of something steamy that she desperately hoped was coffee. "One packet of the pink stuff, right?"

"Yes, thank you. What time is it anyway?" The demand was in her voice, and she mentally scolded herself for talking to Ethan as though he were her assistant. Speaking of assistants, Addie was probably frantic. Chelsea had never been out of touch this long. They talked a bazillion times a day. "Where's my phone?"

"And a fine good morning to you too, buttercup." Ethan held out one of the cups. "Coffee first; questions after."

The warm cup felt good in her chilly hands. The temperature had gotten considerably cooler at night, and her hands always ached when it was cold. "Thank you." After a few sips, she said, "I need to get moving soon. I've got a lot to do today."

"Big plans?" he asked, moving to the kitchen as she followed.

"Chuck Austin and I are recording our song."

"Damn, that's right," Ethan said. "Brad asked me to babysit Words and Music this afternoon." He leaned against the counter, sipped his coffee, and stared at her over the rim of the cup. "I'll get Russ to pinch hit for me."

"Why? Are you still too sore to work?"

"I'm fine," he snapped.

The topic of his injuries was clearly verboten. "Why can't you go to the restaurant?"

"You're recording."

"So?"

He glared at her as if she'd just asked a ridiculous question. "With Chuck."

"Again...so?"

The last time she'd seen the perturbed look he was shooting her now, he'd walked away from the bar to let her fend for herself as bartender.

"I don't understand why you're upset," she admitted. "Why do you think you have to be there?"

* * *

Ethan caught himself right before he answered her question honestly. "Figured you'd want me there." That sounded a lot better than *I don't want you alone with that pretty boy.*

His thoughts smacked of jealousy, which was not something he was willing to admit to her. He'd barely acknowledged the emotion to himself.

Jealousy and caring were both so new. Ethan still hadn't accepted either of them totally.

"I think I can handle laying down a couple of tracks of a song." Although she didn't roll her eyes, her condescending tone was plain.

"Brad wants me to come," he blurted out.

"Brad wanted you at Words and Music."

She had him there.

Setting her cup aside, she moved to stand in front of him. "What's going through that crazy head of yours?" Her eyes searched his. "Ethan, what's wrong?"

Trying to avoid the conversation, he stepped to the side to escape and downed the last of his coffee. He rinsed the mug and tossed it in the dishwasher. Then he turned around to find Chelsea with her arms folded under her breasts, leveling a hard stare at him.

"What?" he asked.

"This will never work if we're not honest with each other."

"Oh, come on. I just thought you'd want me there."

"Bullshit. This isn't about me or Brad or..." Her eyes widened. "Chuck. It's about him. You don't trust Chuck. You don't trust *me*."

"I'm getting dressed," he announced and fled the kitchen.

She was right on his heels. "You're jealous?

"No, I'm not."

"Yes, you are. And you've got no reason to be." Her hand snaked around his upper arm and dragged him to a halt. "Look at me, Ethan."

Although he probably looked as pouty as a two-year-old about to be punished, he did as she asked.

"I wish you'd tell me the truth," she said.

"Fine. I'm jealous."

"Which means you don't trust me."

He shook his head. "I don't trust him. I mean, he's got one of the worst reputations in Nashville. He's almost as bad as . . . well, as bad as . . . as . . ."

"As bad as who? You?"

"Yeah, Chelsea. He's as bad as me. At least as bad as I *was*."

"Glad to hear you've put your serial dating behind you."

He couldn't help but grin at the polite way she'd referred to his less-than-stellar behavior, and he was grateful she wasn't holding it against him. Then a frown swiftly followed. "I don't want you hanging around him."

Her frown matched his. "So you really don't trust me."

"I told you, I do."

Since the discussion was becoming as futile as a cat chasing its own tail, she let him go to his room by himself.

* * *

This wasn't an issue she was going to drop, so Chelsea checked the time to see if she could pin him down after he got dressed or if they'd have to have the discussion later. It was close to nine, so she could afford to wait. Assuming he'd listen to her.

Damn, the man was stubborn.

Good thing she was too.

Ethan came back to the living room, tucking his shirt into his jeans.

"Ready to talk now?" Chelsea asked, finally spotting her phone. She grabbed it off the end table and parked herself on the sofa. A quick look at the screen showed several missed calls and a slew of texts, but she wasn't addressing those until she and Ethan worked through their problem.

"I need to feed the horses," he insisted.

"Joe will handle it."

He kept casting yearning glances at the door.

Why were men always so hesitant to talk about important things—like feelings? She wasn't letting him escape that easily. "Do you know Lance Watson?"

"The actor? Didn't you date him?"

She nodded. "Not for long, though. Wanna know why?"

"'Cause he's a dick?" Ethan tossed her a smirk.

"Actually, yes. Because he's a *jealous* dick. An uber-jealous dick. I can't handle another jealous boyfriend."

The smirk shifted to a fierce frown.

"He made my life a living hell. I couldn't go anywhere without him grilling me on who I was with or what I'd been doing," she explained. "Lance never trusted me. If I was out of touch, he'd start calling everyone to find out where I was. My mom. Dad. Addie. My agent. Once I got pulled over by a cop when I was driving down I-24. Found out Lance had told that poor cop that I'd been kidnapped or something asinine like that. Just another instance of Lance trying to hunt me down. He alienated everyone and I didn't need a stalker in my life."

Ethan's scowl had faded as she told the story. "He really *was* a dick."

"Still is, according to his ex-wife. She tracked me down after they eloped to Vegas. Two weeks with him and she wanted out. Like he'd make it that easy. I had to hire a private detective to keep tabs on him for a while because I was terrified of him. Ironic, isn't it?"

"Didn't you write that song about him?" he asked.

"'Back Off, Bubba'?" A smile formed on Chelsea's lips. "Yeah, I did. He wasn't too happy about that." She let the smile fade. "I'm not living like that again, Ethan. Never again."

"I won't be like that," he insisted. "I was just..." He raked his fingers through his hair. "Look, all this is new to me. Okay? I've never...I don't know how to...I'll keep a lid on it."

What she got from his aborted sentences was that Ethan had never been jealous of anyone before. The thought that he hadn't been in love, that there'd been no woman about whom he cared enough to be jealous, hit her hard.

Was she his first?

Her phone distracted her, vibrating against her palm. She checked the screen then took the call. "Hi, Mom."

"Are you okay?" her mother asked. "I called last night. Got kinda worried when I didn't hear back from you."

"I...um...stayed at Ethan's last night." Although she'd told her mother a little about the budding relationship, Chelsea still kept some things to herself. Much as she cared for him, there were times in the three weeks they'd been together that she wondered if they were doomed from the start. Nothing had come easy to the two of them so far, and that showed no signs of improving.

He perked up, probably at his name. "Who's that?"

The question smacked of more jealousy. "My mother."

"Oh..." After letting out a resigned sigh, he said, "Sorry. That sounded bad didn't it? Jealous, right?"

Chelsea gave him a curt nod. "I have to get going, Mom. What did you need?"

"I didn't need anything, honey," her mother replied. "Just hadn't talked to you in a while. I guess I was a little...lonely."

Guilt draped over Chelsea. "Sorry. I've been so busy. I had three songs to finish for the December album, and now I need to start on the duets." Which was partly the truth. But she admitted to herself that she'd allowed her budding relationship with Ethan to dull her pain from the loss of her father. Her mother didn't have that luxury. "How about I come over tomorrow?"

"Lunch would be nice. If you're not too busy..."

"I'm never too busy for you, Mom. Love you."

"Love you too. See you at home tomorrow." Chelsea ended the call.

Ethan sat next to her on the couch and took her free hand in his. "I'll try to rein in the jealousy. I promise."

"That's all I ask." Perhaps the time had come to let Ethan know a little more about her world. If he was developing feelings for her as quickly as she was for him, she needed to share more of her life with him. "Why don't you come to lunch with me tomorrow? To, you know, meet my mom."

"You want to introduce me to your mom?"

"Yeah, I do," she admitted.

"I'd like that."

One more issue needed a solution. "How about you handle Words and Music today, and if you get a lull in the action, you can come to Brad's?"

He didn't appear too happy, judging from his frown. But he nodded. When she tried to stand, he pulled her back to the couch. "Thank you."

"For letting you come to the recording session?"

"For taking such good care of me yesterday." He brushed a kiss over her lips.

She wanted more, so she put her hand behind his head and held him still while she gave him a much deeper and more satisfying kiss. By the time she ended it, she found herself straddling his thighs. The man had the skill of making her forget herself.

"I should go," Chelsea said softly. Regretfully. Her resolve to wait a little longer before they got too intimate had cracked in wake of Ethan's kisses.

He wrapped his arms about her and stood, acting as though she weighed nothing.

With an appreciative sigh over his strength, she put her feet on the floor.

"I've got chores," he announced in a husky voice that brought a smile to her lips.

On tiptoes, she gave him a no-nonsense kiss. "Then let's get this day started."

CHAPTER SIXTEEN

Things weren't going well at all, and Chelsea was struggling not to let her frustration show.

Chuck Austin might've come from good stock, but he couldn't sing worth shit. Take after take, he went flat. Or sharp. Or couldn't keep the beat. She'd heard better singing at high school musicals.

The man wasn't exactly tone deaf, but he came pretty close.

Brad's voice buzzed through the headphones. "How about we take a short break and get something to drink? Then we can try one more take." He shot Chelsea a consolatory look.

She only hoped the rest of the duets weren't this much of a challenge. "Sounds good, Brad."

"We've already done... what? Twenty?" Chuck asked.

Closer to thirty, but since he sounded perturbed, she struggled to pacify him and reminded herself that he'd agreed to do this for charity—for her father's memory. "Brad's right. We could use a short break." She glanced through the glass at

Brad. "Maybe we could listen to a couple of the takes? See if we can do a little tweaking that might help?"

"Might be a good idea," Brad replied.

With a shake of his head, Chuck pulled off his headphones and set them on the music stand. "I'm getting a beer. Maybe that'll help."

Chelsea gave him a smile. "Sure, Chuck. Whatever you need."

He headed out of the booth and up the stairs.

Putting her own headphones aside, she checked her cell. She'd turned it off to minimize distractions, and once she powered it up, several text messages appeared. Addie asking questions that Chelsea tried to quickly answer. Her mother checking in. And Ethan.

She'd been pleased that he'd gone ahead and worked at Words & Music instead of hanging around, scowling at Chuck and probably intimidating him. Ethan's text asked how things were going. She replied honestly.

Slow. Really slow.

His reply came quickly.

Sorry to hear that. Mind if I stop by to see if I can help? WM is dead tonight.

Considering the trouble they were having recording this song, she was more than happy to have his support.

"I can clean things up a lot," Brad said when she joined him at the control table. "But probably not enough."

"Yeah . . ." She glanced at the stairs to see if Chuck was close enough to hear them. Thankfully, he was probably scrounging around the kitchen for a beer. "I'm getting really depressed."

"Hard to believe he's Vivian Austin's son. The woman had golden pipes."

"I was thinking the same thing." The more she thought about it, the more she wondered if Ethan might be able to help. If nothing else, he could be moral support for her, because at the moment she feared she'd bitten off more than she could chew. "Would you mind if Ethan came over?"

"I wondered if he'd be able to stay away," Brad said with a laugh. "Sure, have him come over if he's got stuff covered at Words and Music."

"Thanks." After firing off a quick text to Ethan to ask him to come whenever he could get away, Chelsea let out a sigh. "I could use a drink. Want me to grab something for you, Brad? A beer?"

"No, thanks. I'm gonna play around with this," he said. "I've got a couple of ideas I wanna try."

"Like what?" she asked.

"I'd like to make it more up-tempo," he replied. "It's a great song, but when Chuck sings it, the thing drags."

She nodded. "Might be a nice way to bring it into our era. Think you can take a little of the emphasis off the steel guitars? That might give it a more contemporary feel, too."

"Absolutely. That's a good idea, Chelsea."

Now she understood why he'd wanted to prerecord the instrumentals. Each individual part of the band was now in his control. If he wanted more horns, then all he had to do was adjust a toggle.

She set a hand on his shoulder. "Thank you for doing this. It means the world to me."

"My pleasure." He put his headphones back on and started fiddling with his equipment.

Voices drew her upstairs. Maybe Savannah had finished helping her daughter with her homework and was talking to Chuck. When she hit the top step, Chelsea recognized one of the voices through the open door.

Ethan's here.

"Well, well," she said when she entered the kitchen. "That was a quick drive, Mr. Walker."

Good Lord, the man's smile had the power to make her stomach somersault.

"I hit the speed of sound," he teased.

How long had he been sitting in the driveway, waiting for permission to come in?

The waiting made all the difference, though. Ethan was proving not to be like her ex. And that was all that mattered.

Sidling up next to him, she loved how he put his arm around her waist and pulled her closer. Then he dropped a kiss on the tip of her nose.

Chuck was leaning against the large kitchen island and he stared at them with knit brows. "Didn't know you two were an item."

Savannah set a longneck in front of Chuck. "No one knows, so please keep it to yourself, Chuck. Okay?"

"Sure thing," he said, still watching Chelsea and Ethan

closely. "Can't imagine Ethan ever settlin' down. Would be a helluva surprise."

"An understatement if I ever heard one," Savannah said with a wink to the couple.

Something about Chuck's tone raised Chelsea's antennae, but she couldn't exactly put her finger on why she was so concerned.

Paranoia, maybe? So far, with the exception of some rumors that had started when Ethan had attended her Black Stallion concerts, the media had pretty much left them alone. Addie fielded a few calls as reporters asked for confirmation of the juicy story, but Chelsea's social media accounts weren't loaded with questions about whether she and Ethan were really together. So far, Chelsea had kept silent, hoping some other celebrity would do something stupid to draw the attention their direction.

Ignoring Chuck, Ethan gave Chelsea a squeeze. "How are things going? Did you put the song to bed?"

"Not yet," she replied. "We're having a little trouble."

Savannah frowned. "That doesn't sound good. I think I'll head down and see if Brad needs anything—some tea or a snack." She headed down the stairs and out of sight.

Ethan turned Chelsea to stare into her eyes. "What's causing you trouble?"

While she wanted to tell him that Chuck couldn't seem to carry a tune in a bucket, she simply shrugged.

"Would you care if I go listen to a couple of takes?" Ethan asked.

"I'd like that."

Chuck glared at her. "Too many cooks spoil the soup, you know."

It took all Chelsea's control not to roll her eyes. She sent up a quick prayer that the rest of the duets wouldn't be nearly this difficult. At least most of the other children of Nashville stars she'd lined up to work with had experience singing. Hopefully, those recording sessions wouldn't be as agonizing as this one.

"Oh, come on, Chuck," Ethan said. "Sounds like this has been uphill so far. Maybe a new ear can help."

"Couldn't hurt," she added.

"Fine, whatever." He chugged the rest of his beer and set the empty bottle aside. "I'm hitting the john, then we can do a couple more versions." He made a point of checking his watch. "After that, I gotta go."

Alone with Ethan, Chelsea opened up. "I'm not sure a couple more takes will be enough."

"That bad?"

She nodded. "Brad and I are switching a few things up. Maybe that'll make a difference."

* * *

Hearing Chelsea sounding rather resigned for the first time made Ethan angry. Whatever was going wrong with the song had to be Chuck Austin's doing, because Chelsea could sound fantastic singing the phonebook.

When they made their way downstairs, she quickly turned and kissed him, making him smile against her lips. Not only did he enjoy her expressions of her feelings, he'd grown accustomed to them. Chelsea was so open with her affection, so giving. She made him want to be the kind of man who deserved her.

When she pulled away, Ethan snaked an arm around her to tug her back. Setting his lips against hers again, he nibbled and teased until she opened her mouth. He thrust his tongue inside.

His desire was consuming him whole. She was all he thought about day and night. The taste of her lips. The warmth of her skin. What she'd feel like when he was buried deep inside her.

There'd never been a woman who'd made him wait this long before he could make love to her.

Make love?

More like fuck.

Even comparing Chelsea to the other women who'd drifted in out of his bed was like putting grape juice up against Dom Pérignon. They weren't even in the same league. When he was with her, it would truly be making love—maybe for the first time in his life.

Chelsea would like hearing that.

He wanted her and he hoped to hell she'd feel the same by the time they were at Brad and Savannah's upcoming wedding.

Savannah's chuckle made him end the kiss, but he still held Chelsea close. "We'll continue this later," he whispered.

"Absolutely." Wiggling out of his arms, Chelsea hurried to Savannah, and the two of them started chatting as Chelsea made her way downstairs.

"So you two really are a couple," Chuck said as he strolled back in. "Lucky man."

Chuck had never been one of Ethan's favorite people. In fact, he was exactly what Ethan despised—the kid of a music star who acted as though he deserved fame because of his mother's hard work. When Chelsea told him Chuck had agreed to sing with her, Ethan's first thought had been that Chuck never did anything nice—not without an ulterior motive. That was the root of Ethan's jealousy, which he'd mostly gotten under control once she'd brought him to his senses.

But he still wondered exactly what was in this for Chuck...

"Shouldn't you get back to work?" Ethan asked, ignoring Chuck's comment. What was happening between Ethan and Chelsea was none of Chuck Austin's fucking business.

"Damn fine-looking woman," Chuck said as he headed toward the studio.

Ethan followed, wishing the recording was done so he could get her out of there. At least now, Savannah had joined them. She was sure to offer some great suggestions to improve things.

After giving Brad a friendly slap on the back, Ethan took the seat next to him while Chuck joined the women in the booth. "How bad is it really?"

Brad turned to give him an exasperated frown.

"That bad, huh?"

"That bad."

"Shit." Ethan sat back and stared at Chuck through the glass. "What are we gonna do about it?"

"Now that *you're* here," Brad replied. "I have an idea..."

* * *

"One more time?" Chuck asked and Ethan refrained from punching him in the nose.

Instead of giving into that impulse, he sang the verse again. Then he waited—with what little patience he had left—for Chuck to repeat it. At least he was on melody this time.

Brad was right. As usual. When Ethan sang first, showing Chuck exactly how the notes should sound, Chuck was able to repeat it reasonably close.

Brad had also been right about adding Savannah backup vocals as well. That had been done in two takes, then they'd focused on getting Chuck's tracks down. If they could only get Chuck to nail the last verse, Brad would be able to blend together one good version of all of Chuck's fits and spurts of decent singing.

Technology was going to save this song.

"Ready?" Brad said, his tone revealing his lost tolerance.

"Ready," Chuck replied. As the music played, he sang the last verse for the fourth time.

"Got it!" Brad said, pulling off his own headphones and setting them aside. Ethan was amazed his pronouncement wasn't followed with a "Hallelujah!"

Chuck extended his hand to Ethan. "Thanks, buddy."

Since he seemed sincere, Ethan shook his hand. "You're welcome."

Anything for Chelsea...

She'd taken off her own headphones, as had Savannah.

While Savannah headed out to talk to her fiancé, Chelsea joined Ethan and Chuck. After taking Ethan's hand, she smiled at her duet partner.

"Thank you so much for doing this," she said. "I'm sure you'll love the finished product."

"Trusting Hitman to polish it up pretty," Chuck replied.

Although he hated it, Ethan didn't make a peep when Chelsea kissed Chuck on the cheek. She was only thanking him.

"How 'bout a quick selfie?" Chuck asked, jerking his phone from his pocket. He sidled up to Chelsea and she obliged him with a picture. He waved Ethan over. "All three of us."

Ethan would've sooner had his arm broken, but Chelsea's weak smile made him change his mind and give in to Chuck's stupid request. Instead of a decent smile, he did an open mouth, wide-eyed campy expression.

"I need to run," Chuck said, pushing his phone back in his pocket as he left the booth. "Got a hot date who's probably tired of waiting on me."

"Have fun," Ethan said, glad to see the guy head up the stairs.

Savannah followed close behind.

Alone with Chelsea, Ethan asked, "Are you hungry, baby?"

"I'm starving! How about we go get some pizza? I've been dying for Luigi's deep dish. We can pick it up and go someplace quiet."

"Luigi's it is." He kissed her forehead.

Before they could step out of the recording booth, Brad

pushed the intercom and his voice filled the room. "Could the two of you do me a favor? Please?"

"Of course!" Chelsea replied before Ethan could. "What is it?"

"Sing the damn song just once so I can hear what it should sound like? All I can hear in my head right now is Chuck sounding like a scalded cat."

About to refuse, Ethan bit back his words when Chelsea turned her pleading eyes on him. They clearly weren't getting out of there until Ethan sang with her.

He narrowed his eyes at Brad, who grinned in return as he put his headphones back on. Chelsea did the same, so Ethan gave in and donned his own set.

"I only need it once," Brad said.

"Because you're recording it," Ethan drawled. "As usual."

"Absolutely."

"Asshole."

"Takes one to know one." With a grin, Brad started the instrumental playback.

* * *

Singing always touched a part of Chelsea's heart. It was one of the reasons she felt so blessed that she could earn a living doing what she loved best in the world. Even if she'd never been anything more than a backup singer, she would've been content.

Before Ethan came into her life, singing had been wonderful; with him, it seemed as close to heaven as she could get here on Earth.

One take was all they needed, because performing the love song had her heart reaching for his. And his heart had reached back.

Savannah had returned to sit at Brad's side. When the recording ended, she'd wiped away a tear.

Chelsea wasn't at all surprised to find one of her own tears had spilled over her lashes to trace a lazy path down her cheek.

Ethan brushed it away before giving her a smile that made her realize her life was never going to be the same.

I'm falling in love him.

Hurrying into the booth, Savannah hugged Chelsea. "That was awesome." Then she turned to Ethan and playfully swatted his chest. "You missed your true calling, my friend."

"She's right," Chelsea said. "You shouldn't waste that voice, Ethan. It's a damned shame."

"Not wasting it," he retorted. "I'm gonna sing a duet with you, remember?"

"That's not what I mean, and you know it."

Savannah chimed in, "You two really should record an album. Double platinum. Guaranteed."

"When hell freezes over," Ethan insisted as he led the women out of the room.

After setting his headphones aside, Brad rose and stretched. "God forbid that he ever deign to follow in Crawfish's footsteps."

"You remember what Brad suggested before, Chelsea?" Savannah asked. "Now's the time to start the buzz with a few teaser videos."

"I remember. And it's a great idea, but which version

should we use?" Chelsea asked. "I mean Brad can probably clean up Chuck's, but I'm sure it'll take some time."

"Ethan's version, of course," Savannah replied. "Not the whole song. Just thirty seconds or so..."

Brad fiddled with his controls. "Could have it up later tonight, if you'd like. What d'ya think, Chelsea?"

"If it brings in more sales, then it raises more money for cancer research. So what's to lose?" Then she realized she needed a bit of advice. "I probably should check with my publicist first."

Ethan rolled his eyes. "Seriously? Something this silly needs to go through your publicist?"

Bristling, she frowned before realizing he was right. It was just a few bars of a song. "No, I guess not..." She made a mental note to tell Will the next time they spoke.

Grateful for all Brad and Savannah had done for her, Chelsea said, "We're heading for pizza. Let me thank you both by buying you a very late supper."

A low growl rose from Ethan.

"What?" she asked, hoping he wasn't going to pitch a fit about a few seconds of his gorgeous voice being released.

Leaning down, he whispered in her ear, "I want to be alone with you."

"You're not mad about Brad releasing the song."

He shook his head and whispered, "I'm mad we're not alone."

His warm breath caused a delicious shiver to race through her. But her revelation that she was falling in love him made her vulnerable. Selfish as it might be, she wanted a little more time to win his heart before they lost themselves in what was sure to be a consuming physical relationship. Once they were at the wedding and away from Nashville and the paparazzi, they would have more privacy anyway. It seemed like the perfect time to take the next step in their relationship.

She crooked her finger to bring him close again. "We'll have plenty of alone time tomorrow after lunch with my mom," she whispered. "Promise."

Savannah seemed concerned as she shifted her gaze between them. "We could take a rain check..."

"Nope," Ethan said, making Chelsea smile. "Let me get the munchkin. We're all going out for pizza."

CHAPTER SEVENTEEN

The four-story building housing Chelsea's condo was a fortress. To even get close to the entrance, Ethan had to pass through a parking lot security gate manned by a guy with massive arms and no neck. After parking his car, he entered a two-story lobby and had to sign in with two uniformed security guards, one of whom checked his ID against a list of approved guests. The younger guard eyed him suspiciously while the older one gave him directions to Chelsea's condo.

Since she was on the first floor, Ethan had to wander a long hallway to reach her front door. He pushed the doorbell. His finger had barely touched the button when the door swung open. He grinned at the notion that Chelsea had been watching through the peephole for him to arrive.

After pizza last night, she'd been exhausted, so he hadn't pressed the point. Thankfully, only a few people had bugged her for autographs or pictures, probably because the restaurant was all but deserted by the time they got there. Chelsea and Caroline had both yawned through the whole meal.

She'd needed rest and he was still pretty stiff and sore. So he let her get some sleep, no matter how badly he'd wished they could have had some time to themselves. Now, he faced lunch with her mother.

What would *that* inquisition be like?

Unfortunately, the face that frowned at him through the now open door wasn't Chelsea's. A woman who couldn't be more than five feet tall with short spiked brown hair and glasses with thick purple frames swept Ethan a hard look that started at his face and stopped at his hands. "Where's the package?" the irritated brunette asked.

He quirked an eyebrow. "Package?"

"Yeah, the package you were supposed to—" Her mouth shifted to a surprised O. "You're not the pharmacy delivery guy."

"I'm not the pharmacy delivery guy."

She covered her glasses with her hand and bowed her head. "Fuck. Please tell me that you're not—"

"Ethan!" Chelsea called from where she'd stepped into the tiled foyer of her condo.

"Hi, baby." As he stepped across the threshold, the brunette backed up to give him room. Hoping to put her at ease, he smiled. "You must be the infamous Addie."

"I am," she replied. "And you're Ethan Walker." She stuck out her hand in greeting. "Pleasure to meet you." She cocked her head at Chelsea. "She's told me a lot about you."

"She's told me about you, too," he said. "You've gotta know she really depends on you."

Quaintly, the woman blushed. He was surprised she didn't drag her toe across the tile and say, "Aw shucks." Instead, she said, "Thanks."

"What were you ladies expecting to be delivered?" Ethan asked.

As though the question were a cue, Addie sneezed. "Allergy medicine," she replied before sniffling.

"Hard frost predicted tonight," he said. "Should give you some relief."

Addie shook her head. "It's not hay fever. It's the cat."

"Cat?"

Chelsea nodded. "My cat. Loki." Turning, she called down the hall, "Here, kitty, kitty, kitty."

The tinkling of a tiny bell announced the animal's entrance before it appeared. Loki was a black cat with a heart-shaped patch of white on his chest. After an affectionate rub against Chelsea's leg, the cat sat, wrapped his long tail around his paws, and focused intense yellow eyes on Ethan.

Why did he feel as though he were being judged?

The women seemed greatly amused by the cat's inspection, grinning at each other before Addie let out another sneeze.

"Why would you get a cat if your assistant is allergic to them?" he asked.

"I didn't," Chelsea replied.

"I got it for her," Addie said.

Ethan knit his brows. "You got it? That makes no sense. Why would you want a cat hanging around here when you're allergic?"

"She wanted a pet and cats are easier than dogs." With a

smile, Addie said, "I'm allergic to most of those, too. And goldfish are so fucking boring."

"Potty mouth," Chelsea said, scooping up Loki.

"Like a sailor," Addie said with a wink. "It's what you love best about me. No bullshit when Addie's on the job."

With a flip of her wrist, Chelsea motioned to him. "C'mon in, Ethan. I was almost ready to go."

It wasn't as if he was in a hurry to get to her mother's home. He had no idea what he was going to say to her or how she'd react to her daughter dating a guy who might have one of the worst reputations in Tennessee. Since Chelsea never seemed to judge his rather sordid past, he hoped that meant she'd come to terms with it. But what about her mother?

Instead of admitting his anxiety, he followed Chelsea from the foyer into an enormous living area with high ceilings.

Considering the place was all white, glass, and chrome, he was shocked Addie would choose a black cat. The only color was found in the dark hardwood floors and the vibrant red and royal-blue pillows and throws on the plush sectional. Floor-to-ceiling windows looked out over a lake.

"This place is awesome," he said. "From the outside, you'd never know how huge it is in here. Just looks like an apartment building."

"Yeah, surprised me, too. I toured it thinking it wouldn't be anything special. But it was. The complex is built into a hill, so its size is deceptive—looks small outside but is huge inside. And I love the security here." A smile blossomed. "Do you know who my closest neighbor is?"

Considering the tight security he'd pass through, he

wouldn't be too shocked at any celebrity she named. "No, who?"

"Grace Burns. You know, the author."

Ethan knew the name well. The woman wrote some of the best thrillers he'd ever read, horror stories mostly. "That doesn't scare you?" he teased. "I mean, the stuff that woman dreams up... After I read her last book, I had to sleep with the lights on for a week."

When Addie giggled, he grinned at her.

"Actually, it did at first," Chelsea replied. "Some of her stories give me the willies." She set Loki down on the sofa and stroked his back as he arched to meet her touch and let out a rumbling purr.

"He loves you," Ethan commented. "All my cat does is hunt mice in the barn. If I tried to pet him like that, I'd lose some skin."

"Loki's a pet, not a barn cat. I love having him around. Gives me company when I get—" She frowned. "I need to grab my jacket. Boy, when fall hits in Nashville, it hits with a vengeance, doesn't it?"

"When you get what?"

"Lonely," Addie said, skirting around the sofa to show Chelsea something on the tablet she held. "This work for you, boss?"

After considering whatever was on the screen for a moment, Chelsea nodded. "Be sure and see if Brad is fine with that time too. Glad Marie is on board."

"Already on it. Emailing him now." Without a backward glance, Addie hurried out of the door, disappearing back into what looked like an office on the far side of the room while Chelsea dug around in the coat closet.

Hearing that Chelsea was lonely felt like a punch to the gut. Sure, Ethan had great friends like Brad and Russ. Plus there was always Joe hanging around. Yet there were a lot of nights where the four walls seemed to close in around him and he wished he weren't so alone...

Wishing didn't get you anywhere. Men like him were fine all on their lonesome.

Bullshit.

Not surprisingly, the voice in his head sounded a hell of a lot like Joe. Come to think of it, Joe's voice was often his conscience as well as his common sense. Which was logical. Joe had been more of a father to Ethan than Crawfish Walker could've ever claimed to be.

"Here it is." Chelsea pulled a purple jacket off a hanger and closed the closet door.

Ethan helped her don the coat just as the doorbell chimed, which sent a sneezing Addie scurrying out of the office.

"Better fucking well be my Benadryl," she said as she hurried past. "Sneezing my skinny ass off here."

The woman made him smile.

On tiptoes, she peeked out the peephole. "What the ass?"

"Who is it?" Chelsea asked as she zipped her coat.

"Jason." Addie opened the door to reveal one of the uniformed security guards, the one who appeared barely old enough to shave. "What's up?"

Leaning to his left, he looked past Addie. "I wanted to bring you your medicine, Ms. Harris. The guy who brought it looked kinda... suspicious, and you already have a guest. So I sent him on his way." He directed a rather hostile glare at Ethan. "Didn't want anyone disturbing you. Anyone *else*."

Addie snatched the sack. "Thank you. And goodbye." She shut the door in his face.

Since the kid was clearly crushing on Chelsea, Ethan was glad to see him gone. "Best assistant in the world," he said as Addie passed him, jerking a box of Benadryl from the gray sack.

"Fuckin' A." She turned left in the great room and disappeared, probably looking for something to drink so she could take the allergy meds.

"I should've given you a tour of the condo." Chelsea checked her watch. "But I told Mom we'd be there by noon. How about I show you around when we get back?"

"Sounds like a plan." Besides, he always faced problems instead of avoiding them, which meant he wanted this trial by fire over and done.

"Why are you scowling at me?"

"I'm not." Hand on the small of her back, he guided her to the door. "Let's get this show on the road."

* * *

The whole drive to her mother's, Chelsea worried that she'd made a mistake in inviting Ethan to meet her mother. His mood was sour and she wished she knew if that was because he was being forced to meet her mother or if there was something else bugging him.

Every attempt she made at conversation was deflected by Ethan with the expertise of a NHL goalie. By the time he pulled his truck into the driveway, she was ready to have him turn it around and take her right back to her home.

When he popped his seatbelt and reached for the door handle, she grabbed his arm. "Wait. Please."

"What?"

"Can I ask you something?"

He nodded.

"What's got you so pissy today?"

She'd expected him to get angrier because of the question, especially her rather abrupt wording. Instead, his features softened and he let out a small sigh. "I *was* being kinda pissy, wasn't I?"

"Yep. Care to explain why?"

Another sigh. "This is new to me."

His pensive tone made her smile. "What's new?"

"Meeting the folks. I've never actually done something like this before."

"Never? You didn't have a girlfriend who made you meet Mommy and Daddy?"

"Not a one. Hell, I never got past a couple of dates before."

Chelsea couldn't help but tease him. "Virgin territory, then? You know for a guy with your reputation, you seem to be rather...um...inexperienced."

At least Ethan chuckled. "Yeah, I suppose I do. This relationship stuff is new to me."

She took his hand and gave it a squeeze. "It's only my

mom, Ethan. This isn't a big commitment or anything. You're just meeting my mom."

"You're right." After returning her squeeze, he reached for the door again. "Ready?"

"Absolutely." Unlatching her own seatbelt, she opened the door before Ethan could come around to do it for her. She took his hand again and led him to the front door.

Her parents' house hadn't changed in years. When they'd moved away from Nashville, they'd kept the house, renting it out until they finally returned. She'd sat on the same swing, run laps on the wraparound porch, and sung her heart out to the birds in the weeping willows. It was so easy to picture her father raking leaves or her mother hanging out the sheets on the clothesline.

Thankfully, Chelsea's publicist, Will, had foreseen the intrusive nature of the press and convinced her parents to put the house into a trust so their real names weren't on the deed. No one seemed aware that this was the house where Chelsea Harris had grown up. Back then, she'd been known as Chelsea Maddox, a name she'd chosen to leave behind. Harris had come to her by accident. She'd been tossing around possible stage names with her agent, who happened to say she hoped Chelsea's career soared. That image made her think of spaceships, which made her think of *Star Wars*, and then an image of Harrison Ford popped into her head. When she said she liked the name Harrison, her agent suggested shortening it to Harris, and Chelsea Harris had been born that day, leaving Chelsea Maddox and her Welsh roots behind.

Never in her wildest imagination had she expected that

she'd have the career she now enjoyed. Sure, there was the constant hassle of the press interfering in her life, and yet the love from the fans nourished her like blood fed a vampire. Until she'd met Ethan, she hadn't considered reporters to be anything but a nuisance. Now, judging by his deep hatred for publicity, she fretted about whether they'd ruin any chance she had for something long-lasting with him.

When he reached up to knock, Chelsea brushed his hand aside. "Family doesn't knock." She pushed the door open. "Hi, Mom. I'm home!"

* * *

There was so much joy in Chelsea's voice that Ethan couldn't help but smile.

A plump middle-aged brunette, complete with apron and fuzzy slippers, came out into the hallway where he was helping Chelsea take off her jacket. "Chelsea!" She quickly wrapped her daughter in a warm hug.

The aroma of home cooking filled his nostrils, and he breathed in deeply. When he'd been growing up, those wonderful smells had meant his mom and dad were back from whatever trip they'd been on. Once in her own kitchen, which wasn't often, Dottie had gone crazy roasting and baking, probably trying to make up for being an absentee mother. Ethan would always stuff his belly and then try to hang on to his mom as much as possible before she and Crawfish went on the road again.

"You must be Ethan," the woman said after she'd turned her daughter loose.

"Yes, ma'am." He held out his hand.

"Ethan Walker," Chelsea said, "this is Betsy Maddox."

Instead of shaking his hand, Betsy grinned and hugged him.

Dottie had been a thin, tall woman. Not this lady. She was full-figured and her hug gave him a weird sort of comfort. He even hugged her back.

"Why don't ya'll come into the kitchen? I've got fresh coffee. God knows my Chelsea runs on the stuff." She patted her daughter's arm and then shuffled off in her purple slippers. "Fresh cinnamon rolls just came outta the oven."

"So that's what smells so wonderful," he said, following her. When Chelsea pulled out one of the bar stools at the big kitchen island, he did the same. A few moments later, they both had a mug of coffee in front of them.

"Would you two like some rolls?" Betsy asked.

"No, thank you, ma'am," Ethan replied. "I'll save mine for after lunch. Everything smells great." He turned to Chelsea. "So Harris isn't your real last name. You never told me that."

As she poured sweetener in her coffee, she shrugged.

"Is it even Chelsea?"

"Yeah, that's my real first name. Chelsea. Chelsea Lorraine Maddox."

"Lorraine was my granny," Betsy added. She poured herself a cup of coffee then turned to face the couple. "You'll forgive me if I seem a bit... nervous, but Chelsea has never brought a beau home to meet me."

He stared at Chelsea. "Never? *Now*, who's in virgin territory?"

Her cheeks flushed pink as her mother chuckled.

"Since her daddy's passed..." All the humor seemed to flee from her features as Betsy leveled a hard stare at Ethan. "It falls to me to ask the question—what exactly are your intentions toward my daughter, Ethan Walker?"

CHAPTER EIGHTEEN

Mom!" Chelsea felt as though she were blushing to the roots of her hair. "Stop being so silly!"

"I'm silly? To worry about my only daughter?" Betsy feigned innocence, pressing a hand to her bosom. "I'm wounded to the core, Chelsea Lorraine."

The smile on Ethan's face helped Chelsea relax. He'd taken the question for teasing. Oh, it might be disguised by exaggeration, but she knew better. Betsy Maddox looked and acted like Susie Homemaker for Ethan's benefit, but she was as sharp as a tack and guarded her daughter like a tigress.

"Not silly at all," he said. "As for my intentions—"

Chelsea put her hand over the one Ethan had rested on the counter. "Stop." She glanced to her mother. She narrowed her eyes at her mother.

With an airy chuckle, Betsy let her hand drop away from her chest. "I should stop teasing the poor man. He's not used to the Maddox warped sense of humor."

The comment made Chelsea smile. Her father had always been irreverent and sarcastic, a trait shared by his wife and offspring. But that still didn't excuse her mother's thinly veiled fishing expedition.

"On the contrary," Ethan said. "I speak the same language since sarcasm is Uncle Joe's native tongue."

"Uncle Joe?" Betsy asked.

While Ethan enlightened her about Joe's role in his life, Chelsea settled back to sip her coffee. The ice was broken and he appeared no worse for the wear.

Having drifted off in thought about what to wear to the wedding, she was startled when Ethan nudged her. "So am I really the first guy you ever brought home?"

Betsy chimed in. "Absolutely. Why, even in high school, she was too busy singin' to date. Skipped her senior prom."

Ethan chuckled. "A late bloomer, huh?"

Before Chelsea could think of what to say, her phone rang. *Saved by the ringtone.*

"It's Addie. I better take it." She slipped out of the kitchen to answer her assistant's call. "What's up?"

"Did you know the Hitman was going to release a fucking video of you and Ethan singing?" Addie's tone was agitated, which was a rare thing. One of the reasons Chelsea loved working with her was that she was virtually unflappable, even if she cursed a bit too much. The woman was solid as a rock.

"Yeah, I knew," Chelsea replied. "I forgot to tell you and Will. Brad said it would help preorders on the album. It was only supposed to be a minute or so, not the whole song. You know, good publicity and all."

"Oh, it was definitely *publicity*." Addie snorted. "*Good* might be another story."

"What are you talking about?"

"I've been flooded with a shitstorm of calls, text, emails. Every fucking entertainment reporter in the country wants confirmation."

"Confirmation of what? That I'm doing a charity album? That's old news."

"They want confirmation that you and Ethan are engaged," Addie replied.

"That's crazy," Chelsea insisted. "Why would a duet video make people think we're engaged?"

Addie didn't have to answer, because Chelsea's own naiveté stung her like a slap across the face. She'd been so thrilled with how great she and Ethan had sounded together, and so focused on making money for cancer research, that she hadn't thought about other repercussions, especially how the press would react.

"Chuck the Asshole Austin," Addie said with venom in her voice. "*He's* why."

"Chuck?" Chelsea asked. "What does he have to do with this?"

"He blew up his social media this morning with comments about the recording session."

"Like what? The whole thing was a mess. I can't imagine he'd want to post that Ethan had to sing every stupid note before he could carry a tune." The session had been a nightmare. Why would Chuck embarrass himself like that?

"Not a fucking word about himself. All he talks about is how you and Ethan were hot and heavy," Addie said.

"*What?*"

"He said he could barely get his song down because you and Ethan were too busy pawing at each other."

That son of a bitch.

Ethan came stomping into the hallway, a fierce scowl distorting his handsome face. "That son of a bitch."

"I take it Ethan found out," Addie drawled.

Chelsea sighed. "That would be my guess, too."

"Want me to release a statement of denial?" Addie asked.

"No. Not yet, at least," Chelsea replied. "We need to think this one through carefully. For now, our best tactic is probably silence."

"For the short term, I agree. Let me talk to Will and see what he recommends."

Since Will Laurence was a fantastic publicist and had done some great work for her and her career, he would definitely have some ideas on how to put out this fire. He was sure to be pissed that she hadn't told him about the video. "Good idea," Chelsea said. "I'll get back to you after I talk to Ethan."

"Damn right, you're talking to me," he said with a scorching scowl.

"Stay off all your social media accounts," Addie advised.

"Absolutely." Chelsea ended the call, her head spinning.

Despite her promise, the first thing she did was open one of her apps. Addie had meant to refrain from posting but there was no reason Chelsea couldn't take a look to see if her assistant had been exaggerating the news. This whole engagement tale couldn't be a big thing. All he was trying to do was start a stupid rumor. No one would care.

Chelsea was trending.

So was Ethan.

So was their "engagement."

"Fuck a duck," he said as he stared over her shoulder at his screen. "When I see Chuck, I'm gonna strangle him with my bare hands."

Since she was inclined to do the same, she didn't scold him for the threat. It took all her willpower to not start posting that Chuck Austin was entirely full of shit.

The nerve of the guy…

"What's going on?" her mother asked as she joined them. "Thought we were getting ready to eat."

"Remember the song I recorded with Vivian Austin's son last night?" Chelsea asked.

Betsy nodded.

"Ethan and I sang the same song after Chuck Austin left."

"Why on earth would you do that?" her mother asked.

"Chuck sounded like a braying donkey," Ethan said. "So after he left, Chelsea and I sang it together."

"Ah. Sort of cleansed the palate, huh?"

"Something like that," he replied.

Chelsea wanted to scream in frustration. Seemed like every step of the way, this album had been nothing but a headache.

The road to good intentions…

"And now…?" Betsy coaxed.

"Chuck is all over Twitter, saying Ethan and I are engaged," Chelsea replied.

"Are you?" Betsy's question was thankfully followed by a wink.

"Why would he do this?" Chelsea asked, not caring if either person replied. All she wanted was to get Chuck to stop being a jerk. Unfortunately, the damage was done, and a bell couldn't be unrung.

"My guess," Ethan said, "is that he's pissed."

"Why would he be pissed? I was so patient with him last night. I sang until my throat hurt even when he kept screwing up!"

"He's pissed because we put our version online, and it was a helluva lot better than any of his million takes of the song."

That made perfect sense and also made her feel entirely stupid. "Everyone knows it's his mom's song. Why didn't I think of that?"

"We showed him up," Ethan said. "He knows everyone will compare his version to ours, and his will come up short. *Way* short."

"I'm an idiot. I didn't even think about that."

"Quit beating yourself up. Neither did Brad or I."

Chelsea gave her full attention to her phone, wanting to see the damage Chuck had done. Her time line was clogged with fans asking if the rumor was true. There was no way she could answer without making the feeding frenzy worse. If she and Ethan were seen together in public, everyone would just assume they were lying should they deny the engagement. Every eye would be on them if they did something as simple as get a bite to eat or go see a movie.

"That's a good one," Ethan said, pointing at a post as he returned to reading over her shoulder. "What an asshole."

"What's it say?" Betsy asked.

"That Chelsea should demand I be tested for STDs before the wedding."

While she wanted to keep reading simply out of morbid curiosity, Chelsea closed the app and slid her phone in her pocket.

"Hey!" he protested. "I was reading those."

The majority of what she'd read had been adamantly against the marriage, and she not only didn't need to see that kind of negativity, she didn't think Ethan did, either. The comments she'd read ranged from calling him the Hugh Hefner of Nashville to out-and-out insults on how people believed he was mishandling his parents' legacy.

She'd come to terms with his past. Whatever he'd done, he'd done it before he'd met her. How could she hold that against him?

At least the public seemed to love the duet Brad had released, although it was the only thing about her pairing off with Ethan that they seemed to support. Even worse, that duet was the reason they were in this mess.

Ethan jerked his own phone out of his pocket and started scrolling.

"I didn't know you had an account," Chelsea said, a bit shaken that he participated in any kind of social media.

"I don't. But I have an account to follow some people. It's private, so no followers."

Great. So he could see all the vitriol directed at him.

Having never stopped to consider the reaction people might have to her and Ethan being a couple, she was taken by surprise at the adamancy of her fans. Sure, the man had a bit of a reputation with women. But so had a couple of her other boyfriends.

So why was everyone dead set against the two of them?

Her phone rang again, so she fished it out of her pocket and answered Addie's call. "What did Will say?"

"He said he wants a raise," Addie quipped.

"Addie..." Chelsea scolded.

"No fucking sense of humor. He said we have two choices. We can ignore it and hope it goes away, which he doesn't think is likely. Or—"

"Or what?"

"Geesh. A little patience there, boss. Or...we can try to get ahead of the fucking storm. You know, spin it in our favor."

How like Addie to say "we" and "our" as though this nightmare was happening to her, too. "How does he want to do that?"

Ethan tapped her on the shoulder.

"Addie, I'm putting you on speaker."

"Will says we need to get our own information out there, but he wants to meet with you first."

"Who's Will?" Ethan asked, obviously not remembering that she'd mentioned him before.

"My publicist," Chelsea replied. "Why does he need to meet with me?"

"He didn't say," Addie replied, "other than to tell you to keep your trap shut until you do. Otherwise, he said you could easily step into a huge pile of shit."

"Will doesn't curse," Chelsea reminded her.

"I paraphrased."

"Call him back and tell him I can come in within the hour."

"What about lunch?" Betsy asked.

"I'm going too," Ethan insisted.

"Are you both coming?" Addie asked. "Not a bad idea. He'll want the two of you to be on the same page. Assuming..."

"Assuming what?" Ethan asked.

"Assuming we decide to go on the offensive."

The scowl on his face was hot enough to melt an ice cube while it was still in the freezer. "Great. Just great."

It wasn't as if Chelsea needed someone to tell her what had him so pissed. The last thing in the world Ethan wanted was publicity—of any kind. The notion of trying to handle the backlash of Chuck's absurdity by launching a social media campaign was probably the least appealing thing he could imagine.

"When I get my hands on him..." His hands were clenched into tight fists.

"I get first shot," Chelsea said, hoping to defuse a little of his anger. "Giving him a nice black eye sounds mighty appealing."

Not even the hint of a smile.

"What's the verdict?" Addie asked.

"I should talk to Will." Chelsea locked eyes with Ethan. "My condo? An hour?"

He gave her a curt nod.

"See if that works for him," Chelsea told Addie. "Call me back if he can't swing that."

"You got it."

Ending the call, Chelsea turned to her mom. "Let's wolf down that lunch. Then we need to run."

"Wolf down, my fat fanny." With a wave for them to follow, Betsy turned to head toward the kitchen. "You'll both eat a proper lunch so you can deal with this little hiccup."

* * *

The lunch hadn't been the disaster Ethan had feared. He found that he enjoyed talking to Betsy Maddox. In her easygoing way, she put him at ease, even with her joking questions about his relationship with Chelsea. He knew quite well that she was serious about him treating her daughter well, but he'd felt nothing but welcome in her home.

Then he remembered Chuck Austin and got angry all over again.

The same security guards were in the lobby when they got back to Chelsea's place, and the younger one still gazed at her with puppy-dog eyes. She smiled at them as they passed the checkpoint and made their way through the complex to her front door.

Chelsea let them in, tossed her coat on the foyer bench, and reached for Ethan's jacket. "Addie?"

"In here," her assistant called. "Will's here too."

Taking Ethan's hand, Chelsea led him to the cavernous living room.

His first thought was that any guy with a "man bun" was too prissy to handle the kind of tempest coming their way.

Then the man's eyes caught Ethan's. There was steel in that gaze, so he decided to hear him out to see what they could all do to stop Chuck's rumors.

"Hi, Will." Chelsea inclined her head at Ethan. "This is Ethan Walker." As the men shook hands and then sat, she flopped on her sectional as her cat came to curl up against her thigh. She ran her hand over his fur almost absentmindedly. "Addie said something about going on the offensive?"

"That's the plan," Will replied, grabbing his tablet from the glass coffee table. He typed in a few commands. "But I wanted to talk to you first. To be sure that's really what you want to do."

"What I want," she replied, "is to go back a few days and tell Chuck that I didn't need his help on the album."

"That album is in your favor," Will said. "You're doing it entirely for charity, for cancer research. That brings a lot of goodwill." He stared at Ethan. "What are your thoughts?"

"My thoughts are that if we just ignore the gossip, people will find some other bandwagon to jump on," Ethan replied.

"That's one tack we could take." Will touched his screen a few more times. "But then we have no chance to spin any of the chatter our direction."

"You think you can control a rumor?" Ethan asked.

"In some ways, yes, I do. The right information gets out there, the more people will carry the message. Chelsea has an extraordinarily supportive fan base. If we release something about how happy she is, how much this relationship means to her, those fans will grab it and run."

"But we're not engaged," Chelsea said.

"That's what we announce," Will explained. "We make it clear that you two are dating but haven't gotten too serious."

"Like they'll believe it just 'cause we say it," Ethan said with a shake of his head.

He hated the idea of exposing his relationship with Chelsea to public scrutiny, but if they didn't say something that scrutiny would probably continue to be nothing but people warning her away from him.

The posts he'd read had been brutal, a few hitting him like a punch in the gut. One of the things he hated about the Internet was the general lack of civility. Posts were often juvenile, petty, and downright cruel—like a bunch of bullies on a playground. The more anonymous the account, the worse the postings.

"You'd be amazed." Will cast a wary glance at Ethan before turning to Chelsea. "The question I need to ask is this: Are the two of you serious?"

Chelsea cocked an eyebrow. "Serious?"

"Yeah. In a committed relationship," he replied. "If we start sending information that the two of you are together... Wait, you're not engaged are you?"

"No," she replied in a soft voice.

"Then we need to clarify that by telling them exactly what's happening. If we keep your fans in the loop, so to speak, they aren't as likely to pay attention to outrageous stories like Chuck's."

"What you mean by 'clarify' is to invade our privacy," Ethan said, resisting the urge to growl at the man for being so damned nosey.

"I don't mean to be digging into your business," Will explained. "But if we decide to hit this hard and get her fans on your side, you two need to be genuine."

This time, Ethan did growl—only his irritation eased and the sound ended abruptly when Chelsea took his hand. Funny how she kept having that kind of calming effect on him.

A bit of a miracle, that.

"We *are* genuine," she told Will. "The question isn't whether we're in a relationship. The question is whether we want to open up and share that with everyone. I'm not sure Ethan's ready for that."

Her statement told Ethan everything he needed to know about her opinion on the subject. Judging from Addie nodding to almost everything Will said, she felt the same. They were all prepared to blab private business.

Looks like I'm the only one who doesn't want my love life paraded around the whole fucking world. . .

"Ethan?" Chelsea asked quietly. "We can still hope it all just dies down. I don't want to do anything that makes you uncomfortable."

He didn't say anything, because he didn't want to show her his anger. She knew how he felt about publicity, especially about his private life. But he was angry.

And getting angrier by the minute.

But angry at whom?

Chuck? *Absolutely.*

Every gossipy asshole on the Internet? *No doubt.*

But why was some of his anger directed at Chelsea?

Because she was famous, and no matter how much he

wished she wasn't, her life was never going to change. And if he wanted to be a part of that life, he was going to find himself in the public eye. The last place in the world he wanted to be.

CHAPTER NINETEEN

I *sure stepped in it this time.*

Chelsea huffed out a long breath, then realized she'd let her frustration with Ethan show. His fierce frown told her as much.

No wonder. Here she was dictating to him how *she* wanted to handle this crisis—a crisis that involved him as much as it did her. Having made decisions on her own for so long, it was hard to get accustomed to considering someone else's point of view.

"I'm sorry," she said, taking his hand. "I didn't...Look, this time we'll play it your way." She glanced to Addie and then to Will. "We're going to let this rumor burn out on its own. No postings. No going on the offensive."

Addie's brows knit, an expression Chelsea knew well. It was the same look her assistant gave her every time she thought her boss was making a big mistake. "Chel, are you sure that's what you want to do?"

Not at all. I want to meet it head-on like I do everything else.

"This should be Ethan's call," Chelsea replied, swallowing her own apprehension.

Why wasn't he saying anything? He had to appreciate her gesture, right?

Oh, who was she kidding? This was the kind of nightmare he'd always feared, had always wanted to avoid. And she'd plopped him smack dab in the middle of it. Amazing that he wasn't running for the hills.

Which meant he must really care for her. She'd do her best to make this right.

"Seriously, Will," she said. "I want Ethan to make the choice. I'm used to this kind of bullshit; he avoids it like the plague."

"If we decide to maintain silence," Will advised, "then you're both gonna have to lay low. Really low. Stay out of the public eye. 'Cause if we act like you're not together, and people see you two out and about, you'll lose every ounce of credibility you've ever had."

"But we *are* together," Ethan said, his tone stern.

"Not in public, you're not," Will said with a scolding lilt. "In fact, if we stay silent, the best thing you two can do is go your separate ways—at least for a while. You can't be seen together."

The words were like a knife to her heart. She'd barely begun to win Ethan's affections. Every ounce of patience she had was used in waiting to hear what he would say to Will's suggestion. But she needed to know his answer. If he was willing to stay apart simply to avoid publicity, he wasn't the man she thought he was.

Ethan shook his head. "Nope. Not happening. We're together. Just because we're not engaged doesn't meant we need to hide like a couple of criminals. Shit, I hate the press."

"Don't we all?" Will gave them a sardonic grin. "Then let's use the vultures. I can release a statement. You know, tell the public you're dating, for want of a better word. Better yet, the two of you should sit down with a reporter and— Why are you shaking your head now?"

"I don't talk to reporters," Ethan said. "Ever. That's off the table."

Thrilled that he'd so adamantly insisted that he wouldn't leave her behind just to avoid some publicity, Chelsea tried to solve this rather troublesome puzzle. How could they be together but not let everyone know they were together? Silence didn't seem to be the right tack, but it wasn't what Ethan wanted.

"So any press is out?" Will asked. "Not even a quick statement."

"Absolutely nothing about Chelsea and me. No interview. No statement. *Nothing*," Ethan replied, glancing to Chelsea. "If I'm still making the choice."

She nodded.

Will shut his tablet cover with a loud snap that made her wonder if he'd shattered the screen. "Well, then . . . I have only one piece of advice left." He stood. "Get out of Nashville."

Chelsea jumped to her feet, sending the cat seeking a new place to lie down. "What? Why would we leave Nashville?"

"I didn't mean forever," Will said with the easy smile that she was more accustomed to seeing. "I mean until the heat dies down. If you two go on a vacay, no worries about being spotted. Right?"

"I don't get why it even matters," Ethan said, pulling her back down beside him on the sectional. He kept a tight hold of her hand. "Who gives a shit whether we go out for tacos? Hell, it might even help since they'll see she's not wearing a ring. Engagement rumors come to an end."

"I know it doesn't seem like something important," Will replied. "But Chelsea has a lot of goodwill with her fans, because she's always been so open about herself. She doesn't make a statement about the rumor and then starts parading around the city on your arm, it looks like she's lying to them."

"How can she be lying when she doesn't say anything?"

"A lie by omission," Will countered. "I know it sounds stupid, but that's the way fans are. They feel as if they have a stake in her and her life, like they're part of the family. She runs around Nashville with you without a word about your two being in a relationship, they're going to damn her for her silence. So if you don't want to stay away from her, then my advice as her publicist is to get the heck outta here for a while." He grabbed the coat he'd draped over the arm of the chair next to his. "Besides, it's supposed to be majorly cold the rest of this week. Go somewhere warm. Get some sun. Eat some seafood. We'll do as you want, Ethan, and see if things die down."

Addie walked Will to the door, mumbling about "fucking press bastards."

Chelsea squeezed Ethan's hand. "We could go down to

Jekyll early. I mean, we are heading south for the rehearsal and the wedding, right?"

At least he smiled. "Let me book a couple of airline tickets and see if—"

Will called back from the foyer. "Did I hear airline tickets?"

"He's got ears like a bat," Chelsea whispered.

"No planes!" He hurried back into the living area. "You can't book under false names, because you have to show ID. You two book seats under your names, it's on the Internet ten minutes later. If *that* long…"

"Then we'll just have to take a road trip," Ethan said.

"Addie, anything on my calendar that can't be cleared before the wedding?"

Will kept shifting his gaze between Chelsea and Addie. "Wedding? I thought you two weren't even engaged."

"Cool your jets," Addie said. "They're attending Savannah Wolf's wedding. Don't get your tighty whities in a bunch."

"That wedding will be covered by entertainment reporters," Will said.

Chelsea shook her head. "They don't want any press there."

"She's marrying the Hitman and they don't expect press?" He let out a chuckle. "Good luck with that."

"Trust me," she said. "They want nothing to ruin it. They rented out a whole resort just to keep things private."

"Then I suggest you and Ethan do your best to keep whatever you do every bit as private."

As Addie escorted Will out—again—Chelsea waited for Ethan to say something, to give her some idea about what he wanted to do now. The idea of them going away together was appealing. *Very* appealing. She needed him to take the lead, though. How odd, since her whole life she'd kept the reins firmly in her own hands.

Perhaps that was what being in a relationship was all about, or at least supposed to be about. Caring so much for someone else that you let them call the shots.

* * *

It was hard for Ethan to gather his thoughts and decide what to do now. He was still in a stupor at realizing that Chelsea had allowed him to dictate how this mess would be handled.

The idea that they would, as Will had put it, "go on the offensive," was repugnant. Shit, by the time the press was done, Ethan would be seeing his picture everywhere. He'd look like a fool, standing a few paces behind the great Chelsea Harris while she dazzled them with her smile and wit.

What a nightmare.

When he got his hands on Chuck...

No, that would only give the asshole more ammunition. All it would take was a quick picture of the black eye and bloody nose Ethan would give him, and Chuck would get fifteen more minutes that he didn't deserve.

Ethan would be a good boy and get Chelsea the hell out of the city so he could spend some time alone with her. Exactly as though they were real people and not public property.

Addie came back to stare at them. "So? Where you two going? I need to get to work on finding someplace uber-private. Start naming destinations. And...go!"

"I suppose we could go to Jekyll," Chelsea said. "I mean, we need to be there Friday anyway, right?"

"Probably not as private as you think," Ethan replied, "when the whole resort isn't rented out like it will be for the wedding."

"You've been there?" Addie asked.

"Once or twice. There's more people there than you'd think. We need something more like a cabin on a private beach—somewhere with no neighbors."

Addie looked to Chelsea. "Budget?"

"It's on me," Ethan insisted. "After all, we're doing this because I wanted to keep things on the down low."

"Okay then." Rubbing her hands together, Addie trotted toward her office. "Sky's the limit!"

"Addie," Chelsea said in a motherly tone. "Keep it reasonable."

"I don't care how much," Ethan said. "Just find someplace warm and away from prying eyes."

While Addie was in her office, he stood, hauling Chelsea to her feet. "This could be fun." Her wan smile made him worry. "What's wrong?"

All she did was shrug.

Tugging her into his arms, he covered her mouth with his.

Every time he kissed her, it felt like the first time—such a surprise to feel her soft lips against his own. His desire rose swiftly and fiercely, and somewhere in his distracted brain, he realized this would give them alone time. A lot of alone time.

His tongue found hers, and the kiss began to get out of control as his hands slid down her back to cover that shapely ass. He pulled her up hard against him so she'd have no doubt about how much he wanted her. For a moment, he flippantly considered thanking Chuck for giving them a reason to go someplace private.

Only Addie loudly clearing her throat restored any sanity. Thankfully, Chelsea was breathing every bit as hard as he was. Saved him some embarrassment over feeling like a teenager who'd been caught necking with his date.

"Sorry to interrupt..." Addie chuckled. "But I think I have the perfect place."

"Where?" Chelsea asked.

"It's an island."

"An island? You can rent a whole island?"

"Fuckin' A," Addie replied with a smirk.

"I said be reasonable," Chelsea said.

For once, Ethan didn't give a damn what something cost. To have a whole island to themselves? That would be..."Amazing, Addie. Good work."

"It's all the way in the Keys," Addie said. "You're looking at a twenty-hour drive, but I think I might be able to get you there faster. Working on a private plane, something that reporters couldn't track. Let me keep working on it. You two ready to go in the morning?"

"Yep," Ethan replied.

"Absolutely," Chelsea added.

"Then I'm on it." Addie hurried back to the office. "Pack your swimsuits."

"A whole island," Chelsea said, a bit breathless. "Peace and quiet."

"No press. No social media. No Chuck's bullshit." Pulling her close again, he nuzzled her neck, loving the soft sighs she gave him in response. "I can't wait to get you alone."

She just hummed and tilted her head, giving him more of the soft skin of her neck.

Nibbling and licking, he couldn't help but think that despite what Chuck had put them through, one good thing could come out of it. He and Chelsea would have a chance to be completely alone. With an entire island to themselves.

This was going to be epic.

CHAPTER TWENTY

W ho's Mary Todd?" Ethan asked Chelsea as they approached the forty-something woman holding a tablet with that name.

With her brown hair pulled into a severe bun and dressed in a navy-blue suit, the woman looked the consummate professional.

Who wears a suit in the Keys?

"I'm Mary Todd," Chelsea replied.

He turned a skeptical gaze her direction. "Pardon?"

"Addie always uses names of former First Ladies when she reserves stuff for me."

He chuckled as they went to the woman in the suit.

"I'm Mary," Chelsea said.

The widened eyes followed by a full-blown smile on the lady's face told Chelsea she'd been recognized. Hopefully, that wouldn't be a problem, especially in light of what Will had said about lying low. Addie had surely paid this person well for her silence.

"I'm Sharon. Nice to meet you, Ms. . . . Todd. I'm going to take you and your guest to the house." She glanced at the bags they carried. "Need to wait for more luggage?"

"No, thanks," Chelsea replied. "We're good." She inclined her head at Ethan. "This is Abe." Then she tossed him a silly grin, hoping he got the joke.

"Hi, Abe. Since we're all ready, let's go!" Sharon led the way, talking over her shoulder. "Won't take long to get to the house."

Chelsea was pleased to see Ethan had a bemused smile on his face. "How long?" she asked Sharon.

"Only a fifteen-minute drive to the dock," she replied. "Then about twenty minutes in the boat."

"Boat?" He chuckled. "Never thought I'd be staying some-place that was only accessible by water."

Sharon led them to a black Expedition. After she opened the back so they could store their bags, she crawled behind the wheel while Ethan and Chelsea got in the backseat. The whole drive, she chatted about the house and the amenities on their island getaway. Great beach. Swimming pool. Hot tub.

The place sounded amazing. Addie could work miracles.

"Once you get there," Sharon said, "you won't have to leave unless you want to. The kitchen is fully stocked. Plenty to eat, drink, whatever. There are a few nice bars and restaurants not far from the dock. I'll leave my card and if you want to come back across, just text or call. I'll have a ride for you in a jiffy."

The boat was what Chelsea would've expected people used to waterski, something she'd never had the chance to do. It was tied to a small dock and she was surprised that Ethan seemed so at ease with helping release the tie-ups and even keeping an eye on Sharon as she started the motor and sent them flying through the water toward the small island in the distance.

The closer they drew to the island, the more Chelsea relaxed. Everything around her was beautiful. The rolling water. The swaying palm trees. The scent of salt water. As the tension left her body, she began to realize that she'd been under a lot of pressure lately. Between the loss of her father, the stress of the last year's packed concert schedule, and her budding relationship with Ethan, she'd gone through the ringer.

This vacation was exactly what she needed—what *they* needed. And to be able to share time with the man she'd grown to love while they were out of the ever-intrusive eyes of the press?

Paradise.

* * *

Ethan held out his hand, happy to see Chelsea's beaming smile as she stepped off the boat. She was so beautiful, he couldn't help but give her a quick kiss before turning her loose so he could grab the bags that Sharon was passing him. Once their luggage was resting on the dock, he helped Sharon out as well.

Still chattering on about the house's many amenities, she led them inside. All he wanted was for her to wrap it up and get gone. They could explore things on their own and he had something else he wanted to concentrate on.

Chelsea.

"And here's the key," Sharon finally said, with a slight chuckle as she held out a keychain. "Not that you'll need it. This place is all yours. Anyone wanting to bug you can only get here by boat."

Ethan took the key, nodding at Sharon. When he saw Addie again, she was due a huge hug and a present. Perfume, maybe? Not only had she found them the perfect place, she'd arranged for the kitchen to be stuffed full of groceries so he and Chelsea wouldn't have to leave the island until they headed to the wedding.

Chelsea was staring at her cell and frowning. "No service?"

With a shake of her head, Sharon said, "But there's wireless by satellite. The password's on the kitchen counter. Once you're signed in, you can use that for calls as well. If there's anything else you need"—she plucked a card from her pocket and handed it to Chelsea—"just call or text."

"I think we're good," Ethan said with a glance to Chelsea.

She nodded. "Need any help with the boat?"

With a dismissive wave, Sharon said, "Not necessary. Please contact me if I can help in any way. I'll see myself out."

Finally alone with Chelsea, he had to resist the urge to toss her over his shoulder like a sack of grain and march immediately into the bedroom. "Wanna look around some more?"

The seductive smile she gave him made his insides tighten. "I want to see the bedroom. And I want to see you. Naked." The sultry tone of her voice when straight to his groin.

Exactly the invitation he'd needed. Before another moment went by, he had her in his embrace and his mouth captured hers. He drank her in, tasting the sweetness of her mouth by plunging his tongue inside. When she grabbed his lip gently between her teeth and tugged, he growled deep in his chest and pulled her harder against him.

She coiled her arms around his neck, tangling her fingers in his hair as she ground her pelvis against his erection.

Ethan gripped her hips and lifted, pleased and relieved she knew what he wanted. Her legs wrapped around his waist, and still kissing her, he carried her down the hall to the master bedroom. The only notice he gave of the room was that there was a king-sized bed, which was exactly where he was heading.

He dropped her back against the mattress, following her down, careful to brace his weight on his elbows. While he wanted desperately to start removing her clothes, he couldn't seem to stop kissing her.

Everything about her—about this—was different. Normally, he viewed foreplay as a necessary means to a pleasant end. Except now, he wasn't in a hurry. In fact, he was enjoying the anticipation, savoring each stroke of her hands against his back, his hips, his ass.

Finally tearing his mouth away, Ethan kissed his way across her soft cheek to her ear, where he ran his tongue around the delicate shell. Then he licked the warm skin of her neck, nibbling as he slid his hand between their bodies to find the buttons of her silk blouse.

Easing himself to his side, he watched her face as he opened each pearl button. The way her cheeks flushed and her breathing hitched made his own breath catch. "You're so damn beautiful."

She lifted her hand to brush the back of her knuckles against his face. "And you're so damn handsome. What did I do to deserve you?"

A chuckle slipped out. "Since that was supposed to be a compliment, I won't tell you that you must've fucked up something royal to get stuck with me." After the last button was undone, he slipped his hand under the silk to caress one of her full breasts. "I want you, Chelsea."

She covered his hand against her breast with her own and rubbed it in a circle. "I'm yours, Ethan."

Relishing the words, he kissed her again, a lazy exchange of stroking tongues that made fire shoot to his cock. She moved restlessly as she tried to tug his shirt out of his waistband. The shirt was being stubborn.

Ethan smiled at her as he stood and jerked his shirt over his head. "I need to get the condoms."

"By all means..."

He hurried to grab the box he'd left in his bag down the hall.

* * *

Chelsea smiled at the speed of his exit, his enthusiasm matched hers perfectly. To move things along, she got up, pulled back the covers, and then kicked off her shoes. She'd slipped off her pink top and was draping it over the chest at the foot of the big bed when Ethan came back, holding some condoms.

"How many did you bring?" she asked with a wink when she saw the large box.

His eyes raked her from head to toe, settling on her lacy bra. "Seeing you looking like that? Probably not enough."

"Flatterer." She crooked her finger, calling him closer.

After tossing the box on the night table, he came to stand in front of her, their bodies close to touching. He cupped her face in his hands and gazed down at her.

The tenderness there made tears sting her eyes. Then he slowly lowered his head until their lips met. A gentle kiss that he ended to look into her eyes again. "Let me make love to you."

A smile bloomed as she nodded. A gasp followed as he swept her into his arms and carried her back to the bed.

Ethan unzipped her jeans, and she helped him remove them. Soon, they were tossed on the floor as he worked on getting his own pants off.

Staring was in order. When she'd held him, she'd felt the ropy muscles, but to see them paraded in front of her was almost too much to take in. Thick biceps, sinewy forearms, even a real six-pack. It was all she could do not to drool. "How 'bout you take off those boxers and get in bed?"

His lopsided smile only added to the enticing package. Hooking his thumbs in the elastic waistband, he dragged the baby-blue underwear off his hips. A rather impressive erection sprang forward, pointing right at her.

"Oh, my . . ." Chelsea patted the mattress. "C'mere."

A couple of running steps, and he jumped up on the bed.

She let out a little squeal that turned into a giggle when he landed so hard on the mattress that she bounced. The giggle ended abruptly when her hand made its way to his cock. The heat of him against her palm, the silky skin against her fingertips, made her eyes close.

* * *

Ethan's breath caught. The way she gently stroked him was almost more than he could bear.

This whole experience was new and unexpected. Mostly dressed and up against a wall had always pleased him just fine.

Now, he couldn't believe the wealth of feeling—both physical and emotional—that rocked him. Something as simple as her gently moving her hand up and down his erection had the power to send his senses reeling.

Although he would've been content to let her play, he suddenly wanted to see every inch of her. "My turn." He gently brushed her hand away, gripped her shoulders, and pressed her back against the bed.

With a quick flick of his fingers, he opened the front clasp of her bra and her lush breasts bounced out. Full and round, they were tipped with pink nipples that had hardened to tight buds. Leaning in, he drew one between his lips, loving how her hands went to the back of his head as though she wanted to hold him there.

Since he was in no hurry, he lavished her with attention.

Suckling, licking, and kissing the warm valley between them. He let his hand glide over her stomach to slide under her silky panties, past the soft hair on her mound, until he could slip his fingers between her wet folds.

Chelsea let out a low moan and restlessly moved her hips. Ethan took that as approval and decided to play until he could make her crazed. He loved how she tugged at his hair, how her breath came in little hitches. Her hands moved to his back, where she dragged her nails across his skin.

Yeah, baby.

But he needed to see all of her the same way she'd seemed to need to see all of him. He helped her shrug off the bra and wiggle out of the pink panties. Then he drank her in.

The woman was exquisite. From her bright green eyes, to her voluptuous hips, to the patch of red hair at the apex of her thighs. "God, you're gorgeous."

"Not so bad yourself, mister." Chelsea took his cock in her hand again. "Where are those condoms?"

Ethan grabbed the box, opened it, and tore one from the sleeve. After playfully tossing it at her, he dropped to the mattress on his knees and crawled toward her until he could kneel next to her. "Want to do the honors?"

"Gladly."

She opened it with her teeth, and he had to grin when she seemed to have trouble rolling it on. Once the job was done, all his amusement fled as desire grabbed him.

He blanketed her body with his, rubbing his cock against her core, mimicking the act without quite completing it. Everything about her flooded his senses—the sweet scent of her arousal, the heat teasing him through the thin sheath, the enticing smile as she opened her arms to him.

"You're right, you know, I really *am* a virgin," he said with a smile.

"Why this time?" she asked, her voice husky and low.

"Because I've never taken this long to make love to a woman."

Her eyes widened.

"I'm serious."

"I love a man who takes his time." She cupped his neck and pulled him into a kiss.

Damn, did she kiss him. And kiss him some more. Each time her tongue stroked his, he lost another thread of his control as the need to be buried deep inside her rose higher inside him. As she lifted her knees, he finally eased into her tight heat.

* * *

Chelsea nearly screamed for him to come to her, but then Ethan was suddenly there, moving in a slow, maddening slide into her body. She wrapped her legs around his hips to pull him deeper and scored her nails across his shoulders.

She felt full. Complete. But she also needed more. She needed him to move.

Now.

Before she could tear her mouth away to tell him, he seemed to finally catch on. The rhythm he set was fast and hard and absolutely perfect.

She'd waited so long for this that it seemed as though she couldn't wait a moment longer. Everything inside her tightened as he drove her higher and higher until she shattered, his name on her lips.

CHAPTER TWENTY-ONE

Ethan had no idea how long they'd slept after the most satisfying sex of his life. When he'd awakened, the room was growing dark, and he was aware that his stomach was rumbling as though he'd just completed a forty-day fast. It let out a particularly loud growl, which was followed by a giggle from the sexy naked woman lying against his side.

"A little hungry there, Ethan?" Chelsea pushed herself up on an elbow, her red hair in beautiful disarray, her eyes full of life.

He suddenly thought it might be a good idea to make love to her again. To test the waters, he cradled her cheek in his palm and brushed a soft kiss over her lips.

Then his stomach complained again.

"How about I whip us up some supper?" She traced the line of his jaw with her index finger.

"That sounds great." With a quick jerk, he pulled the sheet

away from her and drank in every luscious curve of her body. "Although...we could—"

Damn if his stomach didn't interrupt.

"That settles it." She bounced off the mattress. "Something to eat comes first."

Ethan let out a chuckle. "Pun intended?"

There was a twinkle in her eyes that held promise for more delights to come. "Absolutely."

After she tugged on her panties, she looked around the room.

"Want your bag?" he asked, crawling out of bed.

Whatever she'd been searching for was evidently forgotten, because her mouth curved into a smile as her gaze raked him from head to toe, settling on his groin. "Much as I hate to ask..."

A smile on his own face, he bowed at the waist. He picked up his boxers, slid them on, and went to fetch their bags.

* * *

Chelsea stared at him as he left, wondering what really good thing she'd done in her life to deserve a guy like Ethan.

It wasn't his exquisite body she was thinking about, although it was as close to perfect as she'd ever seen. No, she loved the whole package. His humor. His wit. Even his stubbornness.

Perhaps he'd been right about the press after all. She'd thought it was the wrong call, but she hadn't been angry at him for making it. Giving him his way had been her choice, and knowing what she did about his past, she could understand why he'd decided to keep their personal lives private. The only nagging doubt clouding the horizon was that they would have to face the music eventually, especially if they hoped to share a future together. Experience had taught her that postponing the inevitable only made it more difficult.

He trotted back into the room, a shirt draped over a shoulder. After handing it to her, he tossed their luggage on the bed.

Shaking the garment out, she found a worn T-shirt with a red Coca-Cola logo. "What's this?"

"I want you to wear it."

"Why?"

"Because it's mine."

"That's not a reason."

He shrugged, so she went ahead and put it on without asking anything more. The faster they ate, the faster they could get back to doing exactly what she wanted to do, which was get right back in bed.

He smiled. "Looks a lot better on you than it does on me."

Taking his hand, she led him into the kitchen. "Let's see what we've got to choose from."

"Doesn't matter to me. Let's just make it quick."

As Chelsea searched through the pantry, Ethan came up behind her and pulled her back against him. After nibbling her ear, sending chills racing over her skin, he whispered, "I'm still hungry."

She leaned back against him, stroking his forearms and

humming in pleasure. Suddenly, food didn't seem all that important. "So am I."

His teeth tugged her earlobe. "Want to cook?"

"Hmm?"

"I asked if you wanted to cook, or do you want me to?" Sounding a bit disgruntled, he backed away from her before giving her ass a playful swat. "Told you, I'm still hungry."

The man was going to drive her crazy. "You're nothing but a tease, aren't you?"

"I'm not teasing. I'm starving."

"Fine. I'll cook." Opening the refrigerator, she was pleased to see that Sharon had done a great job stocking it with food. While she could've put together just about anything, she grabbed the carton of eggs and the butter, wanting something she could whip up quickly. "Scrambled eggs sound okay?"

He moved to block the door when she tried to close it with her hip. "How about an omelet? A big omelet. We can share."

"Fine." As she set the eggs on the counter, he placed ham, cheddar cheese, onions, peppers, and some cherry tomatoes beside them. "Can you please hand me the milk?"

Ethan did as she asked, putting the milk carton next to the vegetables. "Want me to chop while you mix?"

With a nod, Chelsea searched through the island and was pleased to find a mixing bowl as well as a frying pan. She put the bowl on the granite counter and set the pan on one of the burners.

He popped a tomato in his mouth before grabbing a chopping block from where it rested next to the sink. "This is a great kitchen."

"Yep." She cracked open an egg, letting the yolk and white sluice into the bowl. She let her gaze wander the large kitchen. "I love this place. We'll have to come back here sometime. I hate Nashville winters."

"Works for me. I hate 'em too."

Fragrant aromas filled the air as a gentle breeze blew through the open windows—melting butter, fresh onions, salt water. Chelsea breathed it all in, grateful to be doing something as normal as preparing a meal for the two of them. For the next few days, there would be no performances, no autographs, no recording, no press. Only the two of them in a place about as close to paradise as she could imagine.

It wasn't easy to cook with him constantly touching her, but she soldiered through, knowing that as soon as they'd satisfied their hunger they would be satisfying other needs. By the time she slid the omelet from the pan onto the plate, she wanted nothing more than to wolf down a few bites and drag him right back to bed.

She fed him a forkful of omelet, and he returned the favor. And she didn't feel silly, although to anyone watching them, they probably looked like a couple of goofy teenagers in love.

But that was exactly what she was—someone in love.

For a moment, she flirted with the idea of telling him how she felt. That impulse was discarded as rapidly as it formed. Ethan was still like a green colt—easily spooked. Should she utter those three infamous words, he'd probably bolt that same way a colt would when he got skittish.

As wonderful as it was to be alone with him in this beautiful place, and romantic as the atmosphere might be, this simply wasn't the right time. Not now. Not yet.

How would he react when she told him? Would he brush her declaration aside? Would he admit he felt the same? Would he fall on his knees and ask her to marry him?

She snorted a laugh at the silly romantic image of him begging for her hand.

"What?" he asked.

Instead of telling him how absurd she was being, she just waved a flippant hand.

Setting aside her fork, Chelsea let him finish the last bites of the omelet as she polished off the orange juice left in her glass.

Ethan let his fork drop to the empty plate and turned to grin at her. "That was great. But I want dessert."

She arched an eyebrow. "And what exactly would you like for dessert?"

"You," he replied in a husky, low voice that sent electricity racing through her all the way to her toes.

In the blink of an eye, he pushed himself off the bar stool, scooped her into his arms, and headed back to the bedroom.

* * *

Ethan couldn't wait to have her soft, warm skin pressed against him again. Although he'd loved seeing her in his T-shirt, feeling as though that marked her as his, he tugged it over her head and discarded it on the floor. His own boxers quickly joined it.

Slipping his hands down her hips, he looped the elastic waistband of her panties with his thumbs and dragged that bit of lace and satin down her thighs. The thatch of red hair beckoned him, so he tossed the panties aside, gently spread her thighs, and kissed her exactly where he'd dreamed of kissing her.

She tasted sweet, womanly, and he kept up his assault, forcing her to take the last steps to the bed. All he needed was a gentle push against her stomach to get her to fall back against the sheets. Spreading her thighs wider, he licked between her folds, finding the jewel he sought. He pulled it lightly between his teeth and then drove her crazy with his tongue.

Each moan, each arch of her back, drove him higher until his cock felt so hard he wasn't sure how much longer he could last. Easing back, he ripped another condom off the strip and quickly rolled it on. Positioning himself between her thighs, he lifted her knees, encouraging her to wrap her legs around him before he drove inside her.

Chelsea matched him so perfectly, matched his passion, his rhythm. Moving inside her again and again, Ethan felt himself tighten and knew his release would be soon. A moment later, she cried out his name, the sound of wonder in her voice pushing him over the edge. One last thrust, and the world around him swirled as his orgasm raced through him.

After a hasty cleanup, he crawled back into bed as she lifted the sheet and patted the mattress beside her.

Exhausted and satisfied, he hauled her up against him, loving how she draped her leg over his thighs.

He fell asleep with a smile on his face.

* * *

Waking up in Ethan's arms was something Chelsea wanted to get used to.

Her body felt sated and her mind content. This vacation had been exactly what she needed—what *they* needed.

Morning was here, and she was ready to greet it with a cup of coffee. After breakfast, she wanted to explore their island.

A yawning Ethan came into the kitchen when the coffee was just about done. They ate their breakfasts in quiet companionship that she could also get used to.

After cleaning up the kitchen, she decided it was time to start their exploration. They wandered around the island under the canopy of tropical trees, watching the birds and wildlife and then marveling at the variety of flowering plants. As the heat began to build close to lunchtime, she suggested that they should spend some time on the beach.

Back at the house, Ethan slathered her with sunscreen again and she returned the favor. Just to be sure she didn't burn in the strong midday sun, she also took one of the floppy straw hats that hung in the mudroom and put it on. She grabbed a blanket and the picnic lunch she'd taken a few moments to pack for them.

"Ready?" he asked, flicking the brim of her hat.

"Ready. Here . . . " She handed him the basket. "Take this for me, please."

It was only a short walk to the beach, practically right outside the big French doors.

She spread the blanket out over the hot sand and turned to catch the sun.

"Careful, ginger," Ethan said with a smile as he put the basket on the blanket. "You've already been out, and you'll burn in the blink of an eye."

"I know, I know. We won't stay out too much longer. Shouldn't you be wearing a baseball cap or something?"

"Nah. I never burn. Just get tan."

"Famous last words." She stared at him as he jerked his shirt over his head and dropped it on the picnic hamper. Damn if her thoughts weren't already turning to making love to him again. He'd reached a part of her that she'd never known existed, a part that seemed to be a bit of a sex maniac—probably because she loved him so damned much.

And things were sure to get better and better.

"God, I love the sounds of waves," she said. Then she tossed him a grin. "Race ya!"

Running toward the water, she squealed when he caught her from behind and swept her off her feet.

Ethan hit the waves, holding her just above the surface. "Want to cool off?"

Struggling to hold on to her hat, Chelsea replied, "Don't drop me!"

"What was that you said?" he teased. "You want to go swimming?" He feigned dropping her only to pull her close and press a quick kiss on her lips. "Later, perhaps." Setting her on her feet, he held her hand as they both let the waves lap against their legs.

"This place is so beautiful," she said in a reverent whisper. When she glanced at him, he was staring at her. "What?

"*You're* beautiful."

She thanked him with a kiss before she took his hand. "C'mon. I've got a surprise for you in that basket."

She sat down cross-legged on the blanket. Flipping open the lid of the picnic hamper, she pulled out the bottle of champagne she'd packed. It had seemed the perfect choice since she felt like celebrating. For the first time in just about forever, she was truly happy—as if she were able to be herself and not have to wear some kind of mask.

He plopped down beside her and took the bottle. "Let me." In no time, the loud echo of the popping cork echoed through the air.

Holding the glasses while he poured, she tried to catch as much of the bubbly overflow as she could. After he propped the bottle in the sand, he offered up his glass. "A toast."

With a smile, she held hers aloft as well. "To what?"

His gaze wandered the beach. "To this island. To this amazing island." He turned his eyes to her as a slow smile bowed his lips. "To the best woman I've ever known." With a quick lift of his glass, he drank down the champagne.

Not sure whether to drink to herself, she held her glass a little higher. "And to the best lover I've ever had." Savoring his wide-eyed response, she downed the contents of her glass and immediately started choking. After coughing and coughing, she finally expelled the champagne that had gone down the wrong pipe.

"Not a drinker?" he asked with a sexy wink as he refilled her glass.

"Not used to the bubbles," she replied.

They shared the lunch she'd thrown together. Nothing but sandwiches and chips, but it tasted wonderful.

Everything was perfect. Until she looked out over the water and saw the boat.

And the photographer.

CHAPTER TWENTY-TWO

Shit." Chelsea scrambled to her feet and started gathering up the things they'd taken out of the picnic hamper.

"What?" Jumping up, he grabbed her by the upper arms. "What's wrong?"

She tossed her head at the intruder. "There's a guy on a boat out there, taking pictures."

His head whipped toward the horizon, then his eyes narrowed. "Son of a bitch." He released her and started to toss things back into the basket as well.

When everything was stored, she bundled up the blanket, not caring if she also scooped up half the sand on the beach with it. "How...?"

"Sharon," Ethan hissed. "It had to be her. I thought she recognized you."

"So did I, but...I'd hoped..."

"Yeah, I'd hoped too." He nodded at the house. "Let's get

inside. I'm sure he's got plenty of pictures by now." Turning, he flipped the bird in that general direction.

"Oh, come on, Ethan. Don't do that. It'll be all over the place within the hour," she scolded, angry and hurt. The situation was bad enough. The last thing they needed was for him to make obscene gestures for posterity. Those images would be worth even more than the pictures of them together at an isolated beach retreat.

"Like I give a shit," he said with a roll of his eyes.

That's because you don't have a career to worry about...

Ethan had to be livid at the intrusion. She was fighting her own fury, having a hard time not ranting and raving at the invasion of their privacy. His absolute revulsion to publicity probably made his rage burn hotter than her own. But didn't he realize he was only making things worse by letting the guy know how much he'd pissed them off?

Once inside, she slammed the door behind them. The idiot in the boat was probably already firing up his motor and heading back to someplace he could get Wi-Fi access and sell his bounty to the highest bidder. There'd be plenty of buyers, with *Nashville Chat* most likely at the front of the line. No doubt their lead would be a picture of a fuming Ethan with his middle finger extended while she stood right behind him, scowling.

Will would be apoplectic. So would Addie. They had both agreed with Chelsea that she and Ethan should've tackled the engagement rumor while that was all it had been. A stupid rumor. Once those pictures of her with Ethan hit the Internet, her credibility with her fans would be in the sewers.

She should've trusted her gut, but she'd capitulated to placate him. Never again. He might've been born to parents who understood Nashville and the publicity that came with being stars, but he clearly didn't have a clue how to make that publicity become an asset rather than a liability. Chelsea understood and was a master at that game. She'd never second-guess herself again, nor would she bend to Ethan's will as a way to please him. She'd be damned if she'd turn into some simpering female who let the male call all the shots.

Her anger became self-directed, so she took a deep breath and tried to get a hold on her tumultuous emotions. She wasn't going to be of any good to anyone if she kept up this train of thought. The pictures were taken; now she needed to deal with them.

A few calming moments later, Chelsea got her act together. "I should call Addie." It dawned on her that she had no idea where she'd left her phone. The moment they'd gotten there, she'd been so focused on Ethan that she hadn't even thought about checking her messages. Hunting through the house, she finally found the phone resting on the kitchen island.

I'm pathetic. A fool in love.

"Yeah, she might be able to put a lid on those pictures," Ethan said.

"Are you serious?" She put her hands on her hips and glared at him. "There's nothing that can stop that bozo from selling those pictures. He'll make a pretty penny for them too."

"Then why do you need to call Addie? What good can she do if she can't squash this guy?"

"I need to tell her what happened. Then she can talk to Will and get a quick press release out. We need to get ahead of this."

"*That* again?" he said, his volume rising. "So there are some pictures of us together? Who gives a damn?"

"You really don't get it do you?"

"Get what?"

"This is what Will warned us about," Chelsea said, having a hard time keeping the scolding I-told-you-so tone from her voice. "I should've listened to him in the first place. And I should've trusted my own judgment. All we had to do was release a statement that we were in a relationship and these pictures wouldn't mean diddly shit. They'd just show the world that we'd told the truth. Now, they're going to be a hot topic, because it looks like we were hiding something."

"Then we just ignore them," Ethan insisted.

"For God's sake...don't you see that we're *past* that? We were past that before we left on this trip."

"What do you mean 'past that'?" he asked.

Closing her eyes for a moment, she bowed her head and pinched the bridge of her nose. She needed to gather her thoughts and tamp down her anger. Neither was an easy task. "In this day and age, when a rumor starts churning, you can't bury your head in the sand. The best thing to do is go on the offensive and tell the truth behind the rumor. Once someone started saying we were getting married, we should've been honest and put out a quote or two about us being a couple. If we'd done that yesterday, the pictures that asshat took wouldn't be anything juicy—they'd just be confirmation of what people already knew. Shit, they'd probably think they were sweet. But because we ran away and never said a word about the rumor, it's going to blow up in our faces."

He merely shrugged. "So what? Let it blow up. I don't care."

"Of course you don't care. You don't *have* to care!" Chelsea realized she'd clenched her hands into fists and had adopted a stance as though she was ready to face an opponent—feet apart and shoulders back. She forced herself to relax again, but the tension inside her was churning.

Judging from the tense frown on Ethan's face, he was every bit as mad at her as she was at him. This situation was crappy enough without them fighting over who'd been right to begin with—even if it had been her.

"Look," she said, proud that her tone had eased as much as her body language, "I don't wanna fight. The pictures are going to get out there. We need to nip it in the bud."

"Whatever," he said, pulling out a bar stool and plopping his butt on it. "For the record, I think you're wrong."

"For the record, I'm not," she said. "Oh, I *was* wrong. I was wrong yesterday when I let you make the call. Today, I'm right. So let me call Addie. I'll have her get with Will and release a statement. We should get some pictures of us together here and send those as well. They'll help."

"I'm not going off the island just to get someone to take our picture."

"Don't have to. We can do a few selfies," Chelsea said. "Those will be fine." When Ethan shook his head, all her calm vanished. "You don't give a shit about me at all, do you?"

He jumped to his feet. "What?"

"This is my career we're talking about here! My life! Do you know how long and hard I've worked to get my fans to support me?"

He fisted his hands against his slim hips. "What's that got to do with you thinking I don't give a shit about you?"

"Something like this could destroy the relationship I have with my fans. They'll never trust me again."

"Oh, come on, Chelsea. Don't you think you're blowing this a little out of proportion?" Ethan took her hand. As angry as she was, she let him keep it, reserving the right to snatch it away if he said something too stupid. "You're not going to lose your fans just 'cause a couple of pictures of us get out there. You're underestimating them."

"Will always says trust is everything, that once a celebrity lies about something, she loses the goodwill of her fans."

He squeezed her hand. "All I'm saying, Chelsea, is that a few pictures of us put together with a rumor that we're engaged doesn't really make *that* big a story."

"You're wrong, Ethan. The world is a lot different from when your parents were singing." She still thought they needed to be proactive, to get something out there before a picture of Ethan flipping his middle finger was all over every gossip magazine being printed. "What a nightmare."

Why the man suddenly began smiling was beyond her. Then he let out a chuckle.

"What exactly is so damned funny?" she asked.

He laughed a little louder.

When she tried to tug her hand away, he refused to let it go. "Stop laughing at me!"

* * *

Ethan tried to stop the humor bubbling up inside him long enough to explain. "I'm not laughing at you, baby. I'm not."

"Sure sounds like it to me."

"It's just... this is our first fight."

Chelsea stopped struggling to pull away and simply stared at him. Eyes wide, she blinked a few times, her face stoic. Then the corners of her mouth rose. "It is, isn't it?" The grin blossomed to a full-blown smile. "I suppose it had to happen sometime."

The anger that had been roiling through him changed. Shifted. Although heat still whipped inside him, that heat became a need to touch her, to take her into his arms. To soothe the hurt. He had a quick flash of Brad telling him about how he and Savannah hated quarreling, but that the makeup sex was fantastic. Ethan had laughed at his friend.

Now he understood.

One pull had her stumbling against him, and he took full advantage, enfolding her in his embrace as he stared down into those hypnotic green eyes. "Are you half as turned on as I am?"

Instead of replying, she rose on tiptoes, threaded her arms around his neck, and put her lips on his. Not a soft kiss, but one that showed she was as full of need as he was. Her tongue thrust between his lips, teasing and coaxing, and he responded in kind, drinking her in.

He forgot all about the photographer.

Lingering, savoring each kiss, he was ready to carry her to the bedroom. But she shocked the hell out of him.

Easing back from the kiss, she reached out and grabbed the picnic basket, jerking it closer. Then she began to fish through it.

"What are you—"

"A condom," she replied.

"In the picnic basket?"

She found what she was looking for, plucking two connected condom packets and dangling them in front of his face. "What can I say? I was hoping to get lucky on the beach."

"Now *that* would've made a great picture to sell." Ethan let out a chuckle. "I love a woman who's prepared."

Chelsea smoothed her hand down his stomach until her palm settled on the front of his pants. "I love a man who's...*prepared.*"

Heat shot through him as they fumbled with their clothes. A shirt here. A pair of shorts there. They stumbled to the couch, and he dropped onto his back, pulling her down on top of him.

Straddling his hips, she quickly rolled the condom over his cock, and then rose above him so she could guide him inside her.

It was fast. Fierce. Full of passion. Ethan held tightly to her hips, helping her move as he felt his climax building inside him. When she threw her head back and cried out in release, he was there with her, thrusting a few more times and then giving in to a consuming orgasm.

Collapsing against his chest, Chelsea gulped in deep breaths.

Ethan trailed his fingers up and down her spine. How content he would've been to be able to stay there all day, just the two of them, sated and happy in each other's arms.

But the world intruded in the form of Chelsea's phone ringing.

"That's Addie's ringtone," Chelsea said as she tried to crawl off the couch.

Plucking her shirt and panties from the floor, she picked up her phone and answered it. Watching her try to dress while talking to her assistant was highly amusing—and more than a little arousing.

"I was just going to call you," Chelsea said to Addie. "The place is great. You did good. But..." Time passed as Chelsea listened. "That all sounds great, but we've got a problem."

While Ethan dressed, he listened to Chelsea's side of the conversation as she told her assistant about the photographer, even going so far as to tell Addie about how immature Ethan had been. Not that he regretted giving that moron the finger. But it had upset Chelsea, so he promised himself he'd try a little more decorum next time.

And there was sure to be a next time. Once those photos hit the Internet, things would change for a while. Their privacy would be royally invaded, and Chelsea was sure to want to be open with her fans.

Glancing up, he caught her eye.

She said, "Hang on, Addie." Then she muted the call and glanced at him. "Look, I know you aren't happy about it, but I'm gonna have Will release a statement about our relationship. Nothing major, just that we're dating."

"Do I even get a say in it?"

"What do you want me to do, Ethan?"

"Same thing as I wanted you to do before," he replied.

"I know, I know. Nothing." She heaved a sigh. "That's just not gonna cut it now. Not with those pictures. Can't you see that?"

Realizing they were never going to agree on the issue of publicity, Ethan finally breathed out a long sigh of his own. His still thought his way was better—that bullies like the paparazzi were better ignored rather than fed. But what she'd said about her career reached him. What had happened to his parents had been so long ago, and the lessons they'd taught him about dealing with reporters might be a bit outdated. Chelsea seemed to have more control over what she shared with the press than his parents ever did. So, for now, he was willing to give in, if only to ease her mind and get back to their vacation. "Fine. Whatever."

The way she narrowed her eyes boded ill, but she nodded curtly and returned to talking to Addie. When she ended the call, Chelsea came to sit next to him on the sofa. She laid her phone on the coffee table and took his hand. "I know how much you hate this."

Somehow, he doubted that. She wasn't the one who'd grown up under the press's microscope. She wasn't the one who'd lost any chance of a normal childhood or adolescence because her parents loved being famous more than they loved their only child.

A photographer hadn't killed her parents.

What kind of life could he and Chelsea have together if she continued to encourage the paparazzi to interfere in everything they did?

"Addie is going to have Sharon replaced, but she thinks we're fine here until we go up to Jekyll."

Unsure what she wanted him to say, Ethan simply nodded.

"You think this is my fault, don't you?" she asked.

The sadness in her voice shook him. "It's not your fault, Chelsea. It's just that... Well..."

"I'm a singer, Ethan. A good singer who has a lot of fans."

"You're a goddamn star," he said.

"Yes, I'm a goddamn star," she said firmly. "A big, fucking star, with the shit ton of nonsense that goes along with it."

"So that means you have to give up a private life?"

"No, but it does mean I need to be available to my fans."

Fearing another fight, he decided to quit the topic. "How about a swim?"

"In other words, you're done talking about this?"

He stood and grabbed her hand. "I've a hankering to try out that hot tub."

Her eyes searched his, but he had no idea what she was looking for. She opened her mouth as if to speak, then closed it. With a brusque nod, she stood and let him lead her away from the room and the discussion.

CHAPTER TWENTY-THREE

Ethan gave their island a nickname.

Utopia.

After spending three mostly carefree days with Chelsea, he dreaded returning to the real world. Their days had been filled with sunshine, warm sand, and heavenly breezes. Nights crept by as they made love and slept wrapped around each other until he didn't know where he ended and she began. And thankfully, there'd been no more intrusions of their privacy.

Chelsea had made a habit of checking her phone only twice a day, something he'd believed would be difficult for her. She'd surprised him by letting her guard down and simply enjoying herself. There were no fans; there was no career. Once, he'd even had to remind her to look and see if Addie had sent any texts.

He hadn't even bothered to check his own phone more than once or twice. No one ever texted him except Brad or Russ, and they knew he'd be too preoccupied with Chelsea to answer them. Besides, what help could he be? The restaurant would be fine until he got back. So would the farm. Ethan wasn't even sure Joe knew how to text.

"I'm gonna go through the house one more time," Chelsea said, pulling him from his reverie. "Need to make sure we're not leaving anything behind."

"We should stay a few more days," he suggested. "Or weeks. Or months."

"Or years?" She winked, and her laughter followed her down the hall.

At least he'd tried. It wasn't as though he'd been totally serious. But had he meant it even a little bit, that they should stay here and let the rest of the world go by?

Yeah. Just a little bit...

Not only did he need to get back to the horses, but there was also another pressing matter. Brad and Savannah were going to be married tomorrow. As best man, Ethan had an obligation to stand at his friend's side. A guy needed his buddy to help him through that kind of ordeal.

Ordeal?

That was the way Ethan had always thought of marriage— as something to be avoided at all costs. The women who'd passed through his life—and his sheets—had tried to become shackles far too quickly. So he'd discarded them all, moving on to greener pastures before a single one of them could tie him down.

Then Chelsea Harris had waltzed into his life, slinging liquor as though she'd always been a bartender and singing

like an angel. She'd become a part of his world too quickly
for him to have raised a single defense. In truth, he hadn't
wanted to stop her. She shared so many things with him. His
love of animals. His need for solitude. Passion. They could sit
and talk for hours and it seemed so natural, so easy. Or they
might be together while she read or he played solitaire, and
yet it still felt comfortable. Right.

He could be himself with Chelsea and know that she cared
for him the way he was because he felt the same way about
her. No games. No pretending to be something they weren't.
Just two people who enjoyed each other's company.

He'd never known someone as giving, a trait that made
him want to give in return.

Now, he believed that finding himself married wasn't so
far-fetched—but only to her. Should he somehow convince
her to take the plunge, he would feel a kind of security that
suddenly seemed appealing. If they were husband and wife,
he would have tangible proof that her feelings ran as deep
as his own. Best of all, he would know that she'd be coming
home to him every night. Just the two of them sharing the
farm.

Oh yes, that all sounded appealing—enough that the infamous question tickled his tongue.

Thankfully, Chelsea reappeared, snapping his mind back
into a normal mode. "I think we got everything," she announced.

What in the hell was wrong with him? He wasn't meant to
be a husband—*anyone's* husband. Especially not Chelsea's. She
needed someone who could support her status as a star, some-

one who didn't hate reporters the way he did. Should they stay together, he was sure to have more embarrassing episodes such as what had happened on the beach. He'd could never put himself in the spotlight the way she'd expect him to.

He tried to convince himself that the marriage nonsense had been nothing more than a romantic illusion cast by being on their isolated island. Like some mirage a thirsty man saw in the middle of a desert. That, and clearly Brad's impending wedding was taking a heavier toll on Ethan than he'd realized.

Marriage?

Fuck that!

"Ready?" he asked, picking up their bags. "Boat's at the dock."

Chelsea nodded and then allowed her gaze to wander the kitchen and living space. "I'm going to miss this place."

"Don't sound so forlorn," he said. "We can always come back."

"Not for a while," she said. "I've got that charity album to finish, and then I have a crap ton of events. And then—"

"I know, I know," he grumbled as he dropped their bags with a loud thud. "You're a busy star. Got to keep those fans satisfied."

* * *

Chelsea dropped her jaw, entirely thrown off center by his swift and decidedly negative change in attitude. The days they'd spent had been so loving, so tender. They hadn't exchanged a single cross word after their fight about the photographer. Their time here had been nothing short of wonderful. Yet now, the man sounded downright petulant.

She leveled a hard stare at him. "I can't read your tone. Are you mad or jealous?"

"Jealous?" Ethan snorted. "Of what?"

"That I might spend some time with my fans instead of with you."

"I..." His eyes narrowed and then slowly softened. "Maybe."

With a shake of her head, she went to him and wrapped her arms around his waist. She rose on tiptoes to press a kiss to his lips.

Her being a star would always be a sticking point between them and she was pretty sure she'd finally figured out why. His whole life he'd been second best to the two people that had mattered most to him—his mother and father. Sure, he'd been lucky to have Joe in his life. Yet how could the love and attention of one man ever make up for what Ethan had missed. His parents had never made him feel wanted and valued.

"You have nothing to be jealous of, Ethan. I'm not like your parents."

"What's that supposed to mean?"

"They let their careers come first. They made you feel like you were second best."

His face hardened, but he said nothing.

"I know how hard it must've been for you," she said. "Watching them leaving for yet another tour. Everyone knows how hard Dottie and Crawfish worked. But what everyone *doesn't* know is what it cost their son."

God, if she could only read him. But his face remained a mask, giving her no clue as to whether she was pushing too hard.

Figuring she was already in with both feet, she pressed the point. "My fans are important, but I will never put them before you. *Never.*" Her gaze searched his. "Understand?"

The words had to be said, and yet they were more than words. This was a vow she was making. What he needed to know was that she meant what she said, every word.

"I promise, Ethan. You are more important than anything else in my life."

Her breath rushed out as he suddenly tugged her hard against him and hugged her as though she were the only thing keeping him from drowning. This wasn't passion; this was love.

In that moment, she would've been happy to confess how she felt. Yet caution won out. She'd laid her heart on the line already, opening up to him in a way that made her too vulnerable for her taste. If anyone was going to admit that what they shared was love, it was damn well going to be him.

Knocking at the front door intruded. "Yoo-hoo!" a feminine voice called with another knock. "I'm here with your boat!"

* * *

Ethan helped Chelsea out of the town car while the driver pulled their bags from the trunk and handed them off to the bellboy, who'd appeared with a rolling cart. After slipping the driver a generous tip for the smooth ride from the airport, he took Chelsea's elbow and guided her to follow the bellboy.

The Jekyll Island Royale looked like a ghost town, albeit an elegant one. There were no other cars in the circle drive at the main entrance, only one vehicle in the parking lot, and no people hanging out on the terraces. Even the pool appeared deserted with nothing but empty white chaises scattered around the deck. Not that he'd expected otherwise. Brad had planned to rent the whole place out, but it was so much bigger than Ethan had anticipated.

This wedding must be costing Brad a fortune.

Having been curious about the place, Ethan had done some digging online. The main building of the resort had been a rich family's extravagant home back in the 1880s. Years later, it was turned into an affluent club. The clubhouse was flanked by three other houses that could only be described as mansions, which now held guest suites.

He smiled when he saw Chelsea gawking as she took everything in. The images he'd found in a Google search had been nice, but he had to admit the place was even more impressive in person. After the wedding, they'd have to spend some time exploring the resort and the island.

He was having a difficult time paying attention to the amenities the bellboy was rattling off because Ethan was thinking about Chelsea. Her insight back on their island had blown him away, mostly because he hadn't even realized that the emotional wounds his parents had inflicted ran so deep. He'd always looked back at their choice to put their careers ahead of him as an annoyance. Turned out, he had an entrenched fear that he'd never be the number one thing in anyone's life. Once she'd pointed it out, he couldn't believe he hadn't thought of it before. Perhaps his hatred of the press and any type of publicity had more to do with his own insecurity than he'd ever realized.

But she'd known. And she'd soothed his worries with her promise that she would put him first. All he had to do was trust her and take her at her word.

Why was that so damned hard to do?

The woman at the front desk greeted them with a smile. "Welcome! I'm assuming you're guests for the nuptials."

Ethan nodded. "Best man."

Chelsea sidled up next to him. "Lowly guest."

With a light laugh, the lady poised her hand over her computer's keyboard. "Might I have the names?"

"Ethan Walker and Chelsea Harris," Brad said as he strode across the floor to cuff Ethan on the shoulder. Leaning closer, he said, "Since the resort's ours the next couple of days, no need to worry about playing games with fake names. The staff was handpicked and given huge tips to keep their cell phones in their pockets and the happenings around here to themselves."

The smile on the clerk's face grew, making Ethan wonder exactly how much that smile had cost his friend. She pecked away at her computer before saying, "I have you two sharing a suite on the second floor. King-sized bed. Two-person jetted tub. Private balcony."

"Sounds nice," Chelsea said, leaning her cheek against his shoulder.

"Almost as nice as our island," Ethan quipped.

"You two are going to have to tell me all about that," Brad said. "Sounds like someplace Savannah might enjoy."

After running two cards through a scanning device, the clerk placed them in a small folder. "The suite is number 220." She handed the folder to Ethan and then plucked a map of the resort from the display on the counter and proceeded to show them the best way to get to their room.

"I'll let you two get settled," Brad said. "We're throwing a big shindig tonight at the pool. Savannah has them putting together enough food for an army. See you two around seven." He waved as he hurried off to greet some other newly arrived guest.

Ethan took Chelsea's hand and they followed the bellboy to their suite. When Ethan tried to tip him, the guy waved him off. "Taken care of, but thanks." He shut the door behind him.

"This place is great," she said, wandering through the suite. "It's bigger than my first couple of apartments."

The living area had a sofa and two overstuffed chairs. A huge television was mounted above a large hearth. He followed her into the bedroom, pleased they had such a big bed. Tall as he was, he tended to find his feet hanging over the end of some hotel mattresses. The two-person tub gave him plenty of ideas for how to entertain her later.

Back in the living room, she fished her cell phone out of her pocket. "I promised to call Addie."

Although he dreaded it, he nodded. Chelsea had been so relaxed when she'd avoided the real world. Unfortunately, contact with Addie would send them both back into a huge pile of bullshit, now that the photos of them together had hit the Internet. At Will's insistence, they'd released a short statement that confirmed he and Chelsea were in a relationship and Ethan hoped that would be the end of it. Once she talked to her assistant, Chelsea was sure to be stressed out over the publicity again.

"Hi, Addie," Chelsea said into the phone. "Hang on, I'm putting you on speaker since Ethan's here."

"I take it you guys made it to Jekyll," Addie said.

"We did," Chelsea replied. "This place is amazing."

"I hope you enjoy the wedding, 'cause things might get fucking crazy by the time you two get back."

"*Now* what?" Ethan asked, flopping into one of the chairs.

"I'm still fielding all kinds of interview requests."

"Nope," Ethan said.

"I know how you feel," Chelsea said. "But I just can't help but think if we answer a few questions, they'll realize there's no story here, get bored, and give up on with the whole thing."

He shook his head. "Not happening."

"God, you're stubborn," Addie said, which only made him smile.

With a sigh, Chelsea said, "After the wedding, I've got a couple of radio appearances for the charity album."

"Like *that's* what they'll want to talk about," Addie said.

"Exactly. After I answer a question or two just to let everyone know that Ethan and I are together, I can redirect them back to the duets."

"It's better than silence," Addie mused.

"You ladies worry too much," Ethan said. "Mark my words, some celebrity will do something stupid soon. Then we'll be old news."

He thought he heard Addie growl like a feral cat. "I need to be honest with you, boss," she said. "What I'm seeing out there ain't so great."

"What's that supposed to be mean?" Chelsea asked.

"That means that most of the stuff I'm reading on fan forums are postings that can deal with the idea of you two being together, but they hate that they think you two are lying, that there's a lot more to the two of you than just dating."

"Fuck 'em," Ethan said. "We can't spend our whole lives worrying about what people think."

"We do when they're Chelsea's fans," Addie insisted.

Evidently, Chelsea was growing as weary with the conversation as he was, because she said, "Look, we need to run, Addie. For now, just do your best to hold down the fort. Hopefully, it'll all blow over soon."

"Don't forget *The Cathy Kay Show* on Monday morning. You have to be at the television studio by noon."

Chelsea frowned. "Crap."

"You forgot," Addie scolded. "Relax, it's only a short segment, and Cathy usually plays softball."

"Yeah, she's nothing but a pussycat."

* * *

After ending the call, Chelsea went to Ethan and picked up his hand. Although she was frustrated at his attitude, she knew trying to change his mind was probably wasted breath. But learning that her fans, the people who'd made her what she was, thought of her as a liar didn't sit well. No, not well at all.

She squeezed his hand. "I know you hate this publicity stuff, but Addie's right. We really should—"

Her words were cut off when he hauled her onto his lap and kissed the breath right out of her. "We have a party to get ready for," he said as he cradled her face in his callused palms. "Can we quit worrying about the world for two more days? Can't we just be together and enjoy Brad and Savannah's wedding? There'll be plenty of time to deal with Addie and Will and whatever the hell people are saying about us when we get back to Nashville."

The pleading in his voice cut straight to her heart. "You're right," she said, turning her face to kiss one of his palms. "Let's go have some drinks and get those two married. What harm can a couple more days do anyway?"

CHAPTER TWENTY-FOUR

The next afternoon, the sky was beginning to turn the most marvelous kaleidoscope of colors when Chelsea took her spot with the dozen or so people attending Brad and Savannah's wedding. She was barefoot, having left her sandals in a long line with the shoes of the wedding party and other guests, back by the gate leading to the resort's pool. She wiggled her toes in the still warm sand, watching the pink, orange, and yellow streaks that seemed to frame the lace canopy waiting for the happy couple.

Ethan waited under that canopy, while Joslynn, holding her bouquet of orchids, was ready to serve as maid of honor. Her off-the-shoulder satin dress was mint green, the hem brushing the sand. Her long dark hair was coiled on top of her head. Attired more casually, Ethan sported a white oxford shirt with the sleeves rolled up to the elbow. His tan linen trousers were crisply pleated and he wore no tie.

Brad said a few words to Russ before he strode to the shelter to take his place in front of the minister. A few moments later, he nodded to the harpist, who began to play a lilting melody.

Chelsea's heart sang as she took in the whole of the wedding scene, enchanted by the beauty around her. The sweet strums of the harp. The vivid colors of the setting sun. The romantic picture of Savannah in a shimmering white sheath dress as she held tightly to her daughter's hand. Caroline cradled a velvet box in her other small hand while Savannah carried a bouquet of orchids. They walked confidently toward the canopy.

Chelsea glanced to Ethan, not really surprised to find him looking back at her. When he smiled, something inside her melted. This man might not realize it, but he held her heart in his tanned hands. She could almost imagine the two of them standing under that swath of lace, her clothed in white instead of the pale pink she now wore. He would, of course, be every bit as ruggedly handsome as he was today.

When Savannah and Caroline reached Brad, he went down on one knee to kiss Caroline's cheek. Then the girl smiled and moved to stand at Joslynn's side, still clinging to the black box. Brad rose to face Savannah and took her hand into his. They faced the minister together.

"What a happy day this is," the man said before glancing over his shoulder at the sunset. "And quite a beautiful day as well."

Then he launched into a fairly typical litany of what marriage was—or more specifically what it should be. After admonishing the bride and groom that the pledges they were ready to make to one another should be sacred, he said, "The couple would like to exchange their own vows."

Judging from the solemn yet happy expressions on Savannah and Brad's faces, they knew exactly what they were getting into and were more than ready to take the plunge.

"Me first," Brad said to Savannah. "I need to spit this out before you say something that derails my train of thought."

Savannah's brows gathered. "What exactly do you think I could say that would throw you off?"

With a broad smile, he tugged her a little closer. "How about 'I love you'? Every single time you say that to me, my mind is filled with nothing but you."

A collective sigh rose from the ladies, which was followed closely by chuckles.

"Here goes," Brad said. He plucked the orchids from his bride's hand and passed them to Joslynn. Taking Savannah's slender hands into his, he gazed down into her eyes. "I promise to always be there for you, no matter what life throws in our path. I promise to take care of you when you're not feeling good and to make your life crazy busy when you are. I don't give a crap whether we've got money or fame, all I care about is making a family with you and with Caroline. I love you, Savannah, and no matter what happens, I will always stay at your side."

Blinking back tears, Chelsea let her gaze find Ethan's. Damn if that man didn't look a bit misty-eyed himself. His mouth rose in a smile, and he gave her an almost imperceptible nod.

With a deep breath, Savannah offered Brad a shaky smile.

"I love you, Brad. From now until the end of time, I'll be your wife. You never have to worry about having someone there to take care of you or to share the good and bad times. I'll be there for both. If God grants us one year or fifty, you can count on me to spend each and every one with you." When a sob bubbled up, she put her hand to her lips and tried to smile.

Dropping her hands, Brad turned to Caroline and called her over with the crook of his finger. Down on one knee again, he opened the box she handed him and let a long gold chain with heart locket dangle from his fingertips. "I have a promise for you, too, Miss Caroline."

The girl's responding smile was as radiant as the sunset.

"I want to be your daddy," he said. "If you'll have me. I want to do all the things a good daddy does for a daughter. Coach your soccer team and tuck you in at night. I love your mama, and I love you, too."

Caroline turned around so that Brad could put the necklace on her. Her lip quivered as a tear rolled down her cheek.

Chelsea lost it right then and there, allowing her threatening tears to fall. Here were all the things she'd ever dreamed of. A man to love her. A family. Once she'd decided that she would focus on her career, she'd all but given up that hope.

* * *

Ethan hated to see Chelsea cry. Even though he was sure the tears she shed were out of happiness rather than sadness, he found his stomach in knots. The fact that he was so concerned about her moods told him something he'd already feared—

that his heart was no longer his own. Chelsea Harris had captured it. Completely. Irretrievably.

He was hers.

The ceremony might have continued, but Ethan wasn't paying much attention. He was too busy watching Chelsea, letting thoughts of the future cloud his mind. The time they would spend together on the farm, riding horses, working in the barn.

For a moment, he even let the notion of the two of them with a kid tickle his imagination.

And if that wasn't proof he was crazy, he had no idea what was.

An elbow in his ribs made him huff out a breath. "What?"

"The ring," Brad said. "Remember?"

"Oh. Sorry." Ethan produced the gold band from his pocket, handing it over to Brad as Joslynn gave a ring to Savannah.

After the couple exchanged their rings, the minister had them join hands. He offered a blessing for a long and happy life together and then grinned. "You are now husband and wife. Go ahead, Brad, and kiss your bride."

* * *

Chelsea set her champagne glass next to the bride's bouquet she'd caught and watched the guests. Some were dancing to the rock 'n' roll that the happy couple had chosen for the celebration. The DJ seemed to know exactly when to give the up-tempo songs a break and insert a slow song that allowed everyone to catch their breath or nibble on their slices of cake.

There were quite a few guests who'd abandoned their fancy clothes in favor of swimsuits. Most of them were in the pool, floating by on inflated rafts as they sipped their drinks. The rest were like Ethan, deep in discussion.

Suddenly feeling hemmed in, she got to her feet. She'd eaten far too much and danced enough to make her feet ache. Her head was buzzing from the noise and the champagne, and all she wanted was a few moments of peace and quiet to settle her mind.

A glance to the beach made her long to hear the waves lapping against the shore and to feel the sand sluicing between her toes. She weaved through the crowd, murmuring greetings to the people she barely knew since they were mostly family members of the bride and groom. Once she passed through the wrought-iron gate that opened onto the beach, she breathed a sigh of release.

Kicking off her sandals, she carried them as she walked toward the surf. Slowly, the music softened, growing fainter and fainter as she moved farther away. As each wave slapped against the beach, she relaxed a little more.

She hadn't realized how much she'd needed a vacation until she and Ethan had found themselves alone on their island. The peace of mind she'd found there, the way her head had cleared and her body had rested, made the idea of returning to the real world seem like a challenge. Knowing that they'd both have to return to Nashville, to the hustle and bustle of their lives, was enough to make her mood take a turn for the worse.

With a shake of her head, Chelsea banished the threatening melancholy and kept walking, heading toward the canopy, where the lace covering still billowed in the night breeze.

The music had faded to nothing more than soft notes carried on the wind when she reached the place where Brad and Savannah had become husband and wife. She dropped her sandals to stand under the canopy before letting her fingers brush the fabric. She couldn't help but wonder if she'd been correct years ago when she'd assumed that her fame had robbed her of any chance at happiness in her personal life.

It wasn't as though she'd expected to meet someone she could love as much as she now loved Ethan. Sure, she'd had a couple of semi-serious affairs, mostly with other famous people. An actor. A singer. A guy who pitched for the White Sox. None had lasted because those relationships were never intended to be permanent. Not only was she more concerned with her career than any of those men, but a romance being scrutinized by the press was more likely to fail.

Until she met Ethan, she hadn't honestly thought about trying to make that kind of personal connection last. The thought of walking away from him made her heart hurt and tears sting her eyes. How could she let what they shared end?

Brad and Savannah obviously had faith that living in the eye of the paparazzi didn't automatically doom a marriage. They'd exchanged vows and were brave enough to at least try.

Could Ethan be that courageous?

Could I?

Chelsea left the canopy to get closer to the waves, smiling when the first bit of water washed over her feet. Without even bothering to lift the hem of her dress, she took a couple more steps, loving the shifting feel of the wet sand beneath her feet as each wave rolled in. Closing her eyes, she wrapped her arms around her middle and savored the crisp salty air. At that moment, she decided that should she ever tire of singing, she'd move far away from the craziness of Nashville and live next to an ocean.

Somehow she knew Ethan was there before his body pressed against her back. His arms came around her, one warm hand covering her own as the other held the bride's orchids in front of her. "Forget something? I mean, after tackling the other ladies to catch the bouquet..."

She took the flowers as she bumped her butt back against him. "I didn't tackle anyone. Savannah tossed it right to me."

"If you say so, but I could've sworn you left a couple of crumpled bodies back there."

Like she'd dignify that statement with any kind of acknowledgment.

He rubbed his chin against her temple. "What'ya doing out here?"

"Just needed a little less noise."

"I know what you mean. After our island, everything feels...I don't know..."

"Crowded?" she offered.

"And loud. I miss the place."

"Me, too."

He hugged her tightly before easing up. "Your dress is getting wet."

"So are your pants."

He laughed at that. His arms fell away, then he took her hand. "Come with me, pretty lady."

Curious, Chelsea followed him as he led the way back to the canopy. Surprisingly, he stopped there and turned to face her. "Ever see us doing something like this?"

Unsure as to the path his thoughts traveled, she couldn't help but ask, "Like what?"

"Like standing together on a beach," he drawled. "Getting married."

* * *

How he'd found the courage to say the words was beyond him, but now that he'd said them Ethan had no intention of taking them back. Not that he was proposing. At least not yet.

Maybe it was the booze. Or the moonlight. Or the romantic setting. He wasn't sure why, but he wanted—needed—to tell her how he felt. Even more, he had to hear her say that she loved him.

Her eyes searched his. "I didn't think you were the marrying kind."

"People change."

"Not in my experience."

The conversation wasn't going at all as he'd hoped, so he decided to take another tack. Pulling her closer, he leaned down to give her a kiss.

His lips touched hers. Once. Twice. Then her arms rose to circle his neck, the orchids pressing against the back of his head as Chelsea slid her tongue between his lips.

Ethan couldn't seem to get enough of her, slanting his mouth over hers again and again, chasing her tongue with his own. All he wanted was to pick her up, march back to their suite, and make love to her until her eyes crossed.

One thing remained to be done, though.

Easing back, he smiled at her bemused expression, the same one she always got when she'd been thoroughly kissed. He cupped her cheek in his hand and worked up his courage. "I love you."

Those incredible green eyes widened. "You do?"

He nodded. "You know, I've never said that before. Not to anyone."

"Ever the virgin," she said, her lips rising in a bewitching smile. "I love you too."

"Since when?" he had to ask.

She let out a light laugh. "Probably since the moment you walked away from the bar to prove your point. God, you're a stubborn man."

"That's what you love best."

Chelsea's smile grew. "Nobody ever said I was smart."

"Maybe not," Ethan quipped. "But you clearly have excellent taste." Sobering, he lifted her chin with his fingertips. "Say it again, baby."

"That I'm not really smart?" Her teasing ended as she let out a telling little sigh. "I love you, Ethan Walker. With all my heart."

CHAPTER TWENTY-FIVE

I made it. I actually got here on time.

Of course Chelsea had needed her driver to break every speed limit to get her to the studio for the scheduled interview. Thankfully, Addie had made great arrangements for the extraordinarily early flight back to Nashville, and there had been no delays at check-in or getting through TSA. Although Chelsea was exhausted, she only had to stay awake long enough to get this interview done, crawl back into the town car, and get home. Then she could finally sleep.

Chelsea let out a lusty yawn as a hand settled on her shoulder.

Cathy Kay, the show's host, smiled back at her from the mirror on the makeup table. "Get those yawns out of your system before we go live. I'd hate for my viewers to think that I bore you. Trust me, you won't have anything to be bored about." She winked at Chelsea.

"Sorry, Cath. Got up at the crack of dawn so I could get back here."

Actually, dawn hadn't even broken when Chelsea's phone had sounded its annoyingly happy little wake-up tune. She and Ethan both grumbled, but while she'd forced herself to haul her carcass out of bed, he'd simply rolled over and gone right back to snoring.

It wasn't any wonder that getting up had been so difficult. They'd spent the night making love, reaching for each other with downright greed. She wasn't sure if their desperation had been born of their confessions of love or the fear that what they'd shared on their time away from the real world would be compromised once they returned to Nashville.

"Yeah, Addie told me you were out of town when we set this up." Cathy studied her hard in the mirror. "Did you have a good time?"

"The best." Another yawn slipped out.

"Can we please get Ms. Harris another cup of coffee?" Cathy called out to no one in particular.

Three production assistants scurried away.

"Now *that's* service," Chelsea said.

With a satisfied smile, Cathy said, "It helps when the show's named after you." She patted Chelsea's shoulder. "I need to go on now, but we'll have lots to talk about on stage."

"Did Addie send you the information about the charity album?"

Cathy's grin changed from genuine to enigmatic right before Chelsea's eyes. "I have absolutely everything I need. See you in a few?"

"Yep."

"And no yawning!" Turning on her heel, Cathy strode toward the set that reminded Chelsea a lot of the setup Ellen DeGeneres used on her talk show. Just a couple of big, comfy chairs, a small table between, and a flat-screen mounted behind the guests.

At least the place made her feel comfortable, knowing there was nothing worse than being on live television sitting in an uncomfortable chair. It always made the guest look fidgety, which implied there was more going on than what was being said.

As another yawn threatened, she gratefully took a fresh cup of coffee from a girl who appeared far too young to be working at a television studio.

"Let's see if I can help get those eyes looking a little less . . . tired," the makeup artist said as he grabbed some concealer.

"Good luck with that," Chelsea said, frowning at the dark circles under each green eye.

The "all quiet" warning went through the studio, and Chelsea settled in to wait for her turn to sit opposite Cathy and talk about her album.

* * *

After watching the taping of two heartwarming stories—one guest was a teenager who'd just had a cochlear implant, the other a sixth-grader who'd sold more Girl Scout cookies than anyone else in Tennessee—it was time for Chelsea's turn with Cathy Kay.

Waiting right off stage, she watched for the cue that would come from the handler on her left.

"Quiet!" the director shouted, which had only a minimal impact on the noise level.

It wasn't until one of the assistants stood in front of the main camera, held up five fingers, and said, "We're live in five, four, three..." She stopped the verbal count, but her fingers showed the last two seconds before the red light on top of the camera illuminated. *The Cathy Kay Show* music swelled through the studio.

Cathy flashed a supersized smile at the camera from where she sat in her chair. "Welcome back!" She picked up a CD case from the table on her right. "My next guest is often called the best female vocalist in country music." She held up the CD, showing the cover of Chelsea's last album. "I'm happy to welcome Chelsea Harris."

The audience erupted in applause that made Chelsea smile. Although she was already walking to the stage, the assistant gave her back a small push, which earned the guy an over-the-shoulder glare. Then she pasted her smile back on and strode toward Cathy.

In her typical fashion, Cathy air-kissed Chelsea's cheeks, then she swept her hand at the two blue chairs. "Welcome! We've got a lot to talk about today!"

"Thanks for having me. I'm really excited to tell you about the new album I'm recording right now."

"Yes, yes," Cathy said, that enigmatic smile firmly back in place. "But first, we want to hear about you and Ethan Walker. You two are the talk of Nashville."

The demand was in the host's voice, and it took all of Chelsea's self-control not to tell the woman to mind her own business. "Ethan and I are dating. It's actually a fun story. We met because of the duet album I'm doing to raise money for colon cancer research."

The flat-screen usually showed nothing but the show's logo, but as the image shifted, Chelsea couldn't help but notice. When she saw what was now displayed, heat rose on her cheeks. She'd imagined what the pictures that moron took of her and Ethan back on their island looked like, but she hadn't actually seen one.

Well, she saw one now. In fact, there was a changing montage of several images. The two of them embracing. Sitting together on the blanket. Wading into the water.

"Tell me all about the house you two stayed in off the Keys," Cathy cajoled. "Looks like you two were mighty cozy."

"It was a really nice place. We were the only two on the island, which was nice. I had a nice time." Great. She was rambling, stuck on the same stupid word.

A picture of Ethan extending his middle finger at the photographer popped up next. "Looks like your man wasn't too happy when he realized the two of you were spotted."

A sigh slipped out before Chelsea could squelch it. "It's always a bit...disconcerting when you have your privacy invaded." She squared her shoulders. "Now that I'm back in Nashville, I'm going to be working hard to get my album recorded. I've got duets scheduled with—"

"Were you able to convince Ethan to sing with you?" Cathy asked. "His parents were such fantastic entertainers."

The image on the TV became the smiling faces of Ethan's mother and father. "Such a tragedy to lose them both. Has Ethan ever told you why he doesn't follow in their footsteps?" She let out a chuckle as she swept her hand to the flat-screen. Ethan was on an ancient cover of some teen fan magazine, bare chested, dressed in very tight gold lamé pants, with a silk scarf around his neck. His hair was long and feathered away from his face. "I'll admit to having such a crush on him when I was a girl. And those songs!" She put a dramatic palm against her breasts. "To die for."

Breathing slowly and evenly to try to keep her composure, Chelsea struggled on how to redirect this interview. Ethan would be livid to be the main topic of discussion. Sure, she'd expected a couple of questions about him since they'd announced they were in a relationship, but this was getting ridiculous. "Ethan has a beautiful voice, but he doesn't want to record for a living."

"Why, how can you say that?" Cathy once again indicated the screen, which now had the video Brad had shot of them singing the song she'd recorded with Chuck Austin. The studio was filled with the sound of Chelsea and Ethan's voices.

Chelsea shot daggers at Cathy Kay with her gaze.

As the music quickly faded, Cathy kept on grinning like the Cheshire Cat. "You two sound so lovely together."

"Thank you. I was able to talk him into singing with me. We'll actually be recording one of his parents' songs on my charity album. Did I tell you why I'm recording it?" Chelsea asked, trying once again to get the upper hand.

"While I'm sure we'd all like to know about that album, I

have to say that there is one other matter we'd definitely like to hear about first." Cathy rubbed her hands together in glee. "We'd all rather hear about your wedding!"

Chelsea's stomach plummeted to her feet. "*What?*"

"I have it from a reliable source that you and Ethan were married last night in Georgia."

Hands clenched, Chelsea had to fight to not grit her teeth as she replied. "I'm not sure who your *source* is, but I can assure you that I am not married. Not to Ethan Walker. Not to anyone."

"Now, don't play coy with me, Chelsea. We're old friends. Everyone is very excited and wants to hear about your elopement with Ethan." She waved her hand at the flat-screen TV yet again.

The image on the screen revealed a picture of Chelsea and Ethan, embracing under the wedding canopy back on the beach on Jekyll Island. Because it was dark when the photo was taken, her pink dress appeared white, and since she was holding the orchids behind Ethan's neck as they hugged, the picture looked exactly like a wedding photograph.

So much for the resort staff leaving everyone alone.

"I know how that looks," Chelsea said. "But we aren't married."

Leaning close, as though she was trying to be nothing but a friend exchanging a confidence, Cathy said, "You can tell me, Chelsea. It looks oh so romantic. I know destination weddings are 'in' right now. This one must have been beautiful."

Although she wanted desperately to say a few obscene words, Chelsea swallowed them. "I know what that looks like, but Ethan and I aren't married. We were attending a wedding of a couple of our friends."

"My source tells me that after *that* wedding, you two had one of your own. How long have you two been in love?"

It took every ounce of Chelsea's fortitude to not rip off her mic and stomp off the stage. Only years of experience in dealing with people who gossiped for a living kept her in that chair. "Sorry to disappoint you, but we're not married. Look, we're dating—"

"Ah, so you two *are* in love. Was this a rehearsal, then?"

"Fine, we're in love, but this wasn't a rehearsal. We were at the wedding of a couple of our friends. That's all."

"You two are only in the 'making plans' stage. Have you talked about starting a family? Can you imagine?" Cathy slapped her thighs with her palms. "Your kids would be mighty talented. I mean, look at their parents—and their grandparents!"

All Chelsea wanted to do was get the hell off that stage. She dug her fingernails into the arms of the chair. "I don't see Ethan and I starting a family any time soon."

"You're right," Cathy said. "Your wedding should come first, don't you think?"

"Our wedding should come first," Chelsea said through clenched teeth, parroting back the stupid words and searching for a chance to escape. She was so angry, she wasn't even sure exactly what she was saying.

Cathy glanced over at the assistant frantically waving with the signal for a commercial break and frowned. "We're talking today with country vocalist Chelsea Harris about her relationship with the elusive Ethan Walker. *The Cathy Kay Show* will be back right after these messages."

"And . . . we're out," the assistant said after the red light on the camera faded.

Standing, Chelsea plucked the small microphone off her collar and started to jerk the wire through her shirt. "I'm outta here."

Cathy slithered over and put her hand on Chelsea's arm. "Now, Chelsea, honey . . . No reason to get in a snit. It was all in good fun."

Instead of snatching her arm away, Chelsea glared at Cathy until the woman got the hint and removed her hand.

Folding her arms under her breasts, Cathy dropped the fake niceness. "If you leave, everyone will think you're being a bad sport. Or that you're lying. Shit, from what I heard, your fans are mighty pissed that you tried to hide the relationship with Ethan."

"Why would you do this?" Chelsea asked. "If you would've asked me, I could've told you those pictures weren't of us getting married."

"I know *that*," Cathy snapped. "But the rumors are running rampant, and when my people had a shot at those Jekyll Island pictures, well, I couldn't pass them up."

"One minute," the assistant shouted.

"Look," Cathy said, "just sit down. Okay? I'll let you pitch your little album now."

Against her better judgment, Chelsea let the tech help her reconnect her microphone. The last thing she needed was more bad publicity.

* * *

Ethan marched up the long Jetway, his bag slung over his shoulder. He'd spent the better part of the day at the Jacksonville airport, waiting to fly standby since he'd been too damn tired to get up to fly home with Chelsea. All he could do was watch several flights leave without him and pass hour after hour playing Spider Solitaire on his phone until the battery gave out. Damn if he didn't forget to grab his charger when he left the room since Chelsea wasn't there to make her "one last sweep." And he knew the moment he walked to one of the airport kiosks to buy a new one, they'd call his name and he'd miss his chance at a flight.

He finally got a seat in coach, which wasn't a lot of fun for a guy of his height. Once everyone was aboard and the door closed, the airplane had taxied out and then just sat on the tarmac for over an hour because of some kind of mechanical problem. And didn't *that* give him a lot of confidence that he'd get back to Nashville in one piece.

Exhausted and starving, he was about as grumpy as he could get. It was probably a good thing Chelsea had left before him, because he wouldn't have been very good company. All he wanted was a meal, a beer, and to watch ESPN.

Nashville had turned cold, judging from the drop in temperature from the plane to the Jetway. Winter wasn't far away, and he already missed the warmth of Florida and Georgia. But this city was his home, and cold or not, his farm was where he wanted to be.

He made his way through the crowded airport, ready to

see this trip end. As he rode down the final escalator to the ground transportation area, he frowned. A half dozen reporters and an equal number of cameramen were waiting close to the exit. One of them locked eyes with Ethan, put his microphone in front of his face, and then started jostling his cameraman with his elbow. He shouted out, "Ethan Walker! Can you tell us about your upcoming marriage to Chelsea Harris?"

Ethan scowled, especially when the other reporters all came to life, grinning at him as they spoke into their mics. When he reached the bottom of the escalator, he tried to dodge to the left, found his way blocked, and shifted right. He was hemmed in on both sides. Worse, the people behind him on the escalator started plowing into his back. Having no other choice, he shoved his way through the reporters, not really caring if he jarred a couple of the nosy jerks as he moved them aside with his shoulders.

They followed him out the double doors, which wasn't a surprise. He tried to hail a taxi, but two of the eager reporters got between him and the first car, so the taxi moved on to the next person.

"Guys," Ethan said, trying not to lose his temper. "I need to get home. Okay?"

"Chelsea Harris said you two are planning a wedding," one reporter said. "Have you two set a date?"

"She did not," Ethan insisted, figuring they were only trying to get a rise out of him.

"On *The Cathy Kay Show*," the second reporter insisted,

"she said you two were in love and have talked about getting married."

"You're full of shit." Ethan tried again to signal for another taxi, and one mercifully screeched to the curb right in front of the reporters.

As he tossed his bag into the backseat, he found a restraining hand on his arm. Turning to confront whoever had the audacity to touch him, he found a smartphone shoved in front of his face. On the screen was Chelsea, seated opposite one of the most annoying talk show hosts in the business. The reporter touched the screen to start the video.

A slew of emotions raced through Ethan as he watched the short tape of the things Chelsea had said to Cathy Kay. Disbelief. Shock. And finally anger.

Without a word, he swept the man aside with his arm and crawled into the taxi. After grumbling out directions to the farm, he changed his mind. "Take me to Words & Music."

"Downtown, right?" the driver asked over his shoulder.

"Right. And I'll pay any speeding ticket."

How could Chelsea put their relationship on parade like that? Talking about planning a wedding... What in the hell had she been thinking?

Hadn't she listened to a goddamn thing he'd said? How could she blabber on about stuff that was so personal? What was wrong with her?

It was probably a good thing his phone was dead, because he needed to get a tight rein on his temper before he talked to her, or they'd both find themselves in the fight of the century.

By heading to the restaurant first, Ethan could talk to Brad and Russ and they could calm him down before he confronted Chelsea.

If they could calm him down...

CHAPTER TWENTY-SIX

W ords & Music had a decent crowd, and thankfully, Ethan didn't see any reporters as he wove his way through the bar to get to his office. After he tossed his bag on the office sofa and plugged the spare charger into his dead phone, he headed back down to the bar to look for his buddies.

The restaurant's manager, Ellie Foster, glanced up from her clipboard and drew her brown eyebrows together. "You weren't supposed to be back until tomorrow."

He shot her a scowl. "Where's Brad? Russ?"

With a shake of her head, she set the clipboard on the end of the bar. "Seriously?"

His scowl deepened.

She folded her arms under her breasts, drumming her fingers against her forearm. "You know what, Ethan?"

"What?"

"Even though I work for you, I need say something."

"Then spit it out. I've gotta talk to my partners."

"You can really be a selfish jerk sometimes."

All he could do was gape at her audacity. While one of the reasons the partners had hired her and loved working with her was her willingness to call bullshit when it was the right thing to do, he hadn't expected her to have the guts to insult him right to his face.

"Did it even cross your mind that Brad is on his honeymoon right now?" she asked. "I mean, you did just attend his wedding, didn't you? Weren't you the even the best man?"

The wind went right out of Ethan's sails. He hadn't remembered. Nor had he remembered, as he did now, that Russ was staying down at Jekyll for a few days to take his first true vacation since they'd updated the restaurant five years before. Instead, Ethan had been nothing but pissed off at his little reception at the airport and all he'd thought about was himself.

He'd been preoccupied with the fear that the annoying gauntlet he'd had to walk through at the airport would be facing him the rest of his life should he stay with Chelsea. That, and his anger continued to grow over the way she'd blabbed their personal business so freely.

But Ellie was right. His ego always led the way.

He let his head hang.

"Like I said," she added, laying a gentle hand on his arm, "you can be a selfish jerk sometimes. But we love you anyway. Anything I can do to help? I'm not Brad or Russ, but I'm a pretty good bartender, which means I'm a great listener."

"I can't believe I didn't remember that they'd be gone," he grumbled.

"Being as it's the first time any of you three have been

away for years," she said. "It's not really that much of a surprise."

"You'd know," Ethan said. "You've been here as long as the place has been open."

"Which means I should probably take my own vacation soon," she quipped.

"You've earned one." Scrambling to think of when the partners had last given the well-deserving employee a raise, he reached for the clipboard to see what management shifts he was scheduled to cover while Brad and Russ were away.

"You get tomorrow," she said. When he glanced at her with a raised eyebrow, she just grinned. "I have the rest of the week..." She winked.

"You read minds now?"

"Nah, only thinking like I would if I was in your shoes." Ellie's smile faded. "I saw the clips from *The Cathy Kay Show*. I imagine some of your forgetfulness was 'cause you were mad."

With a weary sigh, he gave her a curt nod. "Got mobbed by reporters when I was at the airport. I have no idea how they knew I'd be there."

"Are you kidding me? They probably have someone at every airline on their payroll to tip them off, especially since people have to fly under their real names now instead of pseudonyms."

"Bunch of leeches," Ethan said with a growl in his voice.

"That they are," she agreed. "But you better get used to them."

"What's that supposed to mean?"

Ellie let out a long sigh and pulled out a bar stool, which she sat on as she stared at him.

Since she wasn't in a hurry to answer him, he followed suit, taking a load off and waiting for her to work through whatever it was she wanted to say.

"It's probably none of my business..." she began.

"Like that ever stopped you before," he said, giving her a jostle with his elbow to let her know he was teasing. "Say what you need to, Ellie."

"I can see what the two of you are like when you're together. I think there's something...real there. I just worry...Look, I know how you feel about the press. We all do. But Chelsea's a star, Ethan. A major star. Reporters will always be a part of her life."

He shook his head. "She hates the press too."

"She *needs* the press," Ellie retorted. "She might not like them, but she needs their support to keep her where she is. If you two stay in a relationship, one of you is gonna have to change."

"Yeah," Ethan said. "She'll have to learn to freeze them out."

"You think it's that simple?"

"Of course."

The incredulous expression on her face made him wonder if she thought he was stupid. Or perhaps naïve.

"All I'm saying, Ethan, is that I just don't see her being able to do what she does and not have reporters asking her the kinds of questions she had to answer on that show. She is who she is, and you're who you are. People want to know about you both. They feel like they have some kind of stake in your lives."

"Fuck 'em," he said.

"You honestly believe she'll start declining interviews? That she'll dump her social media accounts? Award shows?" Ellie asked. "All I'm sayin' is that if you can't handle her life, well...Don't keep leading her on. You'll break her heart." Jumping to her feet, she plucked up her clipboard. "I gotta go."

As uncomfortable as she'd appeared, he was surprised she didn't sprint to the kitchen. She took off like a mall walker, quick-stepping away from the bar and the conversation.

Probably not a bad idea since it was clear that she couldn't see things through his eyes. Not a surprise. Most people had no clue what a nightmare it had been to grow up famous and to have that fame kill the people he loved most. If he hadn't grounded himself, if Uncle Joe hadn't taught him that he was more than some piece of meat being chewed up by the world, he could've easily ended up like the litany of other famous children fighting drug addictions or making terrible life choices.

Ethan felt as exposed as if he were sitting on that stool naked. He was still fuming at having his confession to Chelsea, something that was more difficult than she could ever know, paraded in front of the world and sundry. If she loved him, if she truly loved him, she should have known how much that would hurt him.

But what else could she do when ambushed by someone as

tenacious as Cathy Kay? What could Chelsea have done in to get the reporter to change the subject?

Probably nothing...

Admitting that some of his annoyance could stem from his exhaustion and the rotten day he'd had so far, he got to his feet. He'd check his phone to see if she'd called, then he'd head over to her place. Once they talked it out, once she understood why her words had wounded him so deeply, they could avoid something like that disastrous interview from happening again.

* * *

Chelsea checked her phone, even though she'd looked to see if Ethan had called less than five minutes before. With a disgruntled huff, she slammed the iPhone onto the mattress she sat on.

Why wouldn't he call her back? Or at least text her? She'd left several voicemail messages and God only knew how many texts.

Something was wrong.

"I keep telling you that everything's fine," Addie said. She leaned her shoulder against the door to Chelsea's bedroom. "His phone is probably dead or something."

"Or something," Chelsea said. "Like him being pissed off about that interview."

"I told you, I doubt he even saw it. He was probably at the airport all day, trying to catch a flight. Besides, even if he did see it, what was so terrible about it?"

"I just can't help thinking he'll be upset. I mean, I let Cathy get the upper hand. I'm usually a lot better at making a host follow my agenda."

"Yes, you are," Addie said with a nod. "But they don't always get so fucking . . . personal. She pushed your buttons and she got you to reveal a little more than you wanted. So what? You tattled that you love each other. Like *that's* a big fucking secret after that picture. I mean, you didn't say anything that was out of line. It's not like you told the world he's got a small dick." She gave Chelsea a lopsided smile. "He doesn't, does he?"

Her phone chimed a text message, and Chelsea's heart leapt to her throat. "It's from Ethan. He says his phone was dead. Forgot his charger in Georgia. Oh, and he's coming over here now."

Why hadn't he called? He normally hated texts. While she was glad he was coming to her, she couldn't help but wonder why he didn't want to go home and check the horses. Was he making her a greater priority? Or was he hurrying over to give her a piece of his mind?

"I can't believe she got that picture!" Chelsea stood and went to stand in front of Addie. "The staff was supposed to keep things hush-hush. Brad said he'd paid them all well."

"Do you have any idea how much some reporters would pay for a picture like that?" Addie chuckled. "Shit, I wish I'd been there to take it. I would've gotten enough fucking money to retire." She patted Chelsea's arm. "Ethan's just going to have to understand, Chel."

"Understand? Understand what?"

"Your life. Your career. What being with Chelsea Harris entails."

Chelsea let out a resigned sigh. "I was hoping that stuff would...I don't know...blow over? Die down? It's not always this insane."

With a discouraging shake of her head, Addie said, "Die down? Not likely. For fuck's sake, when has it *ever* died down? You're a visible celebrity. You're active online. You know how to make all of that work for you, and you've got really loyal fans because of everything you've done to win them over. *That's* what Ethan's gonna have to understand."

"I guess I'm used to it," Chelsea said with a shrug.

"Then he'll just have to get used to it too. I don't understand why he'd be pissy about publicity. He's famous too."

"He tries to forget that."

"The difference is that you embrace it, you make it work for you." Addie's grin returned. "Besides, you and I are both major extroverts, so we let it all hang out."

"Ethan's about as far from an extrovert as someone can get." Despite their teasing, Chelsea's heart was heavy. She was angry at whoever started the stupid wedding rumor. She was angry at whoever took the damned picture. And she was angry at herself for being far too free with her words.

"I should go," Addie said as she pushed herself away from the door frame. "It doesn't take long to get here from the restaurant. I'm sure you two have plenty to talk about." Turning on her heel, she went to her office.

Heading to the kitchen, Chelsea waited for her assistant to grab her stuff and take off.

Addie stopped long enough to pop her head in. "Don't forget your rehearsal tomorrow."

"I won't. And thanks for being there for me, Addie."

"Anytime."

The door closing sounded as Chelsea grabbed a bottle of wine. A little fortification before Ethan arrived couldn't hurt.

Addie's guidance still rang in her ears. As usual, it was good advice. The woman had insight, which she wasn't shy about sharing. Time and time again, she'd saved Chelsea's ass.

But this time, that advice wasn't at all easy to accept.

The stubborn cork finally gave up the fight, so Chelsea poured herself a large glass of pinot noir. Hip against the island, she sipped at the sweet wine when what she wanted to do was chug it. In fact, she wanted to chug the whole damn bottle.

This was a crossroads in her relationship with Ethan, and she knew things weren't going to be simple any longer. Her fear was that loving him and knowing he loved her in return simply wasn't going to be enough. She cherished his declaration, having not expected it from him. While she held his words deep inside her, she was a realist who was grounded in the crazy world she'd chosen to live in.

A world he would never allow himself to be a part of.

The doorbell startled her, and she was a little depressed that she'd lost herself so deeply in her worries. A glance told her that she'd polished off a lot of the wine.

How long had she been moping?

A second chime from her doorbell got her moving. "Coming!"

Knowing security wouldn't have let anyone but Ethan through, Chelsea opened the door to find the man she loved with a frosty scowl scary enough to make her wonder if he'd turned some of her hair gray.

"Can I have some of that?" he asked, nodding at the glass she hadn't realized she was still holding. "Or better yet, got any beer?"

She backed up a few steps. "Of course! Come in, come in."

After he followed her to the kitchen, she got him a long-neck from the refrigerator. He twisted the cap off and tossed it in the trash before tipping the bottle up and chugging a great deal of it.

Smiling, she refilled her nearly empty glass and sipped her wine. Then an awkward silence settled over them. Each second seemed to pass as slowly as an hour until Chelsea couldn't take it any longer. Disgusted with the quiet, she decided they needed an icebreaker. She put her glass down, plucked the beer from his hand, and set it aside. Fisting her hand in his shirt, she said in what she hoped was a sultry voice, "Follow me."

Ethan obeyed, shuffling after her. When they reached her bedroom, she tugged him closer, wrapping her arms around his waist. "Kiss me," she ordered.

His mouth captured hers, and she let the warmth of his lips and the effects of the wine banish any hesitation. The same kind of desperation she'd felt only the night before was still there, prodding and pushing her to grab all the happiness she could while it was still within her reach. Unwilling to let the fear of what was to come dim her passion, she fumbled for his belt buckle, wanting to show him how much he meant to her.

By the time she got his belt off and his jeans unbuttoned, Chelsea was panting with anticipation. As he reached for her, she brushed his hands away. Pulling down his pants, she dropped to her knees. "My turn."

* * *

Ethan stared down at her, wondering exactly how much wine Chelsea had drank. Her kiss had been so forceful, so full of need, and he couldn't seem to get a read on her mood. He'd come to her place braced for a confrontation. Instead, he'd found a passionate lover who made him want her every bit as much as she seemed to want him.

The confrontation could wait.

Perhaps she had the right idea. In all the time they'd been together, they had seemed so natural together. Tonight had been different. Maybe she'd felt that awkwardness as well, and this was her way to get them past the discomfort.

He was more than willing to let her try.

She dragged his boxers down, and he put a hand on her shoulder for balance as she helped him take off his boots and kick aside the clothing. His cock bobbed toward her, and damn if she didn't lick her lips as she stared at it. Her warm fingers closed over the shaft, and he shut his eyes and let the thrill of her touch wash over him.

A moment later, his eyes opened wide as she took him into her mouth. With a strangled moan, he threaded his fingers through her hair and tried to hold tightly to his self-control. The moist heat of her mouth, the way she glided her tongue over his skin, made the need to be inside her almost unbearable.

"I want you," Ethan said, practically begging. When she kept up her tender assault, he took control of the situation. Easing away from her, he hauled her to her feet and fumbled with her pants. Thankfully she helped by wiggling out of them and then squirmed out of her panties. A moment later, he had her on her back. As she wrapped her legs around his hips, he slid inside her, a bit in awe at how wet and ready he found her.

The cadence was fast. Rough. And thoroughly captivating. His release threatened, and he tried to hold back, wanting her to be with him. A moment later, she lifted her knees and gasped. The way her body pulsed around him pushed him over the edge, and his orgasm left him breathless.

CHAPTER TWENTY-SEVEN

Chelsea was the first to stir. She tapped Ethan's back, not because he was getting heavy but because she suddenly felt vulnerable lying there splayed out beneath him.

With a rather insulting masculine grunt he pulled away from her and headed to the bathroom.

As she quickly dressed, she realized that they hadn't used a condom. Not that she was worried. She'd been on the pill for years and Ethan had mentioned he'd been tested not long ago. What bothered her about forgetting the condom was that she'd lost all control, and knowing that he could succeed in making her forget everything was downright horrifying.

She'd admitted to herself a long time ago that she was a woman who needed to be in charge of her life. She offered no apologies for insisting on having things done her way. Her hard work and desire for perfection had helped her claw her way to the top of country music. Even in her personal life, she'd been in total control. No one bossed her around.

She always called the shots. *She* kept the reins firmly in her hands.

And Ethan had snatched them away far too easily. Even though she'd had every intention of discussing their problems and trying to come to some kind of agreement, the moment she saw him, all she'd wanted to do was to touch him and have him touch her.

So much for control...

She was no better off now than when she'd been with guys like Lance Watson. Ethan might not be quite as big a jerk as Lance, but he wanted things to all be his way. In Ethan's eyes, there was no compromise.

But if he wanted to be in her life, to share their lives, he would have to learn how to bend. Otherwise, there was no hope for them as a couple.

Ethan came back into the bedroom and picked up his underwear and jeans. Silence reigned as he dressed. Since he didn't seem to care that they hadn't used a condom, she didn't bother bringing it up.

"I need more wine," she said as she left him there.

In the kitchen, she downed what little pinot noir was left in her glass before refilling it. She was well one her way to finishing the refill when he joined her. They stood next to the island, her working on her wine, him standing there with his hands slid into his back pockets. After a few awkward moments, he finally let his gaze meet hers.

Before Chelsea could start this conversation, she needed to confess her rather loose lips. "I need to tell you about what happened on that stupid interview this morning," she said.

"I saw it."

"You saw it?"

He nodded. "At least some clips."

"So that's why you wouldn't call me back. You're pissed."

"Of course I'm pissed, but I already told you: I didn't call you back because my battery died and I left my charger back at the resort."

She took another long drink of her wine, unsure how to keep this conversation from becoming an argument. He was angry. Over what? Her telling the truth and trying to squelch a ridiculous rumor that had been fueled by a picture taken by some snoop?

Before she could come to any solution, Ethan fired the first shot. "I can't believe you told that bitch so much. Geesh, baby, what were you thinking?"

Her defenses snapped into place. "What exactly was so terrible about what I said? Did I lie? Did I even exaggerate?"

"No, but why would you even talk about our private life? You know how I feel about that."

"I had no choice," she insisted. "Someone took a picture of us on the beach after the wedding. Cathy was trying to convince everyone we got married. I had to set the record straight."

He shook his head. "All you had to tell her was that she was wrong. That's all. Just tell her she was full of shit." After a deep inhale and slow exhale, he continued. "Whatever we feel for each other is no one's business but our own."

Addie had been right. Ethan was going to have to learn to accept that he was in a relationship with a celebrity. "I had to do something to stop the stupid rumors. All I did was tell people the truth."

"You didn't have to say a goddamn word, Chelsea. Let 'em talk. Let 'em say we're married. Who gives a shit?"

"I do. My fans care about me and—"

He scoffed at her. "No, they don't. Trust me. They don't give two fucks about you except to use you. I've lived with it my whole life. Fans are nothing but vultures."

"How can you say that? My fans made me what I am."

"Your voice made you what you are," Ethan said before taking on long pull on what little beer remained in his bottle. "Your fans are just think you owe them something. You don't owe them a damn thing."

How could she put up any kind of argument with someone who was so wrong and so stubborn that he wouldn't even listen?

She had to try. She loved him too much to not at least attempt to get him to bend. "Ethan, if my fans didn't buy my songs, if they didn't support my albums, I would be just another wannabe singer putting her stuff up online and hoping someone eventually discovered me. I owe my fans for their loyalty. They care about me. They care about my life. They want to share my happiness, my sadness, my success."

"They're not your family," he insisted. "They're just... people. People who want a piece of you. They'd pick your carcass clean if you gave them the chance."

This conversation was going around and around and coming back to the same place. "Then I'll let them have a piece of me."

"Funny," Ethan said. "I thought you belonged to me."

The word choice made her cringe. He sounded too much like Lance, and she couldn't stop herself from bristling. "Belong? You think I *belong* to you?"

"Yes. And I belong to you."

Temper rising by the moment, Chelsea shook her head. "If you can't accept who I am, what I do, then maybe... Well, maybe we need to take a step back."

He just stared at her.

"Maybe things just went too fast," she said, her anger giving way to sadness. No matter how hard she tried, it seemed he would never see things her way.

And she would never be able to stop being who she was.

"Maybe... Maybe we need a break."

"No. I love you, Chelsea!" His forceful shout shocked her and made her eyes lock with his. With the exception of the times they'd made love, she'd never been seen Ethan looking so open, so exposed. "I'm not some fucking teenager, Chelsea. I'm old enough to know love when it happens. We might not have been together long, but I know my own mind. This isn't some... some... *fling*. It's not something that I can get over. When I talked about marrying you, I meant it, and I meant forever." His features hardened. "I thought you loved me too."

"I do, Ethan. I love you."

"But you love being famous more," he accused. He'd closed himself off again, the vulnerability giving way to naked rage. "Admit it. You have more than enough money to walk away right now and never want for anything. Right?"

"Yeah, but—"

"*But*. See that's the thing about people like you. There's always a 'but.'"

She set her hands against her hips. "What do you mean by 'people like me'?"

"People who get off on seeing themselves on TV, every time they find themselves on the cover of some magazine." He shook his head. "People like my parents. They loved being famous a helluva lot more than they loved—" His hand clenched into tight fists and his gaze grew hard. "I'm not going through that again. I'm not. Choose, Chelsea."

While her heart went out to him—to the hurt child who never felt as if he had his parents' love—she wasn't about to chuck everything she'd worked her ass off to achieve into a dumpster. And for what?

For the man you love, her heart said.

For him to get his way, to boss you around, her brain argued back.

She had to know exactly what he'd meant. Because if he was willing to walk away simply because she'd been honest with her fans, he wasn't the man she thought he was. "Are you saying that if I keep singing, you're going to leave me?"

"I'm saying that I love you and I want you to share your life with me. But..."

"But?" Chelsea let out an acerbic laugh. "Funny, I thought only people like me said 'but.'"

His mouth drew into a grim line. "*But* I can't deal with the fear of losing you like I lost my parents."

"That's not going to happen, Ethan."

"How do you know that? And I can't live with cameras being shoved in my face. I don't want my children constantly worrying about the shit I had to worry about. I couldn't fucking go to the john without some idiot following me in. No. Not doing to my kids what my parents did to me."

"I would protect my children," she insisted. "Lots of celebrities have private lives. Their kids aren't fair game. Things aren't the same as they were when you were a kid, Ethan."

"Bull. Shit."

Wrapping her arms around her middle, she knew they'd arrived at an impasse. She wasn't willing to stop being Chelsea Harris, and he wasn't willing to let her do what she had to do to survive.

What more was there to say?

A stray tear slipped down her cheek, and she didn't even bother to brush it away. "You knew who I was."

His brows gathered as he scowled, but he said nothing.

"You knew who I was, and you made me fall in love with you anyway." She tossed the words like an accusation, her anger growing like some living thing inside her. "Fuck you, Ethan. Fuck you for doing that to me. And fuck you for doing that to us."

* * *

Ethan gritted his teeth, trying to will his feet to move. He couldn't find the strength.

If he left, if he walked out of that condo, he was never going to see Chelsea again, unless it was on television or at a concert. He almost laughed as he pictured himself years from now, hiding far back in a crowd just to get a glimpse of her and hoping she didn't see him.

He'd become pathetic, letting her pull his strings like he was some puppet. She was demanding that he do things her way without an ounce of compromise. He was supposed to let people intrude on his life, people he didn't know, who had no connection to him. But what did she offer in return?

Not a damn thing.

Chelsea wanted to stay famous and would keep right on telling everyone things that were supposed to be private, something shared between a man and a woman in love. He had a bad flashback to his father jokingly telling a reporter about the time Ethan had been really sick and wet the bed. For God's sake, Ethan had been all of eight at the time, and his father—a man who was supposed to love him—had humiliated him for the sake of a little publicity.

That had hurt. A lot. No way in hell he'd put his children through that kind of ordeal. Nor could he sit around worrying the press would kill Chelsea the way they'd murdered his parents.

Despite the ridiculous things she was asking of him, he didn't still want to lose her. Not like this. He kept trying to tell himself that all he had to do was open up to the world, to let the things he considered personal become public domain. But after the nightmare of a childhood he'd endured, he balked.

Love her or not, he couldn't live that kind of life again.

Chelsea picked up her glass and hurled it against the

wall. Shards of glass rained down on the tile. "Say something!"

"Like what, baby? You've made up your mind."

"Evidently so have you."

His heart dropped to his boots and he forced himself to take a few steps toward her. When she hugged herself in response, seemingly blocking him coming any closer, he stopped and stared down at her.

Tears brimmed her eyes, and Ethan's every instinct screamed to take her into his arms.

But at what cost?

She didn't want him as he was. If he wouldn't change, even though she was refusing to do any changing herself, she was more than willing to let him go.

Ethan reached up to brush away a tear on her cheek with the back of his fingers. Throat clogged with emotion, he tried to find the words.

They wouldn't come.

With a shake of his head, he walked out of her life.

CHAPTER TWENTY-EIGHT

Y̶ou promised her, Ethan," Savannah said. "You told Chelsea you'd sing the duet."

Ethan took the plate of spaghetti she held out to him and shook his head. "She won't want to sing with me."

"The album is almost done," Brad chimed in, pulling out the bar stool next to Ethan's and taking a seat. "'When You Were Mine' was supposed to be the last song, then she can get it released."

"Chelsea will do just fine with seven songs instead of eight." Ethan grabbed his fork, twirled some pasta around it, and took a big bite, hoping their badgering would swiftly come to an end.

"She wants eight," Brad said, "so if you won't do the duet, she's coming tomorrow to do a solo."

"You should sing with her," Savannah said. "It's been long enough that you two should be able to get together for the time it takes to record a song. What's it been? A month?"

"Three weeks," he whispered.

Three weeks. Three agonizing weeks since he'd left Chelsea's condo. And the only time he'd seen her was when the ad for her Saturday concert had popped up on his TV one evening. The damn thing was already sold out, which made the ad a waste in his opinion.

It wasn't as though she acted as if she wanted to see him again. Hell, less than a week after their breakup, a truck pulling a two-horse trailer had arrived at the farm. The driver brought a letter from Chelsea that had a check to reimburse Ethan for anything he might have spent on Hamlet. Despite Ethan wanting to keep the horse close in hopes his owner might eventually show up, the driver had taken Hamlet away to a new home. Angry, Ethan had torn the check up and tossed it into the trash.

Uncle Joe would barely talk to him, going on and on about Ethan being "boneheaded." Not that he needed a reminder.

He missed her. Plain and simple. The way she snuggled against him at night. Her laugh. The sweet sound of her voice. How comfortable he was whenever she was near, a kind of relaxed ease he hadn't enjoyed since.

Now, he had his privacy—for all the good it was doing him.

"Earth to Ethan," Savannah said.

Ethan glanced up. "What?"

She pushed her own plate of pasta away, frowning. "I'm worried about you."

"Why?"

Brad let out a snort. "Why won't you just admit it already? You're miserable without Chelsea."

"I'm fine," Ethan insisted.

In her typical mother hen way, Savannah came to stand at his side and put her hand on his shoulder. "You still think there's no way to make things right with her?"

The same question he'd asked himself a million times. Yes, he could've done things differently. *Very* differently. But only if he would have surrendered himself to giving up his private life. Only if he'd have agreed to do everything on her terms.

No, she'd demanded he prostitute himself to the press. He refused to do that.

"I just don't see how, Savannah," he said with a shake of his head. "Chelsea and I . . . we didn't mesh."

"You meshed fine," she insisted.

"She wanted more than I could give. Okay?"

She frowned as she withdrew her hand. "It's not that bad, you know."

"Pardon?"

"Being in the public eye. It's not as horrible as you think," she said. Then she glanced to Brad.

Her husband nodded in response. "I know things were intense because of the marriage rumors and all . . . But the press isn't always in our faces."

Although Ethan itched to argue with his friends, to force them to see things from his point of view, he refrained. That didn't prevent his brain from scrambling for comebacks to their reassurances. Neither of them was as famous as Chelsea. They were a media draw because they were both in the music business, but Chelsea was at the top of the game, and Ethan's parents had been—as everybody and their uncle liked to remind him—the King and Queen of Nashville. Had he remained with her, they would be hounded to death.

At least that's what he feared...

But God almighty, he missed her. Every single minute of every damn day.

He decided to go right ahead and argue with Savannah and Brad. "You told me just the other day that you were worried about Caroline. You said you don't want her picture all over the place."

"That's not what I said," Savannah scolded.

"Then what were you griping about?" Ethan asked.

"I was, as you so eloquently put it, *griping* about the fact that she would have to get used to seeing herself in magazines. She was getting teased about that *People* magazine article, and she was carrying on about feeling like a freak."

"See? That proves my point," he insisted. "She feels exactly like I do! Reporters are a bunch of bastards, always sticking their noses into stuff that's none of their damned business."

Savannah shook her head. "I can't do what I do and not interact with the press." She glanced at her husband. "Brad hates it. Not as much as you, but even he knows that if a person wants to make it in country music, she can't live in a vacuum. What I was saying was that Caroline needed to understand who her mother is and why she might see herself on magazines or have people who know her talking about what they saw, like she did when one of her friends bugged her about *People*."

"So you're okay with people taking pictures of your daughter day and night?"

Her smile seemed a bit odd. "C'mon, Ethan. Honestly. Day and night? Even reporters sleep. Besides, when the press wants access to me or my daughter, they get it on my terms. There's no reason you and Chelsea can't handle things the same way."

Although he felt as though she might be condescending to him, he recognized his own hyperbole.

Brad set his fork down. "She's supposed to lay down that last track tomorrow, buddy."

The last track. "When You Were Mine." How ironic that she'd chosen *that* song from his parents' repertoire—a tune that lamented lovers moving on while wondering why on earth they'd ever allowed themselves to part.

"What's she singing?" he asked. "She can't do 'When You Were Mine' as a solo."

"We finally settled on 'In My Life,'" Brad replied.

"The Beatles song?"

"That's the one. Said something about the words meaning a lot to her."

"Probably because of losing her father."

Ethan frowned when Brad rolled his eyes. "I'm sure he's not the only person she hurts over losing."

"Brad's right," Savannah said as she rubbed small circles on Ethan's shoulder. "So what are you gonna do, Ethan?"

* * *

Addie was shaking her head as she joined Chelsea in the kitchen. "You're not going to fucking believe this..."

Glancing up from the celery she was chopping for a salad, Chelsea frowned. The last thing she needed was bad news.

Then again, her life was in the toilet. How much worse could it get? "Spit it out."

"Brad just called to tell me that Ethan is gonna do the duet."

Chelsea blinked, not sure exactly how to react to the news. She and Brad had already made plans for her to record the last song for the charity album tomorrow. It was supposed to be the only song that wasn't a duet, and they'd gone through hundreds of songs searching for the right tune. They'd finally found it in the sentiment of "In My Life," which seemed the proper tribute to her late father while also letting her sing about the hurt she'd felt since Ethan had left her. Not that she'd reveal that hurt to anyone but herself.

Now, instead of doing a couple of takes of a song she knew well, she was going to have to face Ethan.

Three weeks. Three weeks of soul-searching and tears and anger. People were supposed to go through five stages when they grieved, but when they made it through, acceptance would eventually come along. Chelsea couldn't help but believe that she would never get there.

Acceptance? Of what? Of making the worst mistake of her life?

It wasn't your mistake. It was his. He *walked out, not you.*

But she hadn't stopped him, hadn't done a damn thing but let it happen. And despite picking up her phone a hundred times to call Ethan and tell him she missed him so much she ached, she always put it right back down without following through. Her wounded pride would always kick in, asking her why she wanted a man who didn't love her as she was, who wanted her to change everything about her life.

Exactly like you asked him to change everything about his life?

God, she wished she could turn her brain off. Her thoughts never let up. Not even when she slept, since Ethan made an appearance in most of her dreams.

"I gave him your new number," Addie said. "Figured he might need to contact you tomorrow before the session instead of always going through me."

"It's fine. He won't give it to Ethan without asking me first," Chelsea insisted. She'd gotten a new cell phone to be sure he didn't contact her. How could she possibly have endured it if a call from him had popped up on her screen and she discovered that he wasn't begging for her to come back, instead he'd only pocket-dialed her.

"Yeah, Brad's a good guy," Addie agreed.

Thankfully, Brad and Savannah didn't hold the breakup against Chelsea. Nor, from what they'd told her, did they make Ethan feel as though he was the one in the wrong. They could be friends to both of them, which made her extremely grateful. Brad was still helping finish up the charity album, and he'd even found someone willing to distribute for her. And Savannah had already reached out to let Chelsea know that she still cared about her and hoped the two of them could stay in touch.

"So you gonna sing with him?" Addie asked, plucking

one of the croutons from the salad and popping it in her mouth.

"Good question." Chelsea shrugged. "Now I just have to figure out the answer."

"Ticktock, Chel." Addie glanced at her watch. "I told him you'd let him know by seven tonight so he could work on getting the tracks prepped. That doesn't give you much time for a rousing mental debate." She winked.

"What time is it?" Chelsea asked. Seemed as though she'd spent the last three weeks in a daze. Addie had constantly reminded Chelsea when she needed to be someplace. Thankfully, her assistant was the queen of organization, and she kept Chelsea on track. If not for Addie, she would've stayed in bed all day, eating frosting straight from the container and alternating between bitching and crying.

"It's almost six." Leaning her forearms against the island, Addie stared at Chelsea. "I've made the last of the calls for reservations. Are you really sure you want to...you know...do this?"

"You mean take a break?" Chelsea nodded.

"I was able to clear your calendar, but it'll cost you."

With another nod, Chelsea scraped the pieces of the celery she'd prepared from the cutting board into the large salad she'd made. Now that it was done, she found she had no appetite. She'd put a lid on the container and shoved it in the fridge, along with the other healthy food she'd whipped up lately that she never got around to eating. She tended to root around to see what kind of ice cream was hiding in the freezer instead.

"It's worth it," she finally said. "I just...can't. I don't know how I'm going to get through tomorrow morning, let alone the concert tomorrow night." She let out a weary sigh. "I wish they would've let me cancel that, too."

"Not when they've sunk a wad of moola into the marketing campaign."

"I know. But like I said, I just...*can't*."

"You don't have to convince me," Addie replied. "I get why you need a break. Everything's booked, by the way. The flight. The car to take you to the dock. Someone with no fucking agenda to ferry you out to the island."

"Thanks."

"It's just..." Addie let out a sigh of her own. "Are you sure you want to go back there? I mean, won't it...hurt?"

Hurt? Of course it would hurt to be on the island again. But for some reason, that was exactly where Chelsea thought she should be, where she needed to be. "I know it's weird, but I can't explain why that's where I'm heading."

"Your choice," Addie said. "You're allowed to go wherever the fuck you want to go. If you wanna get away from Nashville and sun your ass on that island, I say go for it. Go there. Let yourself heal."

All Chelsea did was nod as the crippling sense of loss washed over her again.

For that moment, she let her guard down and looked Addie in the eye. "How am I gonna face him again?" Damn if her voice didn't quiver.

"Oh, honey..." Addie pushed away from the island and came around to give Chelsea a hug. "You'll be fine." She patted Chelsea's back. "You can do this. You're a tough broad."

Tears threatened but Chelsea held them at bay. *Tough broad, my ass.*

Easing back, Addie gave her a wan smile. "Do it for your dad. Just go in there, sing the shit outta that fucking song and walk out with your head held high."

As though it were that simple...

But Addie was right. If Chelsea could get her emotions under control, she'd go to Brad's tomorrow, sing the song, and get right back out.

"The first time's the hardest," Addie said. "Once you see Ethan, once you get this first awkward meeting under your belt, it'll get easier. Besides, the two of you don't move in the same circles. He has his friends; you have yours. Just go, Chel. Go and sing. Then all you have to do is get through that concert, and you're on your way to paradise."

CHAPTER TWENTY-NINE

Chelsea gave Savannah a heartfelt hug. "I'm so glad you're here."

"I wanted to...you know...be a buffer," Savannah said. "I imagine it's kinda weird to see Ethan again."

The understatement of all time. Weird didn't come anywhere close to describing the gamut of emotions roiling through Chelsea at the notion of being in the same room—the same small recording booth—with the man she loved but couldn't be with.

She hadn't slept at all last night as scenario after scenario played out in her thoughts, becoming more and more ludicrous as the wee hours of the morning came and went. Ethan telling her he missed her. Ethan lamenting that he'd made a huge mistake leaving her behind. Ethan falling to his knees, begging her to take him back.

"You okay?" Savannah asked.

With a weak smile, Chelsea nodded. "Is he here?"

"Yeah, he and Brad are downstairs already. You want a glass of wine or something?"

While it would be easy to drown in alcohol, to try to fuzz up her thoughts so this meeting wouldn't be so damned awkward, Chelsea shook her head. "Let's just get this over with."

"Chelsea...don't sound so depressed. Who knows, maybe... Well, maybe—"

"No 'maybe,' Savannah. Ethan and I are done." Firming her resolve, Chelsea headed toward the door to the basement studio. "I'm only here to sing a song. Nothing else."

If only her heart could understand that just because she was here to see Ethan didn't mean anything would come of it. No matter how much she missed him, how much she wanted him to still love her, she had to face reality.

He'd walked away. When given the choice between his life of privacy and being with her, accepting her and the life she was destined to lead, he'd walked away. For three long weeks, she hadn't heard a peep. At least not from him.

The press?

That was another story altogether.

The stories still ran. Speculation about why the two of them were never seen together was phase one. In response, Chelsea had refused to release a statement—in her mind releasing a statement made it all the more official. Instead, she went about her life without Ethan Walker and hoped gossip would die down. Her silence only led to phase two—pictures of her every damn place she went. God forbid that she be anywhere near anyone with a Y chromosome. That only brought about bullshit conjecture about her having a new guy in her life.

So on Addie and Will's advice, Chelsea finally released a quick statement that she and Ethan weren't a couple any longer. All the admission did was ignite phase three, which consisted of rampant rumors over whose fault it was that they'd broken up.

Disgusted, she'd told Addie to clear her calendar. Chelsea was getting the hell out of Nashville, away from every reminder of exactly how much she hated her life without Ethan in it. Although she felt a little guilty leaving her mother, she needed to be alone. When Addie asked where she wanted to go to get away, all Chelsea could think of was finding someplace where she thought she could heal.

The island.

Although heartache probably waited there, that was the place she most wanted to be.

All she had to do now was survive this recording session—which would be a minor miracle—and get through the concert tonight. Then she could pretend she was only some woman living on an island all by herself. No career. No paparazzi.

No broken heart.

"No wine, then?" Savannah asked.

Chelsea let out a chuckle. "One glass couldn't hurt."

A smile lit Savannah's face. "Head on down there. I'll bring it down."

With a nod, Chelsea went down the stairs to face the

one thing in the world she wanted more than anything but couldn't have.

Ethan Walker.

* * *

He heard her before he saw her. Although he couldn't make out exactly what she was saying, his heart sped in recognition. Pounding, the damn thing slammed against his rib cage simply because he'd heard her speak.

How in the hell was he supposed to get through this song? He could barely catch his breath.

Then she appeared, coming down the stairs slowly, as though she were going someplace she dreaded. Which meant she wasn't nearly as happy to see him as he was to see her.

She'd obviously moved on.

Not that he should be surprised. He'd seen the pictures, and he hadn't needed to go out of his way to do so. Shit, he couldn't even go in a convenience store without being hit in the face with another magazine headline that shouted she was with some new guy.

At least he had his privacy back. His name might pop up from time to time, but he didn't have to see his pictures any longer. Just Chelsea with other people. Other *men*. Men who were linked to her. Men who could see her all the time and share her life with her.

Ethan scowled when she gave Brad a quick peck on the cheek. When she glanced up at him, she must have caught his expression, because she frowned in return.

"Let's get this last song done, Chelsea," Brad said, indicating the recording booth with a quick gesture of his hand. "One more, and we can wrap this baby up."

As she walked around the console, she eyed Ethan warily through the glass. When she was standing in the open door of the booth, she stopped and stared at him, reminding him a little of a doe scenting danger. For a moment, he wondered if she would run.

It hadn't been easy for him to be there, either. But he couldn't help but think of how much sadness she'd had over her father's death. This album was her tribute to him, and Ethan had promised to sing the duet. He might be an idiot, but he was also a man of his word.

No, it was more than that. He hated admitting, even to himself, that he'd fantasized about her rushing into his arms, crying and pleading for him to be with her again. Childish fantasies, but they were digging at him nonetheless, making him wish for things that wouldn't happen. Things like being able to touch her, to kiss her. To spend the rest of his life with her.

So here he was, and now he was sure he'd made a mistake. He hadn't been willing to give an inch, why should she? He needed her to stay and get this damn duet done—to fulfill his promise. Then he wouldn't have to face her again. Which was exactly what he wanted.

Or did he? Seeing her standing there, hesitating to be near him, hurt.

Chelsea was never going to stop being famous, and Ethan wasn't willing to share his life with the whole damn world.

End of story.

So why did he feel so empty?

"Hi," she said as she finally stepped into the booth.

She looked tired. And a little thinner. Her wavy hair was pulled into a ponytail, and she was dressed casually. Jeans and a sweater. She took the empty stool and arranged the music on the stand in front of her. Then she donned the headphones.

I'm a fucking idiot.

"You two ready?" Brad asked, his voice buzzing in Ethan's headphones. "Knowing you two, we'll probably strike gold on the first take."

Ethan snorted, drawing a quizzical stare from Chelsea. He'd forgotten how intense those green eyes of hers were.

He wanted to drown in them.

"Ethan?" Brad's voice buzzed in his ear again. "You okay, buddy?"

No, I'm not okay. I fucked up my life.

"I'm fine," Ethan barked. "Let's go."

* * *

Chelsea bristled at his angry tone, straightening her spine until she thought it would snap. There was no way she'd let him know how much it hurt her to hear how desperately he wanted to get away from her. Clearly, leaving her behind had been easy. He was back to his normal cantankerous self, wanting to get as far from music as he could.

"I'm ready, Brad," she said.

As she listened to the intro of "When You Were Mine," she saw Savannah on the stairs, carrying a glass of red wine.

Chelsea wanted her friend to bring it straight into the booth. In fact, she wanted Savannah to go get the whole bottle. Only copious amounts of alcohol were going to get Chelsea through this ordeal.

Ordeal?

No, this wasn't an ordeal. This was open-heart surgery without anesthesia. She felt shredded, and she wasn't sure how she was going to sing at all, let alone sing a song about the regret of lost love.

She closed her eyes, wanting to lose herself in the tune by living in the past. Picturing when she and Ethan were back on that beach at Jekyll Island, confessing their love, she let the music flow through her, lifting her away from the pain that had drowned her from the moment he'd left.

As she sang the first verse—her verse—she felt every single word of regret all the way to her soul. By the time Ethan joined her for the chorus, she'd disappeared into the world of the song.

"When you were mine, when love was what we shared,

"The world made sense, because I knew you cared.

"Now that you're gone, I can't make it through the day.

"I can't live without you, and there's nothing more to say."

She didn't open her eyes until he sang his verse, and when she did, she was shocked to find him staring at her as though he were singing to her. If she hadn't known better, she might've believed the longing in his voice was real.

Part of her wanted to tell him that she understood what

he'd been saying, that he was right about not needing to be so open with the press. She was allowed to have a life, a private life that didn't have to include sharing every single thing she did, every thought, every action. She'd never realized how suffocating the press had become until he'd come into her life. Now, she understood. And she was making changes, including canceling several appearances so she could get away and heal from all the hurt that still thrummed through her—something she would have never done in the past.

But she couldn't tell him any of that. He hadn't wanted her for who she was, and she wasn't going to turn herself inside out just to make him happy. If the man couldn't accept her for the person she was now, then how could she ever be sure of his love? How could she ever know if they'd be able to weather the storms that life was sure to throw their way?

Somehow, Chelsea made it through the song, holding on to the last note for so incredibly long that she was surprised Ethan matched her through the marathon. They ended together, each taking a breath. Then he kept staring at her, an action she mimicked, unable to pull her gaze away.

Brad's voice piping through the headphones made her jump. "That was absolutely brilliant! You nailed it, guys."

Chelsea finally glanced away, finding Savannah, who was sitting next to Brad. Instead of seeing a smile over a job well done, there was melancholy on her friend's face. Savannah clearly knew what the song had cost Chelsea as only another singer could. Part of her heart was forever lost, left behind in that melody and in those lyrics.

And when people listened, they would never know how much of herself she'd shared.

"Wanna go a few more takes?" Brad asked. "Just for insurance?"

"No!" Chelsea fisted her hands and tried to rein herself in. "I–I can't. I have to...go." She jerked the headphones off, set them on the music stand, and hopped off the stool. "I just have to go."

Ethan got to his feet, removing his own headphones. "Chelsea...wait."

She shook her head, practically running out of the booth. She laid a hand on Savannah's shoulder. "I have to go."

Savannah let out a little sigh. "I understand."

When Brad started to stand, Chelsea shook her head. "Don't get up. I can show myself out."

Unable to stop herself, she glanced through the glass to take one last look at Ethan. He stood there, holding his headphones and frowning.

Frowning. As usual, he was angry at her.

If she heard even one word of criticism, she would lose that last thread of her self-control. So, like a coward, she swallowed the threatening tears and hurried up the stairs.

* * *

Ethan had a million thoughts crowding his mind, each blocking the other so nothing could come out of his mouth.

Chelsea was gone. People fleeing burning buildings probably ran with less speed. Clearly, she wanted to get far away from him as quickly as possible. She hadn't wanted to do another take of the song, even though the album she was doing for her father meant everything to her.

He'd hoped she would at least talk to him for a few minutes. Not that he expected to make a lot of headway with Brad and Savannah listening in. But Ethan figured he could get Chelsea to go somewhere so they could start a conversation. Maybe get some coffee, or even grab some steaks. If he could only get his foot in the door...

Instead, she'd let him know she wanted absolutely nothing to do with him.

Brad left the console to stand in the doorway to the recording booth. "How you doing?"

Ethan set the headphones down and shook his head. "I just wanted a chance to talk to her."

Brad glanced back at Savannah. "Hey, honey. Give us a couple of minutes, please?"

On her feet, she tossed her husband a frown. She leveled a hard stare at Ethan, and he could almost see the gears turning in her head. She clearly wanted to say something, but she either wasn't finding the right words or she was hesitating to talk to him.

"Just say what's on your mind, Savannah," Ethan said.

"I'm not sure that's a good idea," she replied.

He flipped his hand, encouraging her to tell him what was on her mind.

"Fine." Folding her arms under her breasts, her stare became a wicked frown. "You should go after her. That woman still loves you. I'm pretty sure you still love her too, but you didn't have the balls to talk to her."

Brad didn't say a word, but the grin on his face as Savannah scolded Ethan was enough to show he agreed with her.

"Well?" Savannah snapped.

"Well what?"

"Aren't you going after her?"

Brad arched an eyebrow.

Ethan shook his head.

"Then you're an idiot." On that pronouncement, she turned to head up the stairs, leaving the men alone.

"Your wife is...*subtle*," Ethan drawled as he sat back down.

Coming into the booth, Brad took the seat Chelsea had used. "My wife is right." He grinned. "As usual."

"You think I'm supposed to go running after Chelsea like some puppy?"

"That depends."

"On what?" Ethan asked.

"On whether you love her as much as Savannah and I think you do."

Over the years, Ethan had shared a lot with Brad—more than he had with any other person. Even Russ. They had history going all the way back to their high school years. Yet in all that time, in all those conversations and shared memories, there had never been a time when Ethan felt so awkward.

"Since you can't seem to answer," Brad said with a bit of a smirk, "I'll assume the answer is affirmative." His grin faded. "Are you going to let her get away?"

Ethan's temper came rushing forward. "What choice do I

have? She loves the fucking press! I can't live like that. I *won't* live like that."

"What are you afraid of, Ethan?"

"You know what it was like, Brad. You remember my *wonderful* career as a singer, right?"

Brad let out a little laugh. "Who could forget?" He sobered so quickly, it took Ethan by a surprise. "I know reporters were jackasses about that, but it was a different world. You weren't being yourself. They made you into some teenage wet dream."

"It was humiliating."

"I know. But the press doesn't know the real you."

"And if I play my cards right," Ethan said, "they never will."

"What do you think would happen if you were with Chelsea? Do you think they'd crucify you or something?" Brad shook his head. "It's not that terrible."

"They'll print lies, just like they did back then," Ethan insisted, feeling his resolve slipping away. Brad's question kept looping in his thoughts.

"What are you afraid of?"

Ethan answered without a moment of thought. "They killed my parents."

"Your parents died in an accident." Brad held up a hand when Ethan started to argue. "The photographer was a bastard for chasing them, but it was your dad who drove into oncoming traffic. You've got to let it go, Ethan. The same thing's not gonna happen to Chelsea, and it was so long ago..."

His hatred of the press was so old and so deep-seated that he'd never paused to consider whether that hatred was even relevant anymore. If he considered what had been circulating around the Internet, talk shows, and magazines about him and Chelsea, he had to admit the rumors hadn't been all that outrageous. And Chelsea seemed much more organized about what she shared with the press—as opposed to his parents, who shared *everything*.

So the press speculated that he and Chelsea would marry. So what? His friends had made the same prediction. And Chelsea had admitted that she and Ethan were in love. Why had that enraged him so much? It was the truth.

Wasn't it?

From his point of view, it still was. Singing that song had been agony. He must've heard that song a thousand times, but he'd never once felt it—not a single time—not the way he had when he'd sung it with Chelsea.

To Chelsea.

The words still hurt.

I'd give everything I ever had, everything I ever owned
Just to hold you in my arms and to kiss your sweet lips again.

"You know what?" Brad popped off the stool. "I want you to listen to something. Put those headphones on."

Not sure what Brad had up his sleeve, Ethan obeyed while Brad returned to the console.

"Close your eyes, Ethan."

He did. A few moments later, the recording he'd made with Chelsea began. He let her honeyed voice fill his ears as the love he heard in her voice filled his heart. The last note made him swallow hard, hoping Brad wouldn't think he was a pussy if he saw the tears in Ethan's eyes.

"That woman loves you, Ethan," Brad's voice buzzed in his ears.

All Ethan could do was nod.

"So what are you going to do about it?"

CHAPTER THIRTY

Checking the monitor to see the crowd again, Chelsea brushed away a stray tear. How she was going to work up the energy she needed for this concert remained a mystery. All she wanted to do was drown in her sorrow.

Until she'd seen Ethan this morning, she'd been able to lie and convince herself that she was fine without him. One foot in front of the other, and her life went on.

But that was exactly what her life was—a lie. Her heart was broken and would probably never mend. Because she'd put her career first, she'd let the love of her life walk right out the door. Ethan was gone. And despite the twenty thousand people out there screaming her name, she was alone.

Addie poked her head in the dressing room. "Hey, boss? You ready?"

Chelsea let out a little scoffing chuckle. "The show must go on, right?"

Addie nodded. "Think you can do this? I know today was fucking rough, and—"

Holding up a hand, Chelsea stopped her. "This is what I chose, remember? So I damn well better learn to live with it."

Gathering up her courage, she took one last look in the mirror and tried to slap on a smile. Dressed in her sequins and leather, she looked the part. Problem was that she didn't feel it.

She scolded herself to straighten up, telling herself that once she started singing, everything would be all right. When she faced the people who loved her, who wanted to hear her voice, she'd get through this.

"Let's go." She hurried through the door, adjusting her earphones and mic to be sure everything was ready. "Testing," she whispered.

"You're good, Chelsea," her sound manager buzzed in her ear. "Turning your sync on now."

Addie waited with her at the bottom of the stairs leading to the stage. The deafening noise of the crowd was muffled by the white noise filtering in through her headphones. She got just enough auditory input to be able to hear her band and her stage director's voice prompts without the ear-damaging cacophony of the speakers and the crowd.

"And... go," the director said.

Chelsea obeyed, conditioned to doing her job. She hurried up the stairs to hit the stage, a grin on her face even though she sure didn't feel like smiling. Waving her arm high, she tried to connect with the fans who'd paid good money to see her sing. "Hello, Nashville! It's good to be home!"

The first song was an unmitigated disaster, at least in her estimation. Normally, performing was a thrill. She craved the adrenaline, the connection she had to the faces staring up at her. Tonight was different. There was a kind of disconnect that left her feeling worse than she had before she'd started the show.

Although the applause was thunderous, she considered apologizing. This show wasn't giving the people their money's worth, and unless she could give herself a mental kick in the ass, things were only going to go downhill from here. Shit, she should probably offer them a refund.

The band struck up the next tune, and much to her horror, they were playing the song she'd specifically crossed off from the list—"When You Were Mine." Before the show, she'd gone over the set list with her musicians, cutting a couple of the songs she'd sung on the charity album, including the Walkers' old hit. The last thing she needed was yet another reminder of Ethan. Now, the melody was infecting her, and she had to swallow hard to force back the desire to weep.

Turning to face the musicians, she made a slashing gesture, hoping they understood and would move on to another tune. Instead, every one of them grinned at her like simpletons, making her want to scream in frustration.

She tried one more tack, appealing to the stage director. Subtly hitting the mute on her mic, she said, "Barry, this song's out. I won't sing it. Not tonight. Get the guys on board."

Guys? Her backup singers were every bit as bad, swaying to the song as they tossed Chelsea hundred-watt smiles.

Barry finally replied. "Too late. Just go with it, Chelsea."

Like she had a choice. The band had already played the intro twice, and she was going to look like the queen of idiots if she didn't start singing soon.

Tears stinging her eyes, she turned back to the crowd and waited for the band to come back around to her cue. She opened her mouth, but before a single note came out, a familiar thundering baritone filled her ears as the audience erupted into cheers, craning their necks to look stage right.

What the hell?

Chelsea whirled to find Ethan marching across the stage, singing in that effortless way that made her a little jealous. She'd always loved his parents' cover of the song, but his voice eclipsed his father's. So clean. So clear. So sensual.

As he drew closer, all she could do was gape. The chorus was coming up, but she wasn't sure she'd be able to sing a note. Her heart was in her throat.

When he reached her, he took her hand in his and inclined his head at the crowd, encouraging her to join him.

And she did, her years of performing rushing to the fore, forcing her to do what she did best.

Sing.

* * *

Ethan had to fight the urge to sigh in relief when Chelsea finally jumped in to sing with him. The look on her face, the clear surprise in her eyes, had been gratifying. But he had a larger goal, one that was a hell of a lot more important than singing a duet.

Brad had asked Ethan what he was going to do to get Chelsea back. At first, he'd been stumped, fearing he might've made a mistake from which there was no coming back. How could he possibly show her that he'd been wrong, that he was willing to open up to her—and to the fans who cared about her?

Baffled, he decided to go to someone who knew her well. Addie. After all, Chelsea had always called her a miracle worker. Well, she'd been correct. Addie had come up with an idea that to some might have sounded over the top. But to Ethan, it had seemed like the perfect gesture. He would show Chelsea that he was willing to share her life, famous as it was, by surprising her at the concert and sharing her stage.

If it hadn't been for Addie's help, he would never have been able to pull it off. She'd handled everything down to the last detail, working with the band, the backup singers, and the stage manager to be sure that "When You Were Mine" was ready. She'd found Ethan a great place to hide backstage, bringing him the headphones and mic so he'd be prepared.

The crowd roared in approval, making him smile despite the case of nerves that had settled on him as he walked over to Chelsea. While many of the original online comments about him had been negative, it seemed Chelsea's fans had actually lamented their breakup over the past few weeks. Even so, he was a bit surprised at the thundering applause when he'd hit the stage.

Addie had led him out of his hiding place and toward the

stage. The intro of the song had made his stomach churn, especially when Chelsea missed the first intro and then the second cue for her verse. By the time he could see her, his own cue had come around and he'd gathered all his courage to bound up the stairs and start singing.

Step by step, he drew closer until they hit the final chorus. He stretched out his hand, hoping she wouldn't snub him in front of the thousands of people watching him eat crow. If she did, he wasn't sure he would ever live down the embarrassment.

Hand out to her, he waited, watching the emotions playing across her face. Heart pounding, Ethan sent up a quick, silent prayer.

A slow, easy smile blossomed on her lips, and she gradually raised her hand, placing her slender fingers on his palm.

He grasped her hand with the intensity of a drowning man groping for a life preserver. Once he had her in his hold, he vowed never to let her get away from him again.

When the song ended, Ethan pulled her close. She hesitated, subtly inclining her head toward the crowd, as though warning him they were being watched. He just grinned at her, well aware of the thousands of pairs of eyes observing them as they hooted and hollered their approval of the duet.

He tugged a little harder until Chelsea came close enough he could embrace her. Then he hesitated, suddenly losing his nerve. There was one more thing he wanted to do. But should she refuse him in front of all these people, his humiliation would be infamous.

Joe's voice echoed in his mind. *"Work up some guts, boy."*

It was now or never.

Fishing in his pocket, he pulled out the small, velvet box, laid it on his palm, and went down on one knee.

* * *

Chelsea froze, unable to process the scene playing out right before her eyes. This couldn't be happening. None of what she was seeing was real.

Was she dreaming? Or was she simply trapped in some sort of fantasy-based delusion?

"Chelsea..." He swallowed hard. "I missed you more than you could know. I...I don't have a life. Not without you by my side." Ethan took a deep breath and squeezed the hand that still cradled hers. "I love you. I want us to be together forever." He extended his left hand, balancing the black box on his palm. "Will you marry me? Please?"

Her breath caught before coming out in a muted sob. There were so many things she wanted to say, so many questions she needed to ask him.

Why here? Why now?

Had seeing her this morning been enough to change his mind? What possessed him to turn up at a sold-out concert to propose when he hated any kind of performing and publicity with a white-hot passion?

"Ethan...I...I..."

Chelsea wanted to scream that she'd marry him. She wanted to throw herself in his arms and kiss him senseless. She wanted to let every single person gaping at them know that she loved him and that she would be thrilled to be his wife.

But the words wouldn't come.

You're afraid, aren't you? You're afraid he'll hurt you again.

A tear spilled over her lashes. "Ethan..."

He stood, taking the last step to her until he could stare down into her eyes. "Marry me, Chelsea. Please. I'm sorry. About everything. I *need* you, and I want you to be my wife." He kissed her once, a quick brush of his lips against hers. "Let me spend the rest of my life making things up to you."

All her fear vanished, and she nodded, no longer fighting the tears that soon wet her cheeks.

Ethan dropped her hand and cupped her face in his rough palm. "Say it, baby. Say you'll marry me."

"Yes! I'll marry you."

Before she could catch her breath, she found herself wrapped in his arms and lifted off her feet. He spun her around in a circle and laughed. The moment he let her feet touch the stage again, he kissed her the way she'd been longing for him to.

The crowd, the band, and the whole damn world disappeared as she lost herself in his kiss.

"Um...Chelsea? Ethan?" the stage manager's voice buzzed in her ear. "Maybe you two wanna do another song? I mean, this is a *concert* after all."

The band took that cue and started in on "Can't Let You Go," the duet the two of them had sung that pissed off Chuck Austin so much.

She grinned at Ethan and took the first verse. By the time

she reached the chorus, he was right there with her. As they held the last note, he pulled the ring from the box and slid it on her third finger.

* * *

The ride to the farm seemed to last forever, and Ethan's patience was at an end. He was still proud of himself for dealing with the multitude of people who'd wanted to get a piece of him and Chelsea after the concert. Thankfully, he got some time to relax and wind down after doing a third song with her. Addie had taken him to Chelsea's dressing room, shown him where the food and drinks were, and headed back out to keep an eye on Chelsea.

He had to give Chelsea credit. She was a pro. No matter how emotional things had been from the moment he'd joined her on the stage, she'd kept right on performing. How she did it was beyond him. His knees were still shaking from dealing with everyone offering their best wishes.

By the time Ethan was able to get Chelsea in his truck, they'd gone after each other like a couple of horny teenagers. Only by strength of will had he been able to stop kissing her long enough to start the engine and point the truck toward the farm. All he wanted to do was rip off her clothes and make love to her as though some primitive drive needed to be satisfied. He wanted to possess her, to bury himself deep in her body and never, ever lose her again.

After throwing the car in park, he hurried around to open her door, but she was already crawling out. He pulled her into his embrace while she draped her arms around his neck. Their mouths met in a frenzy of rediscovery, and knowing he was close to losing control, he lifted her by the hips. She responded by wrapping her legs around his waist. Smiling against her lips, he carried her inside his home.

They didn't even make it to the bedroom before the clothes began to fall on the floor. Unwilling to wait even long enough to get to the bedroom, he sat on the couch, pulling her between his knees so he could pop the clasp on her bra. Her gorgeous breasts were at eye level, and he took advantage, drawing one rosy nipple between his lips as she laced her fingers through his hair.

Chelsea pushed him down onto the couch and straddled his hips, guiding his cock inside her as she let out a hum of pleasure. Leaning closer, she stared into his eyes as a seductive smile blossomed. "Fuck me, Ethan. Fuck me now." She gave his shoulder a stinging love bite.

"I love it when you talk dirty," he said. Gripping her hips, he did exactly as she'd ordered.

* * *

Chelsea was in no mood for restrained lovemaking. She wanted Ethan to be as rough and wild as she felt. There was no finesse, no seduction. This was raw passion, and she reveled in the way he lost control—the same way she surrendered everything to him.

The tension quickly rose to a crescendo, and when her orgasm raced through her, she let out a shout of pure joy. Wave after wave crashed over her until tears formed in her eyes.

Ethan thrust into her a few more times before he let out a loud gasp. The heat of his release deep inside her set off a small aftershock that drew a surprised gasp of her own.

She collapsed against his chest, gulping for breath, pleased to note that he was doing the same. When she finally gathered her wits, she rubbed her cheek against his shoulder. "That was... wow."

A chuckle rumbled from his chest. "Oh yeah. Definitely a *wow.*"

Normally, she wanted to get dressed right after sex. Being naked always made her feel too vulnerable. But after all he'd done for her, the way he'd opened himself up in front of everyone, Chelsea was secure in his love. She didn't care if he saw a pinch of fat or a bunch of freckles.

He touched a kiss to her forehead. "Do you like the ring?"

Holding up her left hand, she finally took a moment to look at the ring he'd slipped on her finger. In typical Ethan style, it was flashy and simple at the same time—a large pear-shaped diamond mounted on a platinum band. "It's gorgeous. Exactly what I would've chosen for myself."

"I'm glad." He gave her rump a pat. "It wasn't so bad, you know."

The change in topic threw her. "What wasn't so bad?"

"The concert. It was kinda fun singing with you. None of my concerts back in the day were like that."

Having seen several videos of him performing in his teens, Chelsea couldn't help but chuckle. The poor guy had appeared as uncomfortable as a kitten in a room full of growling German shepherds. "That's because you got to be yourself tonight. You've got a great voice. Of course it's fun to show it off. But I won't ask you to do anything like that again. I know singing isn't your thing."

"You know what, baby?" he asked, laughter in his voice. "After tonight, I've decided that I love singing."

"Well, won't that make our lives easier? You ready to sing with me at every concert?"

"Not *every* concert. But maybe I can pop on stage with you from time to time," he suggested.

She pushed herself up so she could look into his eyes. "I was teasing, Ethan. I wouldn't ask you to put yourself out there like that. I don't expect you to change. All I want is for you not to hate that I have to do interviews and stuff from time to time. Addie and I already talked about cutting back. You were right. My fans are wonderful, but they're not the most important thing in my life. *You* are."

"Just like you're the most important thing to me," Ethan said, patting her butt again. "I'm glad you figured things out for yourself. I thought a few things through, and I'm doing some changing, too."

"What did you think through?"

"I've always been so sure that the press was out to get me, that they were the reasons my parents died. But Savannah and Brad opened my eyes a little. They made me think about the whole thing differently."

"Meaning?"

"I'm not gonna talk to every reporter in the world, but a

story here or there about us wouldn't be so terrible. Better to have us control the info rather than having them make shit up."

It seemed as if they'd finally found some common ground, and Chelsea couldn't have been happier. "Would you believe it if I told you that I actually canceled everything on my calendar for next week?"

His eyes widened before a grin bowed his lips. "We're really going to make this work, aren't we?"

"I sure as hell hope so. Know what I'm doing in the morning?"

"Tell me," he coaxed.

"I'm going to our island. Care to go with me?" she asked.

He smiled and nodded. "You know what?"

"No, what?"

"I love you, Chelsea Harris."

"I love you too, Ethan Walker."

* * *

Chelsea leaned against Ethan as they walked along the beach, his arm draped over her shoulders. "I never want to leave. God, I love it here."

He kissed the top of her head. "I know how you feel. But...you've got a charity album to get out there. Then you've got that Chicago concert and—"

She stopped and stared up at him. "Aren't you supposed to tell me to forget all that stuff?"

A warm chuckled rumbled from him. "I'm getting married

to a genuine country music star. I won't let myself forget that again."

With a contented smile, she laid her head against him. "And I won't forget that we have a private life that we'll keep to ourselves."

"I suppose the next feud will be about where we live," he teased. "The farm or your condo."

"No feud," she replied. "We'll just keep both and skip the fight."

His chuckle made her smile. "Sounds like a plan, baby."

Satisfied to let the world remain at bay, Chelsea strolled by his side, loving how the wet sand squished between her toes. The sound of the lapping waves was like music, rolling in and out and reminding her that this place was always going to be their own private paradise—a haven to which they could escape when the rest of the world interfered.

"Our friend is back," Ethan said, causing her head to pop up.

A frantic glance to the horizon found the same boat and photographer intruding on their sanctuary.

"Maybe we'll have to find another island," she grumbled.

"Nah," he said. "This place is too perfect. We're just gonna have to give him a few pictures so he'll go away."

To Chelsea's surprise, Ethan raised his arm and waved at the photographer. And this time, he used all his fingers.

A girl couldn't ask for more than that.

DON'T MISS THE NEXT BOOK IN
SANDY JAMES'S NASHVILLE
DREAMS SERIES!

READ ON FOR A PREVIEW OF
CAN'T FIGHT THE FEELING...

Available in spring 2018.

CHAPTER ONE

The last thing in the world Russell Green wanted was to find himself at this miserable place.

He hated the smell of hospitals. Disinfectant and misery. It didn't help that there was nobody there for him to bitch at about his dilemma. Ellie Foster had made sure he was checked in at the emergency room before she'd hightailed it out of there to get back to Words & Music. Since she was the evening shift manager, she hadn't waited for Russ to see a doctor.

Since his bleeding had all but stopped, he had no desire to wait around a minute longer. Unfortunately, a nurse had already taken his vitals, had a good look at the gash on his forehead, and led him back to a treatment room. He might as well see it through, because the hospital was going to charge him now anyway.

He dutifully sat on the gurney despite the nearly overwhelming desire to flee. Before the nurse had left, she'd taken his dirty wad of tissues and handed him gauze to keep pressure on the wound. At least the tissues he'd surrendered hadn't been saturated like the last few.

"I'm fine now. Really," Russ insisted when the nurse peeled off her gloves, tossed them in the trash, and headed back to the sliding door.

She frowned at him. "You're definitely gonna need stitches, Mr. Green. You want that wound to heal well, don't you?" Instead of waiting for her answer, she said, "Be sure and keep a little pressure on that until the doctor gets in here."

"I could just superglue it," he insisted. God knew that he'd done that before. More than once.

"The wound's too large for that to work." A knowing smile blossomed on her face. "The doctor will give you lidocaine, so you don't have to be afraid of stitches."

Russ had to resist the urge to growl at her incorrect assumption. "I just need to get back to work." A lie. Jorge, the head bouncer who was on duty, could handle the Saturday night Words & Music crowd without him, and he sure didn't want the nurse to think he was some kind of coward.

"We're busy tonight," the blonde assured him. "But it won't be much longer." She looked deeply into his eyes. "Still no dizziness?"

"I don't have a concussion," he insisted. "I barely got winged by that bottle."

"You had a blow to the head. I'd expect a concussion screening at the very least. Better to be on the safe side."

"It wasn't a *blow*. Just grazed me."

The phone in her pocket started ringing insistently. A

quick check of the screen brought a frown to the nurse's face as she answered, "Francie. ER." After a litany of yes responses, she ended the call and shoved the phone back into her pocket. "Hang tight. Someone will be in shortly." She pointed to a white remote resting on the patient table. "You can watch TV if you'd like." Then she skirted around the curtain, opened the sliding door, and pulled it closed behind her.

Russ scowled at the empty room, resigned to wasting the rest of the evening in the boring little cubicle.

His head throbbed, but pain never fazed him much. A couple of aspirin would've taken care of that, maybe with an added shot of Jack Daniel's. If his blood hadn't been pouring so freely from the wound, he wouldn't have bothered to come to the hospital. Ellie had taken one look at his bloody face and freaked. The only way he'd been able to get her to stop being a fussy mother hen was to agree to let her bring him to the ER.

The emergency room? For a small gash on his forehead?

He was made of tougher stuff than that. Shit, he'd broken his nose on the football field. Twice. And both times, a trainer only popped it back into place and let Russ get right back in the game.

The door opened, and when the curtain was swept aside, he was surprised to find a familiar and very pretty face.

He grinned. "Well, well. How you doin', Josie?"

* * *

Joslynn Wright took one look at Russell Green and frowned. This man was a partner in Words & Music with her best friend's husband, Brad Maxwell.

She'd only spent time with Russ twice—at Savannah and Brad's wedding rehearsal and at the wedding itself. Well, three times if she counted that he'd seen her finishing a swim workout the day of the rehearsal. When Savannah had introduced them, he'd immediately given her the nickname Josie, something she found a bit endearing. Most people called her Jos or stuck with Joslynn.

"I'm doing well, Mr. Green." She pulled two purple gloves from the box on the wall and snapped them on. Then she gently took the soiled gauze to see what brought him to her that evening. She'd read Francie's notes and knew he'd been hit in the head with a beer bottle. No surprise to find that the man had a rather nasty gash running along his hairline. "It would seem you're not quite as well."

Russ shrugged before he grinned. "It's only a flesh wound."

In all her years as first a nurse and now a nurse practitioner, she'd heard that Monty Python quote more times than she could count. It normally irritated her.

So why did she find it so cute coming from him?

The dimple. That was the difference. The man had the most delectable dimple on his left cheek. In fact, the whole package was rather attractive, something she'd noticed the first time she'd seen him. His body was no stranger to a gym, judging from the definition in his arms, the lean hips, and the firm thighs. She loved that he wore his blond hair in a short buzz cut. It suited him—and it would, of course, make closing the wound easier.

That thought made Joslynn stop gawking at Russ like some girl looking for a date to the prom. She had a job to do.

He'd come to her for help, and she needed to remember that she was a professional. "Since we're acquainted, I could get another person to treat you."

He just smiled at her. "Why would you do that?"

"Some people find it uncomfortable to be treated by a person they know."

Russ scoffed. "Savannah said you're the best nurse she knows. Why would I want someone else?"

"Nurse practitioner," she couldn't help but say.

"Not the same thing?"

She shook her head, resisting the urge to set him straight on how hard she'd had to work to become an NP. The guy didn't deserve a lecture simply because he'd pushed one of her buttons.

"What's the difference?"

Since he'd asked with a tone of curiosity rather than condescension, she answered. "I'm not a doctor, but I do have a lot of the same privileges. I can see patients pretty much the same way, and I can write 'scripts." She opened a fresh gauze, gently pressed it against his wound, and offered him a smile. "And I can stitch up wounds."

He took over holding the gauze in place. "I'd be happy if you'd take care of this, Josie."

With a nod, she said, "Then let me get a few supplies and we'll get you patched up." She peeled off her gloves and dropped them in the trash. Then she pumped a bit of hand sanitizer from the wall dispenser and rubbed her hands together. "I'll be right back."

Sweeping aside the curtain, she left through the sliding door.

* * *

Russ let out a sigh of relief. After all of Savannah's lush praise, Josie was sure to do a good job patching him up.

The door slid open with a whispered swish, and she strode back in, arms full of packages. She set them on a silver table-tray and slid it closer to his bed. Then she handed him a folded light blue garment. "Instead of having you change to a gown, I figured you might like a scrub shirt."

"Thanks. That's very considerate." He pulled the bandage away, looking for where to toss it.

"Let me take that." Josie tossed it in a biohazard container. Then she began to assemble the supplies into some order that probably made sense to her. One of the packages she opened first had tan gloves that she put on with more care than she had the purple pair.

Russ carefully removed his stained polo, donned the scrub shirt, and then sat back on the gurney.

As soft as the brush of the breeze, she touched the wound. "Are you sure you don't want a plastic surgeon to take a look? It's a fairly big gash, and a plastic surgeon will probably leave less of a scar."

"Can't you just staple the stupid thing shut?" He glanced up at her.

How had he not noticed those chocolate-brown eyes before? Or her scent? Something floral and terribly enticing.

"Staples would leave a really nasty scar," she replied. "If you don't want a plastic surgeon..." She cocked an eyebrow.

"Nope."

"Then let me see if I can do better with some tiny stitches. Just relax. I'll have you put back together in a jiffy."

With practiced ease, she went about getting everything ready. After she injected the area with lidocaine, something he hadn't wanted but she'd assured him he needed, she started working on him.

Zoning out so he didn't have to think about what she was doing, Russ focused on the woman who was so close to him that her breasts kept bumping against his arm. Although he was aware that she was Savannah's best friend, he knew little else about Joslynn Wright. His fault, because he'd all but avoided going anyplace with Brad and Savannah when he knew that Josie was going to be there too. That tack had stemmed from Savannah trying to play matchmaker, always chatting Josie up and telling Russ what a great couple the two of them would make.

Hell with that.

The last thing he needed in his fucked-up life was a girlfriend, especially one who was so close to his partner's wife.

But in a moment of honesty, he acknowledged that he remembered the first time he'd seen her with incredible clarity. The afternoon before the Maxwells' wedding rehearsal, he'd been striding across the pool deck, aiming for the tiki bar. A woman had been slowly ascending the elaborate pool's marble staircase. The sunlight had hit her perfectly, and damn if she hadn't looked like a goddess emerging from a forest pond. Her posture was perfect—spine straight as an arrow, shoulders square.

As he'd taken in her slender body, his mouth had gone

dry. High, firm breasts. Slim waist. Just enough muscle to look athletic and utterly feminine. She'd been dressed in a red bikini that was tasteful, yet still enticing, and she sported a small tattoo of an orange butterfly—it peeked out of the bikini top just enough to see it on her left breast—over her heart.

He'd made up his mind to try to get to know her better—up until the moment Savannah had introduced her and Russ had realized this was the woman she'd been trying to push on him.

Gorgeous or not, trying to date her hadn't seemed worth the aggravation.

Now, he wasn't so sure.

The navy-blue scrubs and white lab coat she wore hid that delectable shape, which helped him get a grip on his rampant imagination. Just because Josie was appealing to him didn't make the situation any less perilous. He had no business becoming infatuated with this woman. With *any* woman...

Not with the dismal future he had in store.

She looked down at him, brows kit. "You doing okay? Awfully quiet there."

"Just patch me up, okay?" Russ snapped. He was immediately contrite. His fascination with her bothered him, but that didn't entitle him to take his irritation out of her.

The way she narrowed her dark eyes told him she'd caught his tone. "Alrighty, then..."

He had to hand it to her, Josie was efficient. She'd thoroughly cleaned and then stitched the wound up quickly. "Done," she announced.

Probably a good thing for Russ, because the more time he spent with her, the more he started to wonder if Savannah had been right all along—that this woman might be worth getting to know.

He needed to get out of there.

Then he remembered the manners his mom had beaten into his thick head. "Thanks, Josie."

* * *

"My pleasure." Joslynn started to gather up the discarded wrappers and used supplies. She'd lost track of how many stitches she'd put in place, because she'd done her damnedest to keep them small and even.

A good job, if she did say so herself.

"When do I get them pulled?" Russ asked, jumping off the gurney.

"You don't," she replied. "These will absorb. I also sealed them with skin adhesive. Just don't pick at it. It'll peel off when it's ready."

"So I can shower?"

She nodded and then pointed to the gurney. "Have a seat. You might as well make yourself comfortable because you need the nurse to come and give you discharge instructions, and I think a quick concussion screening might—"

"Nope. Don't have time for that."

"You're already here. You might as well—"

"I have to get back to work." He picked up the blood-stained polo and tossed it into the trash.

Getting angry at his crappy attitude, she didn't press the point about a possible concussion. It wasn't as though someone had smashed a chair over his head. A screening wasn't necessary. "There's paperwork—"

"I've had enough stitches to know what to do." The scars she'd seen before he'd put on the scrubs added weight to his claim but didn't excuse his rude dismissal. "Besides, you just told me how to take care of them."

She hadn't meant to stare when he'd taken off his bloody shirt. But as he'd changed to the scrubs, she'd gotten a healthy view of his torso. Scars. So many scars. His chest. His back. Right shoulder surgery—probably more than one.

Sweet Lord, what kind of hell had Russell Green been through?

It wasn't at all like her to notice a guy's body in any way except clinically, but she hadn't been able to stop from gawking at his arms. His biceps were well developed, straining the sleeves of the scrub shirt. She found herself wondering what kind of sports he played. Football? Soccer? He had what she called a "rugby body"—muscular, sturdy, and exactly what she liked.

With a shake of her head, Joslynn resisted the urge to wag her finger at him as if she were scolding a naughty child. "At the very least, you have to sign the release paperwork." To give him something to do, she popped up the mirror that was built into the patient table. "Want a peek?"

Russ actually came over to see the stitches. After a good, long look, he grinned. "Nice job, doc."

"I'm not a doctor."

"You did better than most probably could." To her great surprise, he kissed her on the cheek. "See you later, Josie."

And he was gone before she could regain enough of her wits to stop him.

Francie came strolling through the open door. "I guess he was in a hurry, huh?" she asked, watching him jog out of double doors to the waiting area. Then she shifted her gaze to Joslynn. "You okay, Jos?"

Her hand fell away from her cheek. She hadn't even realized that she'd been touching the spot he'd kissed. "Fine. And yes, he was obviously ready to depart from our exceptional hospitality."

Francie chuckled. "They always hate waiting on the paperwork." She shuffled through the yellow discharge papers. "Want me to shred them?"

Joslynn's first response would have been to do just that, but she couldn't get past Russ's rude exit.

A better idea popped into her head, and a slow smile bloomed. "You know what? Please put them in an envelope. I'm going to make sure Mr. Green receives them. In person."

ABOUT THE AUTHOR

Sandy lives in a quiet suburb of Indianapolis and is a high school psychology teacher. She owns a small stable of harness racehorses and enjoys spending time at Hoosier Park racetrack. She has been an Amazon #1 bestseller multiple times and has won numerous awards including two HOLT Medallions.

Learn more at:

sandyjames.com

Twitter @sandyjamesbooks

Facebook.com/sandyjamesbooks

You Might Also Like...

In Nashville the stars shine a little brighter, songs sound a little sweeter, and love lasts a lifetime.

Young, rich, and better looking than a man has a right to be, successful songwriter Brad "Hitman" Maxwell was once Nashville's biggest celebrity. Then a heartbreaking loss and a shocking betrayal caused his light to go out. Now, instead of pouring his soul into song, he pours beers at Words & Music. His bar is the perfect escape—a place to forget his past—until the night she takes the stage...

Savannah Wolf used to dream of becoming Nashville's hottest star. Now, as a young single mom, she dreams of a steady income and being home to tuck her daughter into bed. So when Brad Maxwell offers her the gig of a lifetime—playing as the headliner at Words & Music—Savannah discovers the best of both worlds. And she refuses to ruin this opportunity by falling for her sexy boss. Except that Brad suddenly starts writing music again...music inspired by *her*.

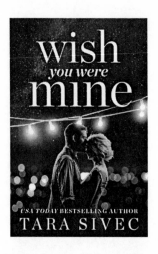

From the *USA Today* bestselling author of *The Story of Us* and *Fisher's Light* comes a new, standalone novel—a heart-wrenching story about first loves and second chances that will make you fall in love all over again...

Five years. I would've stayed away longer if I hadn't received the letter. Not a day has gone by that I haven't thought about her, haven't missed her smile, haven't wished that things were different.

The last time I saw my two best friends, I vowed to not stand in the way of their happiness, even if that meant I couldn't be a part of their lives. Cameron James and her emerald-green eyes were too much of a temptation and I couldn't stay and watch them together. Cameron deserved better than me. She deserved him.

But now that I am back, things are different. I'm not going to stand by and watch the woman I've always loved slip away again. I'm done living my life with regrets and I'm ready to tell her the truth. And I'll do whatever it takes to show her that I always wished she was mine.

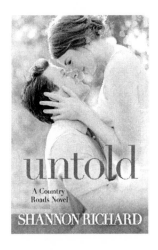

Sometimes love has a plan of its own . . .

Brie Davis came to Mirabelle, Florida, for one thing: the funeral of her birth mother—a woman she never had a chance to know. Now Brie must sort through her mother's life to get the answers she was denied. She plans to leave as soon as she can . . . except the sexy veterinarian makes Brie's pulse beat faster than she's willing to admit.

Finn Shepherd knows Brie's only in town for a short while, but he can't stay away. Instead he finds himself looking for more reasons to keep her close. Finn's already had his fair share of heartbreak, yet Brie makes him want to take that risk again. Now all Finn has to do is convince her to take a chance on him...before she disappears from his life forever.

CPSIA information can be obtained
at www.ICGtesting.com
Printed in the USA
FFOW03n2206120218
45033976-45382FF